I0563760

The Mirror of Dionysus

FROM THE SAME AUTHOR

The Wayward Muse (2005)
The Stones of Camelot (2006)
The New Faust the Tragicomique (2007)
The Shadow of Frankenstein (2008)
Sherlock Holmes and the Vampires of Eternity (2009)
Frankenstein and the Vampire Countess (2009)
Frankenstein in London (2011)
Eurydice's Lament (2015)

The Mirror of Dionysus

by

Brian Stableford

A Black Coat Press Book

The Mirror of Dionysus Copyright © 2017 by Brian Stableford.
Front cover illustration Copyright © 2017 by Mike Hoffman.
Back cover: Midas and Bacchus by Nicolas Poussin, 1630, Alte Pinakothek, Munich, Germany.

Visit our website at www.blackcoatpress.com

ISBN 978-1-61227-585-7. First Printing. January 2017. Published by Black Coat Press, an imprint of Hollywood Comics.com, LLC, P.O. Box 17270, Encino, CA 91416. All rights reserved. Except for review purposes, no part of this book may be reproduced or transmitted in any form or by any means, electronic or mechanical, including photocopying, recording, or by any information storage and retrieval system, without permission in writing from the publisher. The stories and characters depicted in this novel are entirely fictional. Printed in the United States of America.

THE MIRROR OF DIONYSUS

I. A Farewell to Orpheus

I watched the cart carrying the carefully-padded crate containing the completed Orpheus triptych draw away slowly from the door of the house. Although it had more than an hour's journey to make before it reached the residence of the late Marquis de Mesmay, the triptych was now officially out of my hands. The Marquise de Mesmay's steward had taken possession of it, and it was his responsibility to see to its safe delivery—and, I presumed, its hanging.

I had been paid for the paintings, although the money had actually been handed over in Lutèce by the Marquise's man of confidence to my own agent, Myrica Mavor, who would bank the money there. There had been no quibble raised regarding the death of the Marquis, who had actually commissioned the painting; the Marquise had actually come to see me, dressed in full mourning, to see what progress I had made and inquire as to when I might finish. She had seemed enthusiastic to have it done, and although I had not been able to make any sense of her attitude throughout the visit, I was duly grateful for her assurance that she intended to honor all her late husband's debts and carry on his work as best she could.

The resolution to carry on his work might have been slightly ominous, but it was a point I had not dared to press, given that I was not supposed to know that the Marquis had been an important member of the Cult of Orpheus, at the heart of the Duc de Dellacrusca's tangled political conspiracies. It was difficult even to offer formal condolences for her loss, given that the cult were attempting to conceal, or at least to obscure, the circumstances of the multiple murder, even though there had been no other topic of conversation on the island since it had occurred.

Prior to that terrible occasion, I had always thought of the Marquise as a rather retiring figure, eccentric in her pursuit of communication with the dead. with the aid of Vashti Savage and other reputed wise women, and various other mystical concerns. The death of her husband seemed to have galvanized her, and provoked her to all kinds of resolute action, of which seeing to the completion of the triptych was presumably one more item to tick off on a long list of things to be done. I was certainly relieved to have it removed from mine.

The cart seemed to fade as well dwindle in size as it gradually vanished into the gray morning, which was still suffering the gloomy aftereffects of the recent explosion of Hekla, way out in the Northern Ocean. I couldn't help feeling a gnawing regret that I had ever accepted the commission to paint the triptych, and wondering whether there was any clue that I might have picked up capable of dissuading me, had my judgment been better.

I had not known, obviously, when the offer was made, that the Marquis of Mesmay was a member of the so-called Cult of Orpheus. Even if I had known, I would have had very little idea of what that membership implied. Obviously, I was party to the common knowledge that the secret society in question was nowadays merely a cover for political conspirators working within the framework of the Empire, although it still retained a tokenistic respect for the residual trappings of what had once been the Orphic religion, in the centuries preceding the birth of the Empire and the glorious era of the divine Julius. As an artist, I had always considered myself essentially divorced from political affairs, and had made it a deliberate policy to pay no attention to them, in an ostentatiously disdainful fashion.

Had that been a mistake, I wondered? If I had taken more interest in such matters, might I have realized, firstly that the Cult of Orpheus maintained a presence on Mnemosyne, because the influx of summer visitors from various parts of Gaul and even further afield provided a convenient cover for meetings of disparate conspirators? And if I had realized that, might I then have been able to jump to the conclusion—as some other people on the island undoubtedly had—that when the Marquis of Mesmay commissioned me to paint a triptych representing phases in the life of the legendary Orpheus, he was not merely acting as a connoisseur of art, but as an agent of the so-called cult?

Even if I had jumped to that conclusion, I had to suppose, I would not have seen it as a reason for refusing the commission. I would have assumed—and still did assume, in fact—that Mesmay had approached me simply because of my reputation and talent as an artist, which made me, unarguably, the person resident in Mnemosyne best qualified to execute such a commission brilliantly. It was not my usual kind of work, of course, my reputation having been built almost entirely as a portraitist, but it had seemed a useful opportunity to broaden my endeavor, and an interesting challenge, in a purely artistic sense; it would not have seemed unreasonable then to think, even if I had suspected any further agenda on Mesmay's part, that any such hidden agenda was of no relevance to me.

Events had proved otherwise, and catastrophically so, but I really had had no reason to suspect that they might at the time. I was still convinced that the Duc de Dellacrusca, even though he was Mesmay's supposed master within the context of the cult, had had nothing to do with the commissioning of the painting. It was, I still assumed, pure coincidence that the paintings of Orpheus, and my attempts, for purely artistic reasons, to find a imaginative key that would enable me to make sense of his legend and hence to paint him "accurately," had become entangled with Dellacrusca's discovery, in Lutèce, of the long-lost granddaughter for whom he had been searching for years, and his subsequent pursuit of the child to the island...

Except, of course, I reminded myself, that many people believe that there is no such thing as coincidence. The chain of coincidences that had led to the specific circumstances of Lord Dellacrusca's murder, and the corollary murder of the Marquis de Mesmay, certainly seemed so bizarre that it was hard not to imagine the hand of some evil fate being involved therein.

There was a third thread in the chain, which had become intricately entangled with the first two, and in thinking about that, my gaze inevitably wandered from the cart to the house beside the road along which the Orpheus triptych was traveling away, hopefully out of my life forever.

The house in question, which stood between my dwelling, isolated on the headland, and the main body of the island, had been occupied for many years by the reclusive Monsieur Toustain—the ideal neighbor, from my point of view, precisely because he was a recluse, and our relationship had been limited to occasional polite formalities, with absolutely no personal involvement at all. I had never had any reason to suspect, and nor had anyone else, until his death caused his secrets to begin to leak out, that Toustain had been a defector from the Cult of Dionysus, from which the Cult of Orpheus had split in some kind of schism lost in the mists of pre-Julian history, which had similarly endured through the ages, ever a rival to the evolving Cult of Orpheus.

Not had I had any reason to suspect that Toustain had had in his possession an ancient document that seemed to be regarded as a precious relic by the members of both cults, for symbolic reasons. Apparently intent on continuing to keep the document hidden, he had left the book in whose binding it was secreted, along with various other books, to me rather than including it with the rest of his possessions, which had been auctioned for the benefit of the poor. I, of course, had had no suspicion of the existence of the document, let alone that it had been surreptitiously delivered into my custody—but the Duc de Dellacrusca, the master of the Cult of Orpheus and the Gaulish Secret Police, had found out as soon as Toustain's real identity had come to light, and had taken steps to recover it in his customary sly fashion.

Had I known about that, too, I would not have cared, and it would not have occurred to me to think that there might be any mortal danger in the circumstance that members of each of the two rival cults, unknown to one another, had given me commissions of a sort relevant to the long-obsolete mythology of their organizations' supposed origins. Nor would I have seen any hidden significance in the circumstance that Toustain's house, through the intermediary of my agent, Myrica Mavor, had been sold to Charles Parenot, a Lutecian painter who was—not entirely by coincidence, this time—the adoptive father of Elise, the orphan that Dellacrusca, after being introduced to the family by Myrica, had recognized as his granddaughter.

And that, of course, was when things had become seriously complicated, and where the hand of fate, or magic, or Eurydice—however one cared to consider the matter—had become involved. From that point on, events had moved with vertiginous speed and more than a little madness, to the concert after which Dellacrusca had determined, in his underhandedly scheming fashion, to take possession of his musically-gifted granddaughter, and in the course of which he had been hacked to death by maenads who had gained entry by masquerading as musiciennes supplied by the Sister of Shalimar to accompany the performance.

Mesmay's death had apparently been collateral damage, as well as the deaths of three other cult members who had tried to stop the murders, or at least avenge the principal murder. I had got out in the nick of time, with Parenot, after snatching Elise and Hecate Rain from the dangerous crossfire, along with Elise's adoptive mother Mariette, but...

And that *but* was the problem. To all intents and purposes, the affair was over. The Orpheans were, indeed, intent on pretending that it had never even happened, at last insofar as the Lutecian press and the official historical record were concerned, and claiming that their unbeloved leader had died somewhere else entirely, of some other cause. But that mask had to conceal some kind of plan for revenge, or at least for some kind of cathartic violence, of whose details and potential scope I had not the slightest idea.

From my own viewpoint, of course, the whole matter was now concluded. I had finished the paintings to my own artistic satisfaction, assisted by Elise and Hecate, who might or might not have been acting under the influence of the shade of Eurydice, subjectively if not objectively. The triptych had now been officially delivered, and ought to be gone from my life and artistic consciousness forever. The document that Dellacrusca had recovered from me had allegedly been destroyed during the carnage of his murder, and the copies I had made of it immediately after its discovery had been distributed to various parties; I did not expect ever to see them again and did not want to, considering them devoid of any decipherable meaning. Nor did I want to have anything further to do with the rival cults, and would be glad if I never heard of either of them again.

But…would the other parties involved in the affair let me alone, now that I had become accidentally involved in their conflict? Could I be sure that the rival cults were not looking at me suspiciously, each suspecting me of being an agent for the other? And if they did, what might they do about it?

And in that respect, there were other loose ends…

As if on cue, while my gaze was still lingering on what I still thought of as the Toustain house, slightly hazy in the struggling morning light, a black dot emerged from the door that faced my dwelling, and began to move toward me at what I immediately judged to be a slow walking pace: a child's walking pace.

In spite of the poor light, I was soon able see her quite clearly, and she could see me. I recognized her and she recognized me.

I waited for her.

"Good morning, Master Rathenius," she said to me, with scrupulous politeness, when she arrived a few paces away. "May I speak with you?"

As soon as I had first caught sight of Elise, a girl of twelve or thirteen on the threshold of acquiring the particular kind of beauty that pubescent girls begin to acquire, I had wanted to paint her. More than that, I had wanted to paint her in juxtaposition with her adoptive mother, as a study in contrasts—not merely because of the simple fact the Mariette was blonde, a descendant of Northerners, while Elise was raven-haired, testifying to a partial ancestry of what once had been Grecia Magna in pre-Imperial days, but because of the balanced opposition of the child's commencing adolescent beauty and Mariette's adult beauty, now ripened into its full brilliant maturity.

"Of course," I said to her. "Would you like to come into the studio?"

She smiled at that, because she knew it was a privilege of sorts, although, in recent times, circumstances had obliged me to receive rather too many guests in the studio rather than the drawing room, in a fashion that seemed to symbolize the apparent disintegration of the lifestyle that I had built up so carefully and maintained for so long... for too long.

"Thank you," she said, although she must have noticed that I had cast a rapid, slightly quizzical glance in the direction of the Toustain house, because she was quick to add: "Mariette knows I'm here, Master Rathenius. I have permission."

I nodded my head, taking note of the fact not only that she had called Mariette by her name rather than "Mother," that she had not bothered to mention Charles at all, and that her tone clearly implied that she did not think that she needed anyone's permission, being a free agent. She had grown up on Martyr's Mount, where many of the female children of her own approximate age whom she had known since infancy would already have started what they would have called, and doubtless thought of as, "work."

Mariette's mother, if what Myrica had told me could be trusted, had been preserved from that profession until a later age, and had then had been rescued from it when she had taken joint responsibility for Elise with Charles Parenot. It was understandable that she did not see eye to eye with her adoptive daughter as to the extent that she still required protection, and permission to visit artists in their homes. I, of course, am entirely worthy of trust, and I hoped that Mariette had realized that on the basis of our admittedly-slight but eventful acquaintance, but I did have a reputation that might have given her cause for anxiety.

"You should not call me Master Rathenius," I reminded Elise. "We have agreed, have we not, that to a fellow artist like yourself, I am simply Axel?"

She blushed slightly, but went past me in a slightly hasty manner in order to precede me to the studio, in the forlorn hope of concealing the unnecessary embarrassment.

Elise took the spare armchair by the fireplace without waiting to be invited. It was the same chair in which the Duc de Dellacrusca had waited, uninvited himself, prior to our last excruciating meeting.

"I fear that Jean-Jacques has taken the trap into town to renew our food-supplies, and that Luzon has gone with him," I told her, "so I'm alone in the house at present, but if you would like me to make some tea I can do so."

"No, thank you," she said. "I saw the cart leave, carrying the triptych, and assumed that I wouldn't be disturbing you."

"I can give you as much time as you wish," I assured her. "Do you mind if I sketch you while we talk, though? Now that the triptych is off my hands, I hope that I can paint you and Mariette, as I suggested when we first met."

"Feel free..." She left the *but* unspoken, but it had clearly been suppressed.

"Is there some problem with my painting you?" I asked, surprised.

"Oh, no," she hastened to assure me.

I drew the logical conclusion. "Some problem with me painting Mariette, then?" I asked, perhaps a trifle indiscreetly.

Again, she blushed, and again she tried to hide it. I helped her out by turning away to reach or my sketchpad and a stick of charcoal.

"Oh, no," she said, again, but more hesitantly. "I'm sure that she'd like you to." Deliberately or not, that let the cat out of the bag; if someone didn't want me to, it had to be Charles. He didn't know me very well either, and had probably heard far more about my reputation than Mariette or Elise. Myrica Mavor could, of course, have told him that I was completely trustworthy, but whether she would have done so was an entirely different matter. She had entirely commercial notions as to how an artist's reputation and image ought to be managed and massaged, and she also had silly notions regarding the utility of stimulating rivalry between artists.

I didn't take up the question. Instead, I started to sketch, and waited for Elise to tell me why she wanted to "speak with me."

It was obviously something sensitive, as well as something she felt to be important, because she felt a need to work up to it gradually.

"You know that I've been working with Hecate Rain on possible musical accompaniments to hear earlier work, since we improvised the... other piece," she said.

"Yes, I know," I said. "I'm glad. Sometimes, her enthusiasm requires a stimulating spark, and meeting you seems to have provided one."

"She says that if I ask you to tell me the truth, and you say that you will, then you will."

The hand holding the charcoal paused of its own accord, sensing potentially dangerous ground.

I looked her in the eye. "I won't lie to you, Elise," I promised.

She was an intelligent child; she knew the difference between promising to tell the truth and promising not to lie, but she accepted the gesture of good faith. She hadn't finished beating round the bush yet. Whatever she wanted me to tell her the truth about, she obviously felt that some groundwork needed to be laid first.

"Hecate says that you don't believe in magic," she said.

"That's putting it far more bluntly than the question requires," I said. "What I think is that much, if not all, of what people think of as magic not only can be explained naturally but needs to be explained naturally—but that there are aspects of nature that we don't yet understand, some of which are exceedingly peculiar."

"So that when Vashti Savage claims to be summoning the spirits of the dead," Elise elaborated, "the images she's conjuring up actually come from her own mind—from a part of it of which she isn't fully conscious and can't really control."

The hand holding the charcoal was briefly paralyzed again; the ground was definitely dangerous. Elise had been specifically excluded from the séance in which Charles, Mariette, Lord Dellacrusca and I had taken part, but the mere fact of her exclusion must have made her exceedingly curious about what had happened there. Hecate, not known for her discretion, might have told her—but Hecate didn't know the truth of what had happened any more than Mariette did, and I was far from certain that I knew it myself. Eurydice's shade had put in an appearance of sorts, but exactly what that appearance amounted to, or what it signified, I really didn't know.

I forced the hand to move, and to continue sketching.

"That's how I interpret what happens during her séances," I agreed, calmly. "Vashti disagrees, and resents my interpretation, even though I'm always careful to emphasize that I believe her to be perfectly sincere, and that her method produces results that are certainly interesting, and perhaps valuable. She is, in her own way, a genuine artist, with real talent."

"And when people say that you're a sorcerer, they're wrong. Your artist's eye allows you sometimes to see things, and to makes guesses based on what you see, that people who aren't artists can't—but there's nothing magical about you?"

I practically had to grit my teeth to keep my hand moving, even though I knew that she probably had no idea why that particular ground seemed dangerous to me. I wanted to steer her back in the direction in which I assumed that she was trying to go.

"In the same way," I suggested, "that you have an exceedingly good ear, without your being a magician. Lots of people can learn to play musical instruments, and some of them become very good at it through learning—although some, like poor Hecate, find that their capacity is very limited—but others, like you, seem to be born with an innate talent that makes them exceptional almost as soon as they contrive to produce their first note. To many people, your musical ability, precocious as it is, seems magical, or supernatural."

"But you don't believe that it is?" she queried.

"I've seen a great many youthful prodigies of various kinds, ranging from the musical to the mathematical. Many of them seemed marvelous to me, but my inclination is to think that it's a natural, albeit rare, phenomenon." I cursed myself secretly for sounding so pretentious, but she had thrown me off my stride slightly.

We had, however, definitely got closer to the matter that was on her mind. "Sometimes," she said, "it seems to me that I'm as much an instrument as the one I'm playing, that I'm not playing so much as *being played*, especially when I'm improvising rather than playing from sheet music. It's as if the music is coming from outside me...beyond me. Hecate says that she feels the same way about her poetry."

"I know the feeling well," I said. "All artists do. When we're fully involved in what we're doing, it does seem to be happening of its own accord, just arriving, rather than being something we're consciously directing. We can sometimes be surprised by things in our own work—as when you saw something in the unfinished triptych that I'm not sure was really there, but which, once you had called attention to it, I immediately wanted to include, because it was what the work needed.

"In the same way, the music you play does come, at least sometimes, from outside your conscious mind, and sometimes takes you by surprise—but that doesn't necessarily mean that it comes from some kind of supernatural *beyond*. There's a part of your mind where all kinds of urges and impulses originate, which then surface in your thinking mind as feelings, desires and artistic inspirations. The ability to grasp and develop those inspirations is what makes us artists…and the cleverer we become in grasping and using them, the better we are, me as a painter, Hecate as a poet, and you as a musician."

"But you don't believe that music can work magic?"

I strongly suspected that it was a trick question, primed, deliberately or not, by Hecate. I paused, and deliberately removed the top sheet from my sketch-pad and set the sketch aside, to give me time to think. I had promised not to lie to her, and I knew that that might become a difficult promise to keep, especially if she was going where I now thought that she was going.

"I can't say that," I admitted. "I've seen too many strange things happen to the accompaniment of music, or as an apparent consequence of music, to deny it some kind of uncanny power in certain circumstances. What I don't believe is that musicians can work musical magic deliberately. Whatever magic amounts to, in the great scheme of things, it's not something that human beings have yet learned to master, control and direct. I've known people who firmly believed that they could, some of whom certainly weren't liars, but I think that they might have been mistaken about the extent to which they were really producing the effects they observed."

Again, that was overly pretentious, but she was an intelligent girl and she had presumably run through the

argument before, with Hecate, although I could understand that she might have been reluctant to talk to Mariette and Charles about it.

After a pause for reflection, she got to the point.

"Do you remember that hideous discord that my viola produced before my grandfather's murderers drew
their knives?" he asked.

"Yes," I said, refraining from adding that neither I
nor anyone else who had heard it was likely to have forgotten the occurrence, even if they couldn't reproduce
the sound in their minds. "And I know that you didn't
play it deliberately."

"No," she agreed, "I didn't." She stressed the pro-
noun to emphasize that there was a sense in which it
might nevertheless have been deliberate.

I put the sketch-book aside, in order to look as earnest and authoritative as any mere pose could make me
seem. "I promised not to lie to you," I said, "so I won't
tell you that I don't think that that discord had nothing to
do with what happened next, but I'm absolutely convinced that it had nothing to do with *causing* what happened. I think that it was a kind of reaction—a kind of
scream of alarm. Subconsciously, I think, your sensitive
mind had picked up on the fact that something was
wrong, that the appearances around you were deceptive,
and that something terrible was about to happen. I don't
know exactly what clues you picked up, and I assume
that you don't, either, but that seems to me to be the like-
liest explanation of what happened."

She nodded. She didn't thank me, for which I was
glad. If she'd thanked me, it might have meant that she
thought I was trying to spare her feelings.

"I didn't want him dead," she said, baldly. Then she
launched the dagger-thrust. "Did you?"

I met her gaze quite frankly. "No, I didn't," I said. "He was, I suspect, a very bad man, who probably had a lot of blood on his hands, and I didn't like him any more than he liked me, but I wouldn't have wished him dead."

She didn't nod her head again, but I think she accepted it. It was true, after all. Even so, she said: "You reacted very quickly too, pushing my father toward me and pulling Hecate out of harm's way. Perhaps you picked up a clue too?"

"Perhaps," I agreed, "If so, it was subconscious—it wasn't until I saw the knives that I acted."

After a pause, she added: "It was all so *unnecessary*. Why didn't he simply say something when he first recognized the viola? Why didn't he just tell me who I was, tell Charles and Mariette, and then ask me what I wanted to do?"

"That simply wasn't the kind of man he was," I told her. "A lifetime of scheming and employing underhanded ruses to obtain his goals had corrupted him to the extent that he literally couldn't think of any other way of going about anything. When he worked out that Toustain had passed the Orphic fragment on to me without my being aware of it, he could have just sent his sons to knock on my door, explain the situation and ask me to look for it. But that wasn't his way. It probably never occurred to him to do anything but plan some ingenious way of tricking me into finding it for him. As for giving you any kind of choice or say in your own destiny…that probably never occurred to him either, although it would have been sane and reasonable as well as virtuous. Even if his plan had succeeded, he'd have lost by it, just as he lost by treating your mother as he did."

"Did he have her killed, do you think?" she asked.

"I doubt it," I said. "Again, that wasn't the kind of man he was. He'd have wanted her alive, if he's been able to find her, because he'd have wanted to shape her life as he wanted to shape yours, and doubtless felt entitled to do so. Given what happened to you, I think the probability is that your mother died in childbirth—but it's only a guess."

The way she nodded told me that she hadn't finished yet, but she paused. She got up to look at the sketches I'd made. I was ashamed of them—I'd been horribly distracted.

"I can do better," I told her.

She looked down at the first of them—the one that was supposedly complete—with the same interested intensity with which she'd looked at the Orpheus triptych, both before and after it was finished, and I had the uncomfortable impression that, once again, she could see secrets there that I wasn't even conscious of having incorporated into the charcoal lines and smudges.

Then she sat down again.

"Are we in danger, Axel?" she asked, in a soft voice, but with telling bluntness.

I couldn't simply say no; she would have been disappointed in me, and I didn't want to disappoint her, not so much because she was a child, who really did still need a measure of protection, even though she wasn't wrong in thinking herself wise beyond her years, but because she was an artist.

"Not one of the forty-odd people who heard that discord can possibly think that it contributed in any way to Dellacrusca's death," I said. "I honestly don't know exactly how crazy the Orpheans are, but I can't imagine that they're crazy enough to hold any kind of grudge against you for what happened to your grandfather. They might be looking round for someone at whom to lash out at in anger, but they're not the kind of men who'd lash out at a twelve-year-old girl...or are you thirteen?"

"I don't know," she admitted. "There's some uncertainty about my birth date. Does it matter?"

"No," I admitted. "The point is that they think more highly of themselves than that. I can't believe that you have anything to fear from the Orpheans—or from the Dionysians, no matter what kind of garbled account gets back to them of what happened in that hall."

She looked at me steadily. When I didn't go on, she prompted me: "I said *we*."

I felt oddly grateful for the fact that she cared. I shook my head. "I really don't know about me. Unwittingly, I seem to have got caught in the middle of a dispute that has actually nothing to do with me—but none of the disputants know that, and I fear that what they don't know might lead one or other of them to draw the wrong conclusions. I honestly have no idea whether I'm in danger or not, or what I ought to do about it if I am...but for what it's worth, if Charles and Mariette took the view that they ought to try to distance themselves from me as much as possible, I couldn't blame them. If Charles wants to return to Lutèce... well, to be honest, I think he might be wise."

Again, she stood up and went to look at the sketch. This time, her body-language suggested that I'd guessed correctly: that Charles Parenot did want to get away from an island that had so far brought him nothing but anguish. As I'd told her, honestly, I thought he might be wise to want that.

After a further inspection, she said: "I'd like you to paint me. Not like that, but I would like you to do it."

Again, I felt grateful, but it wasn't a time to be self-indulgent. "If Charles wants to leave…," I began.

"He's talking about it," Elise put in. "Mariette doesn't want to go back. They're arguing. If they put it to the vote…but they won't include me if they do, will they? That's not the way these things work. Even if they pretend to take what I want into account, they won't let my vote tip the balance."

"I don't know," I admitted. "I suppose it's difficult for them, feeling responsible for you, and thinking that they know better than you do what's in your best interests—but I can't pretend to know how they feel. I've never had a child."

She looked as if there was a comment or question on the tip of her tongue that she suppressed. In all probability, she was thinking that Charles and Mariette had never had a child either—but she looked at me in a way that was distinctly discomfiting, given the number of other things that she might have thought and asked, and given that she had obviously been encouraged to seek my advice by Hecate Rain. I was, at any rate, sufficiently discomfited to let my tongue run away with me.

"It might not come to that, anyway," I said. "I've been thinking of leaving the island myself."

That obviously startled her, although not as much as it would have startled many people who thought that they knew me a lot better than she did.

"But you want to paint me," she reminded me. "And Mariette."

"That's true," I said, contriving a smile. "But we can't always get what we want, alas."

"Is that a secret?" she asked me, then. "I can tell that it just slipped out, and that you didn't really intend

23

to tell me, but if I can tell Charles and Mariette, it might make a difference to their arguments."

She really was wise beyond her years... or at least clever, which isn't necessarily the same thing. I was ashamed, though, for thinking briefly that there might be a little of her grandfather in her, as well as her real mother.

"It's not a secret," I told her. "You can tell them... but I hope you won't mind me advising you not to try to use it as a weapon in their dispute. You might do well to tread carefully there."

She nodded, as if grateful for the advice, but she didn't say anything about the likelihood of her following it, even though she hadn't promised not to lie to me.

"Nothing I've said is secret, either," she said, "but if someone were to ask..."

"I won't lie to them," I said, with a hint of irony, "but I can be discreet."

"It would be a great pity if you left before painting me, though," she said, pensively. "You'd miss out on seeing Hecate perform her work to my accompaniment as well."

"That would be unfortunate," I admitted, suspecting what was coming next.

It did.

"Have you told Hecate that you're thinking of leaving?"

"Not yet," I admitted, "and you're right that she should have been the first person to hear it. I'd planned to call on her this afternoon anyway, now that the triptych's out of the way. If you happen to see her before then..."

She shook her head. "We're not due to meet until tomorrow," she said. "But even if I were... I can be discreet too. Anyway, she'll talk you out of it... unless you're planning to take her with you...?"

She paused, watching me like a hawk, searching for the answer that I had no intention of giving her.

"No, you're not, are you?" she concluded, correctly, although I was sure that I hadn't given anything away. Immediately, though, she raised her hands and blushed again apologetically, this time. "I'm sorry," she said. "None of my business."

I suspected that it might become her business if I did make the decision. It was some time since Hecate and I had been lovers, but we were perhaps closer now than ever, and when the time came for me to desert her, as it would eventually, it would hit her hard. If Elise were going to become her regular accompanist, if only for a while, she might well have to cope with a certain amount of emotional fallout.

"No apology necessary," I assured her.

The front door banged then, as Jean-Jacques opened it, presumably holding a box of supplies in his arms and unable to muffle its repercussion.

"I'd better go home," Elise was quick to say, "or Mariette will start to worry. Thank you for answering my questions, Axel. When I've thought about the answers, I might have more, though."

"You're always welcome," I assured her. "And let's not give up on the possibility that I'll have plenty of opportunity to paint you. Things are still a little overwrought at present, but perhaps they'll calm down."

I escorted her to the door. Then I watched Jean-Jacques finish unloading the trap. I wanted to talk to him as quickly as possible, about the other commission he'd gone into town to carry out.

II. The Difficulty of Decision

I knew that the news was bad as soon as I got Jean-Jacques on his own. He was a very solid and composed fellow, not given to looking anxious, but he was only human. I took him into the drawing room.

The first thing he said was: "Nobody knows anything, sir. That doesn't stop them talking, of course—makes it worse, in fact, but nobody *knows* anything. My guess is that even those who know that their right hand is steeped up to the elbow in blood are trying to prevent their own left hands from finding out about it."

The point was, however, not so much who knew what as what the people who didn't know were thinking. I didn't have time to intervene, though, before he continued: "The harbor is full of boats, far more than usual for the time of year. A lot of the people who were here when the thing happened have gone back to the mainland, but others have come, mostly strangers. The Sprite is oddly quiet, though, except for the regulars; wherever the newcomers have gone to ground, it's not there. Nobody knows who they are."

"What are people saying?" I asked him. Servants' gossip is always much more prolific, and slightly more reliable, than the gossip of supposedly respectable folk. Jean-Jacques had a firmer finger on the pulse of the island than Fion Commonal, the physician, president of the town council and—it now appeared—member of the Cult of Orpheus.

"Anything and everything," Jean-Jacques told me, unhelpfully. "I defy you to think of a suggestion so crazy that it hasn't been aired somewhere, but it's just hot air. Nobody knows what to believe."

"So be it," I said. "Start at the other end. Do they know what *not* to believe?"

That caught him off guard. "What do you mean, sir?" he asked.

"What I mean," I said, "is: do they know better than to think that the Dionysians murdered Dellacrusca?"

His surprise was only mild, because he jumped to the wrong conclusion. "You've heard that it wasn't, then, sir?"

"No," I said, as patiently as I could. "That's why I sent you into town to discover whether anyone was saying it. I worked it out logically. Nine knife-wielding maenads out of their minds on some kind of drug not on the tariff list at the town pharmacy? Who could possibly believe that the Dionysians would be so stupid, let alone so unsubtle? To anyone with half an eye, it screams deception. That charade required planning, and I doubt that the Dionysians had time to plan it, even if they have agents on the island. They presumably had, even before the mysterious influx of boats to which you referred, if only because the place seems to have been swarming with Orpheans for years, but that operation was too theatrical to have been put together in minutes by a handful of petty spies. Logic suggests to that it was an internecine coup, and that the Orpheans have suffered a serious schism. I don't doubt that they're all keeping their masks firmly on, while looking around trying to work out exactly who their friends and enemies are, and, as you say, everybody's right hand won't even be telling the left hand what it's doing—but one thing they'll surely be doing is sharpening knives and looking for appropriate backs to stab. The question is: how many people have realized that the real murderers are trying to shift the blame, and will they be able to convince the rest?"

He was reasonably quick on the uptake, and he'd been nodding at intervals throughout the speech, but the questions at the end made him frown.

"There are certainly people saying it," he confessed, "and the fact that the Orpheans are denying it, and insisting that it was the Dionysians, probably makes some of them more convinced. There's certainly a lot of talk about a split in the Orphean ranks, but some people are suggesting that it's an argument about how to react to the so-called Dionysian atrocity. As for the Dionysians, well, who can tell? Nobody knows who they are or might be, but there's talk among the people who are contending that they've been wrongly accused of reprisals that they might take. If you're right sir, and I agree that you probably are, there are three sides on the bubbling conflict, none of whose members are sure as to who might be on their side or who might be an enemy."

"Which makes things triply awkward for me," I mused, sourly, "or perhaps doubly triply awkward."

"Why doubly triply, sir?" the manservant asked, puzzled.

"Well," I said, "the Orpheans, or some of them, probably think I might be a Dionysian, because Toustain left me the book, but the Dionysians know I'm not, and might well feel resentful about my handing the treasure to the opposition; hence, my suspected Dionysian affiliation is doubly awkward. As for the Orpheans who killed Dellacrusca, and his remaining supporters, they must both know that Dellacrusca came to see me shortly before his death, when he collected the document from me, but neither of them can have the slightest idea what passed between us, so the murderers probably feel entitled to suspect that I might have been working for him, while his supporters probably feel entitled to suspect that I was involved in the conspiracy against him. Both parties probably wonder whether he might have told me something that might be prejudicial to them: hence, doubly doubly awkward—which, added to the Dionysian situation, makes doubly triply awkward."

"I see, sir," said Jean-Jacques, twisting his lip as if to model the convoluted network of suspicions. "But the islanders, at least, don't suspect you of any involvement at all, or if they do, they don't think it's anything that should worry them. If your name comes up, in connection with the paintings or the way you risked your life to snatch Hecate Rain out of harm's way, the local people scoff at any idea that you might have been in on the murder."

That wasn't encouraging. If gossiping servants knew enough about what had happened at Mesmay's to know that I'd removed Hecate from the path of the knife-wielding maenads or the path of any bullets fired at them by the members of the audience, people with less generous minds might think, as Elise had suggested, that I'd had some prior warning of what was about to happen. That could only add fuel to brooding suspicion

"That shows their good judgment," I was all I actually said, "or at least proves that I've been on the island long enough for the natives to have begun to think of me as one of their own—but it's the outsiders I'm worried about, and what ideas they might have got into their heads."

"Well, I'm not the only one who'll be doing my best to set the rumor-mill right, sir. Things will calm down, given time."

I had already confessed that I was seriously considering accelerating my departure from the island to Elise, so I saw no reason to suppress the information. If there was anyone who deserved to knew the direction of my thinking even before Hecate, it was Jean-Jacques.

"In fact," I told him, "I've been thinking for some time about leaving the island. Now might well be a good time—before any further outbreak of violence."

He raised an eyebrow, in a fashion suggesting that I'd just committed a blasphemy—which, as a good servant, he was obliged to overlook.

"But you never leave the island, sir," he said.

"That's true," I said, "but it's not as if I were under some kind of curse that prevents me from doing so, and I've never had any desire to be buried here—certainly not imminently. This mess might be the spur I needed to stop pondering the question and settle it. What do you think I should do?"

That amazed him. Even as an exceptionally good servant, he wasn't used to being asked his opinion, by me or any previous master. He didn't waste time protesting, though. He spent half a minute or so thinking it over, and then he countered with a question of his own:

"Were you thinking of taking me with you, sir?" he asked.

I hadn't promised not to lie to him, but I didn't think I should.

"No," I said.

He nodded, with perfect equanimity, as if that were simply one more piece in the jigsaw of thought he needed to put together in order to decide what I ought to do.

"Well, sir," he said, finally, "I would advise you strongly not to go."

"And why is that?" I asked him.

"Well sir," he said, still speaking carefully, "for one thing, if you run away, it will only add to any suspicions people might have as to your involvement, and might prompt someone to take action that they might otherwise have decided against. Then again, as you said yourself just now, there are a lot of people on the island who, even if they don't necessarily think of you as a friend, think of you as *one of us*. If they catch wind of any plan to do you harm, at the very least they'll warn you, and many of them would probably try to stop it. As for me, sir, I think you know that if anyone tried to harm you while I was nearby, they'd have to go over my dead body to get to you. So, my opinion is that any enemies you might have will find it a lot harder to strike at you here on the island than they would on the mainland, alone and among strangers. These cultists are said to be cunning, and I don't say that we could stop them if they really did sent assassins after you, but I believe you have a better chance of avoiding trouble here than anywhere else, unless there's somewhere you can go, and can reach, where you're certain of being safe."

He didn't bother to question me as to whether there was. Of course there wasn't. I hadn't left the island for three decades. The places I'd been before arriving on Mnemosyne would probably have changed out of all recognition, and the people...well, if I did leave the island, I wouldn't be going back to any place I'd been before.

I suspected that what Jean-Jacques had said was sound advice, but there were factors in the background of which he was unaware. Could I continue feeling at home here, I wondered, now that all this had blown up?

I was about to ask Jean-Jacques for more details about the precise content of the gossip he'd heard, but the doorbell rang, and he went to answer it, leaving me alone in the drawing room with my thoughts for a few seconds.

He came back to tell me that "Madame Parenot" was asking to see me. He knew perfectly well that Mariette and Charles weren't married, but he would never have dreamt of denying her the appellation on that kind of technicality.

I had been half-expecting her, and I knew that I would have plenty of opportunity to question Jean-Jacques further about the remaining trivia. "Show her in," I said, "and ask Luzon to make some tea."

I stood up to receive Mariette, but she seemed slightly embarrassed by the formality. She might have preferred it if I'd taken her into the studio. She took the proffered chair, however, and accepted the offer of tea. Then she hesitated before saying:

"You've seen Elise."

"She had your permission," I said, confidently.

"Yes she did," Mariette agreed. "I hoped you might be able to put her mind at rest about…certain things."

I was mildly surprised by a slight hint of annoyance in her tone. "I was under the impression that I had," I admitted. "I'm sorry if I failed."

"I'm not sure that you did," she said, "at least, with regard to the…matters about which she came to question you, I certainly don't think you did any harm…"

"But?" I prompted.

"You told her that you're thinking of leaving the island."

"I did mention it," I admitted, "but I didn't think that the news would disturb her, even though she seems to be looking forward to my painting her portrait. In fact, I revealed the information—a trifle carelessly, I admit—

because she had pressed me to confess that I don't feel entire secure at present, even though I don't see any reason why she should feel unsafe herself. The point I was trying to make..."

"Is that she might be even safer if you weren't here?"

Now that she put it so bluntly, I could see, as I had not quite seen before, that the suggestion might have had exactly the opposite effect to the one I'd vaguely intended. Was there no end, I wondered, to the possible complications of the situation?"

"I'm sorry if I upset her," I said. "It was unintentional, I assure you."

"I know," she said. "You weren't to know. There are things...."

She was about to tell me that there were things I didn't know, although I suspected that I did know, and that any account that Elise had given her of our conversation had been replete with discreet omissions. Jean-Jacques brought the tea in at that moment, however, and while he served it, the exchange lapsed. When he had gone, Mariette didn't continue the suspended sentence. Instead, she said: "Charles has been talking about leaving the island too."

"You can't have formed a very good impression of it," I said, sympathetically. "To be caught up in so much intrigue, menace and violence within days of your arrival...I'm sure that if I were you, I could hardly wait to return to the reassuring hubbub of Martyr's Mount."

"I never want to go back there," she said, flatly. "I certainly don't want to take Elise back there. If it had been practical—or if Charles had been prepared to admit its practicality—we would have left years ago, but my...position didn't entitle me to demand it."

"I see," I said, after a sight pause. "I suppose that's understandable too..."

"For myself," she said, "I don't think it matters greatly, but for Elise...we haven't been here long, and it has, as you observe, been an exceedingly turbulent time, but it seems to me that I've perceived nevertheless that Elise belongs here, and needs to be here. She needs the company of people like Hecate Rain, and yourself, and the musicians to whom Hecate has promised to introduce her. There are artists a-plenty on Martyr's Mount, you might say, and you'd be right, but you know better than anyone what a unique society Mnemosyne has to offer, when it's not beset by conspiracies and murders."

"Indeed I do," I conceded. "Unfortunately, for the moment, it does seem to be beset by conspiracies, and I'm not at all sure, alas, that we have seen the last of the murders."

"So you agree with Charles that we ought to run away...and that you ought to run away yourself?"

"It's not for me to take sides in a dispute between yourself and your husband..." I began, perhaps foolishly.

She cut me off abruptly. "He's not my husband. You might have told your servants to address me as Madame Parenot, and you might have gone out of your way, in your gallant fashion, to tell me that there's no such thing as a whore, but it doesn't affect the fact that I am his whore, and that everyone knows it."

"You shouldn't insult yourself, Mariette," I said, mildly, "no matter how angry you are. It does you no good, and it hurts me to hear it."

She seemed surprised for a moment, and then decided that I was still being merely gallant. "It's no good your being kind," she said, with a slight sigh. "But

34

you're doubtless right. Hecate says that you usually are. Have you told her that you're thinking of leaving?"

"No," I said. "I had formed a swift intention to mention it this afternoon, in order to save Elise from feeling that she ought not to say anything about it, but I must admit to being a trifle confused now, and am beginning to wish that I hadn't mentioned the possibility to her."

Mariette nodded. "She has a gift for catching you off guard like that, and saying more than you intended," she observed. "When she wants her own way...she doesn't want to leave the island either, and she doesn't want you to leave either, not just because she wants you to paint her but because...well, I'm not exactly sure. In the past, it never seemed to matter that Charles and I aren't her real parents, but now...well, things are at risk of becoming fraught."

"I can understand that," I said, blandly, merely trying to sound sympathetic.

"I'm not sure that you can," she countered. "What you told Elise is the truth, though, isn't it? You really don't think that she's in danger?"

"It's the truth," I confirmed. "No one can possibly suspect that Elise had anything to do with the planning of her grandfather's murder. No one planning any kind of revenge will mark her down as a target, simply because, unknown to her, she was his granddaughter. She's not an inconvenience to anyone."

"What about Charles?" she asked. "He was present in the hall when the murders were committed, and you and he acted very quickly to get Elise out of harm's way. He was present at Vashti Savage's séance too, and Dellacrusca is known to have visited us in Lutèce. Is he safe from suspicion, do you think?"

That was a good question. Remembering Jean-Jacques' argument, I said: "It won't decrease any suspicion that anyone might have if you all leave—quite the reverse." Unfortunately, the rest of Jean-Jacques' advice was irrelevant to Parenot. In the eyes of the islanders, he was an outsider, far more likely to come under suspicion in servants' gossip than I was. I made a mental note to ask Jean-Jacques about that.

Mariette nodded—not because she agreed with me, but because she thought that it was an argument she could use in the battle to persuade Charles not to take them back to Martyr's Mount, a notorious haunt of assassins for hire as well as whores and starveling artists. The sorest part of the problem, I could see now, was that Charles Parenot, given what Mariette delicately referred to as her "position," didn't have any right to take them anywhere, because Mariette wasn't his wife and Elise wasn't his daughter.

I knew—or thought I knew—that Charles loved Mariette and that Mariette loved Charles, and they certainly both loved Elise, but in the present situation, that might not be enough to hold them together, as it apparently had done for the last decade and more.

I wanted to help, but I really had no idea how I could. Even if I had been prepared to give Mariette advice, I wouldn't have known what advice to give her.

"I don't have permission, by the way," she put in. "Charles doesn't know I'm here. He wouldn't like it if he did."

It was a provocation, but I wasn't sure what she was trying to provoke or why.

"I can understand that," I said, again, equally blandly, and was swift to add, lest she take the remark the wrong way: "He doubtless considers your disputes private, and would rather they stayed under your own roof."

"He doesn't want you to paint me. Do you understand that too?"

"Yes," I said, and left it at that.

The lack of specification troubled her slightly. Perhaps she had been expecting negative answer. After a slight pause, she said: "I don't."

"All artists are jealous and suspicious of other artists," I told her. "Not so much because of vulgar possibilities, in spite of the rich legendry of artists seducing their models, but for more subtle reasons. I understand that he's painted you a great many times, and that the Eurydice in the Mesmay manse is only one of the mythological roles in which he's envisioned you. He's seen you with an artist's eye, repeatedly, over a period of ten years, seen into you, seen things in you that no one else can see…or, in his view, ought to see."

"You mean he's afraid that you might see something in me that he hasn't?"

"I doubt that, unless he's unusually modest—although I, of course, as a monster of arrogance, have not the slightest doubt that I would see you more accurately and more profoundly than any other artist in the Empire. But he feels a…proprietorial interest. He wants his insights, real or imagined, to be his alone. Although artists aren't real magicians, any more than musicians are, there is a magic of sorts in art, just as there is in music. Consciously or unconsciously, Charles suspects that if I paint you, there will be something more in the artistry of my representation than a mere image, like a passive reflection in a mirror."

"You really mean all that, don't you?" he said, sounding slightly amazed. She didn't know me very well.

"Of course," I said.

"Well," she said, "you are an artist. I'm not. I think he's just scared that I might sleep with you."

"I'm hurt that he doesn't trust me," I said, "but I do have a reputation, which Myrica Mavor has always tried to foster, and he doesn't know me very well, as yet."

She laughed. "I see what you mean about being a monster of arrogance," she said. "It's not you he's worried about—it's me."

I didn't know what to say to that, so I tried to make light of it. "I'm entitled to describe myself as a monster of arrogance, by way of flippant self-deprecation," I said, "but for you to repeat it..."

"Is impolite," she cut in. "I apologize. I'm not polite, I fear—badly brought up."

"You're abusing yourself again," I pointed out, with a sigh, "and quite unnecessarily. Elise is a perfect model of politeness, and where could she have learned that, if not from you?"

Her mouth twisted awkwardly. "It's the aristocratic blood in her, I expect," she said. "Now that she knows that her uncles are two of the richest men in Lutèce..."

And that, obviously, was another reason why Mariette wasn't enthusiastic to return to the capital. Tommaso Dellacrusca had been on his very best behavior when he had talked to her after his father's murder, but she hadn't been taken in by the act. She knew his reputation, as well as mine. She wanted to be as far away from him and Lorenzo as was humanly possible, without giving the impression that she was trying to remove Elise entirely from their line of sight.

I was convinced, personally, that Tommaso was a better man than his reputation suggested...but I also knew that in the present circumstances, he would be seething with wrath against his father's killers, whom he was doubtless trying his utmost to identify, and that they would almost certainly have him and his brother at the top of their list of further targets; there was potential for an imminent bloodbath in the twins' vicinity. On that score, I thought, Mariette might be right to want to stay on the island...at least until Tommaso and Lorenzo came back, bringing the potential bloodbath with them.

"I'm sorry this is all such a mess," I said.

"It's not your fault," she said, accurately enough.

"Perhaps not," I said, "but Myrica Mavor and Lord Dellacrusca, between them, seem to have entangled your lives with mine, inextricably, and I wouldn't want anything bad to happen to any of you as a consequence."

She was overwrought. Whatever she said, and however badly she'd been brought up, she wasn't impolite—but that didn't mean that she wasn't prepared to say things she shouldn't.

"If Charles were to go back to Lutèce," she said, "and Elise and I were to stay..."

I cut her off, impolitely. "It won't come to that," I said.

"Why?" she asked, bluntly.

"Because Charles loves you," I said, equally bluntly. "No matter how good his arguments are, or how angry he feels about being contradicted, at the end of the day, you can twist him round your little finger. Even without Elise's support, you'd be able to get your own way. With it, there's no contest. Let him argue, let him blow off steam and let him sulk; in the end, you'll win…and because of that, you have to be certain that you know what you want."

"Do you really think you know us that well, after a matter of weeks?" she asked, a trifle sharply.

"Do you really suppose that you're so very different from the rest of humankind?" I countered—but I smiled, in an attempt to take the edge of the sharpness. "I have an artist's eye, remember, and the eye of an artist of genius. I can see more in a glance than many people in a lifetime of study. And that does make me a monster of arrogance, but it doesn't affect the fact that I'm right."

She smiled in her turn, perhaps a little in genuine amusement, but mostly because she was hoping that I was right. She wanted the reassurance that she could get her own way—and for the moment, at least, she was overlooking the warning about having to be certain that she knew what she wanted.

"If we are in danger," she said, after a momentary hesitation, "it might be better if we were all to face it together, might it not?"

"I might be suspected, wrongly, of being implicated in the assassination plot," I told her, "and it's not beyond the bounds of possibility that Charles will come under suspicion too, equally mistakenly, but I really can't believe that anyone could suspect you or Elise of having a hand in it."

"You don't believe in magicians," she said. "You don't believe that the discord Elise played or what happened at the séance had anything to do with the assassination either…but other people do believe that people can work magic, and other people might."

That was an intelligent observation, and an appropriate reproach. Other people, I had to admit, did believe that some people could deliberately work magic, and

40

even though Lord Dellacrusca had been as hard-headed as me in that regard, he was the head of the relic of a mystery religion, and the Dionysians were reputed to be even more committed to the magic and mystery in their beliefs than the Orpheans. When I put two and two together I always made four...but I couldn't be certain that the people from whom I might be under threat would necessarily calculate in the same way.

I still didn't think that any sane person could possibly hold Elise in any way responsible for anything that had happened at the aborted concert, and I didn't think it at all likely that anyone could possible hold Mariette responsible for what had happened at the séance...except, perversely enough, me. Dellacrusca had assumed that I was responsible for the manifestation there, and he hadn't been the only one, but I knew that it had had nothing to do with me. I didn't think for an instant that Mariette had been conscious of her own involvement, but I believed, and might not be the only person who believed, that she had been the instrument of whatever force it was that had manifested itself, strangely and obliquely, as Eurydice.

On the other hand, magic is not something that can be figured into rational calculations. Whatever I, or Mariette, or anyone decided about the best course of action to take in our present circumstances, we could only take rational factors into account. If the seemingly-supernatural intervened, that was beyond anyone's anticipation or control.

I took so long to think about those tortured question that Mariette felt obliged to speak again.

"I know that it's indiscreet and impolite of me to say so, Master Rathenius," she said, "but since you've challenged me to think hard about what I really want to

41

do, perhaps you won't might me wondering what *you* really want to do. Do you really want to leave the island?"

The simple answer to that was no—but there were complications in the question of which she had no knowledge, and there were risks in my remaining of which she had no idea.

"You're right," I said, neutrally. "That is something that I, like you, need to be certain about. It will require very careful consideration."

I couldn't help remembering what Elise had said about Hecate Rain being sure to talk me out of it. Just as I was convinced that Mariette, at the end of the day, could exert her own will over Charles Parenot, was apparently sure that Hecate could exercise a similar influence over me. She was wrong…and the fact that she was wrong made me doubt my own judgment about Mariette…except that Charles Parenot wasn't like me. Unlike me, he really wasn't very different from the common run of humankind.

"In that case," Mariette said, "perhaps I'd better leave you to your careful consideration, but I hope you'll bear in mind the fact that you promised to paint me as well as Elise, and that you'll disappoint us both if you fail to keep your promise."

I hadn't actually made any promises, merely expressed desires and broached suggestions, but she knew that.

"I'm truly sorry if I accidentally upset Elise," I said, "but she asked me to tell the truth, and I promised her I wouldn't lie. If I had just given her hypocritical assurances that all will be well, she would have known—she has a musician's ear, and something of an artist's eye. She's a little disconcerting, in her way."

"More than a little," she said, with a sigh. "You haven't managed, or even tried, to set my mind at rest either—but for that I thank you. I wouldn't have appreciated hypocritical assurances."

"You're welcome," I assured her, and escorted her to the door.

I went back to the studio, although I had no demanding work to do there. It was simply the best place to think, for an artist.

III. Hecate's Conclusion

I scrutinized the weather carefully after Jean-Jacques had cleared away the remains of lunch—abundant remains, I fear, for I was lacking an appetite—wondering whether I ought to go into town in a covered carriage. Although the sky was leaden in its grayness, however, it was innocent of any storm-clouds, and it had not so much as drizzled all morning. I decided to walk, because the studio had not brought me any intellectual inspiration, and I thought that a stroll along the solitary road might.

It says something about my state of mind, and the level of my anxieties, that I took care to slip a small gun into my coat pocket: one of the new revolvers that were becoming so fashionable. It would not protect me against assassins carrying firearms of their own, but at last it ought to keep me safe from knife-wielding maenads, were any to cross my path.

I had hardly finished dressing for the journey, however, when there was a knock on the bedroom door.

I was expecting Jean-Jacques, and was quite astonished to see Luzon so far from her culinary territory, and arguably beyond the bounds of propriety.

"May I speak with you, sir?" she said.

Why not? I thought, a trifle impolitely. *Everyone else has.* "Of course," I said, aloud. "Is there a problem in the kitchen?"

She came into the room and closed the door behind her—which was definitely beyond the bounds of propriety.

"I know it's not my place sir," she said, "but Jean-Jacques told me what you had said to him, and what advice he gave you."

"Ah," I said. It was only natural, of course that he should have told her, and only natural that she should have an opinion about it—but that she should take the bold step of coming to tell me what it was, presumably having chosen the time and place precisely to exclude Jean-Jacques from any knowledge of what she was doing, was a different matter.

My first assumption was that she was going to add her voice to his, and assure me that if anyone tried to invade the house that they would have two dead bodies to step over in order to get to me rather than one—but I had misjudged her. How well does any man, even one with an artist's eye, know his cook?

"Jean-Jacques is a good man," she said, "and he doubtless meant every word he said to you, but I felt that I ought to tell you, sir, that I think he's wrong."

I covered my surprise by saying: "And why is that, Luzon?"

"He thinks that the islanders might be able to protect you, sir, and they can't. If the threat came from them, then of course they would, but it doesn't, and they can't. I was in town this morning, as he was. I saw the same things, but I didn't talk to the same people. There's trouble brewing, sir, and it's going to be bad. Clovis has doubled the night-watch, but he only has a handful of men, and he knows full well that they'll be straws in a whirlwind. Dellacrusca's murder was the beginning of whatever's going on between the cultists, not the end. The settlement is yet to come—and if my advice counts for anything by comparison with Jean-Jacques', I think you'd be wise to get off the island this very day, if you can, and not come back until the trouble's over. Even if Dellacrusca hadn't come to see you just before he was killed—and I was the one he forced to let him in, if you remember, so I know full well that there was no conspiracy between you—there isn't any way you could have stayed out of it once that old fool Toustain had passed you the black spot, for reasons that the gods alone know. You're not safe here, for the time being, sir, and I wouldn't want you to think you were because of what Jean-Jacques says. His heart is good, sir, but his judgment..."

She sounded almost desperate. It was easy to judge the extent of the urgency that had forced her to smash the bounds of convention.

I almost sat down on the bed, in order to think, but contrived to remain on my feet.

"Thank you," I said, mostly just for the sake of saying something, although, in fact, my gratitude was perfectly sincere, at least for the fact that she was anxious for my wellbeing.

I obviously didn't sound sincere enough. She thought that I was simply fobbing here off. There were tears in her eyes.

"Oh, sir," she said, "don't think it's because I want you to go. You've been the best master I've ever had, and it will be a bad thing for me if I have to find another, even if I can find one. I hope you might come back, and I certainly wish that you will, but only when it's safe. I don't understand what's going on here—I don't know the first thing about these secret societies—but I know there's something in the air, and I don't mean the volcano, and wiser women than me know it too. It's not my place to say so, I know, but if you're wise, sir, you'll pack your bags now and leave for the mainland on the first reliable boat you can find—but make sure it's a boatman you know, and can trust. Jean-Jacques and I will look after the house as best we can for as long as we can, and do our very best to make sure that you find it exactly as you left it when you come back, but...well, if you won't believe me, ask someone you can believe. The poor old witch who used to live on Snowspur is dead, may her soul be at rest, but there are others. They won't tell you any different."

I stepped forward and put my hands on her shoulders, to steady her.

"Thank you," I repeated, more emphatically, this time. "I appreciate the warning, and I assure you that I'll take it seriously. There are other people I need to consult, and other people I need to take into consideration..."

"I know that, sir," she interrupted, "and I know that the witch-child doesn't mean you any harm, or her mother either, but they can't help you any more than the islanders can."

That was bad news, if not entirely surprising. If the old women of the island who thought themselves "wise" were already referring to Elise as a "witch-child," then my assurances regarding her safety might not be as reliable as I assumed. Luzon was not yet old enough to be considered by herself or others as a "wise woman," but nor was she young enough to laugh at their like.

"There was no witchery involved in what happened to Dellacrusca," I assured her, for form's sake. "It was a simple matter of murder, for reasons of Imperial politics that are far beyond our understanding."

"That's what I'm saying, sir," she argued. "That's why there's no help that can be provided, until all this goes away."

Unlike Jean-Jacques, who had realized with perfect clarity that simply leaving the island would not constitute a safety measure unless I had somewhere safe to go, Luzon had a blinkered view of the situation, in which the danger was local and present, and merely had to be avoided by removing myself temporarily from its vicinity.

"You did well to tell me all that, Luzon," I told her, "and I really am grateful. You had best go back to the kitchen now, though. I can't leave the island today, but if I decide to do so, I'll inform you, and I'll be sure to confer with you and Jean-Jacques as to how the house can be maintained in my absence. I won't leave you without resources."

She almost told me that bluntly that she wasn't concerned about being left without resources, but simply for my safety, but her initial impulse had discharged most of its force, and she felt the weight of my judgment that it would be best for her to return to the kitchen. She went, leaving me in a state of even greater turmoil than before.

Hecate was expecting me, though, and since I'd decided to walk to town, time was beginning to creep up on me.

I set out, therefore, with a resolute stride. I half-expected Charles Parenot to surge forth from the Toustain house to say: "May I speak with you, Master Rathenius," but mercifully, he didn't seem to be ready, as yet, to add to the burden of my confusion. I deliberately refrained from looking at the windows of the house to see whether anyone was watching me from any of them.

The walk calmed me down. The even grayness of the sky and the chill of the sea breeze provided a compound of leaden oppression and iciness that seemed salutary in the circumstances. The sea was very calm, although far too dull to seem mirror-like. There were no small boats abroad in the stretch that was visible to me, but I could see the smoke of three steamships in the distance, whose hulls were mere blurs. They were evidently merchant vessels going about their normal business, serenely oblivious to the troubles of the island and the lingering after-effects of Hekla's eruption.

The great advantage of secret societies, I thought, from the point of view of non-initiates, was their resolute discretion, their determination not to trouble the surface of Imperial life. That determined appearance of everyday tranquility was a great asset to those whose only ambition was to live calmly, whether to carry out the quotidian labors of fishing and housekeeping, or to pursue the ambitions of art and music. And it did mean that, as Luzon assumed, once the temporary turbulence had run its violent course, things would ended return to normal, and the surface would be smoothed again.

Had the cook's view of the situation been correct, and I really could get out of danger simply by taking a boat to the mainland and waiting in some secluded spot for the internal strife within the Cult of Orpheus to run its course, and for the bone of contention that had arisen with regard to the adherents of the rival cult to be settled, than it really might have been possible for me to come back to Mnemosyne and resume the life that I had led there for three decades.

Unfortunately, there remained the other considerations, of which—hopefully at least—no one was aware but me. One way or another, I had to leave the island before much longer, and I would have to do my very best to leave as few loose ends behind me as possible, as well as working out exactly where I intended to go, and who I was going to pretend to be when I got there. Even at the very best, it was going to be a terrible wrench—and not just for me, it seemed.

Jean-Jacques and Luzon, I knew, would cope very well, if I kept my promise not to leave them without resources. The Parenots' problems would probably blow over too, provided that they did not get caught up in the violence, and provided that my judgment was accurate that Mariette would be able to persuade Charles to stay. There were doubtless others who would miss me, but in terms of a strict census of affections, the only one to whom I really owed any responsibility of affection or care was Hecate.

I had never intended to become as closely involved with Hecate as I had, and had assumed, with what had seemed at the time to be good reason, that once we ceased, by mutual agreement, to be lovers in the recklessly passionate sense, that we would simply drift apart and become irrelevant to one another, as former lovers generally do. That hadn't happened, although I was not at all sure why. I had somehow failed to notice, while the situation was developing, that we had not only remained on friendly terms, with a certain residual intimacy, but had also in some sense, remained dependant on one another. We had provided one another with something that we both needed, which went beyond appreciation of one another's artistry, and beyond the ease and affection we found in one another's company.

I didn't have any kind of label that I could apply to the bond between us, although it was certainly love of a kind, but I knew that the bond would not be easy to break. With my customary arrogance, I assumed that the inevitable break, when it eventually came, would be harder for her to bear then for me, but I wasn't foolish enough to underestimate the burden of my own probable regret.

In the town, the streets seemed strangely quiet. The influx of strangers was not visible in any ostentatious way. The people whose paths I crossed as I made my way through the outlying districts to Hecate's house were almost all familiar to me, even though vast majority were people I only knew by sight, some of whom did not even bother to acknowledge me. Although it was only mid-afternoon, and sunset was not yet imminent, the streets already seemed gloomy. Doubtless the port would have been busy, all the more so as the harbor was unusually full, but in the quarter where Hecate lived there was relatively little economic activity, and it seemed to have fallen into a state of dormancy already, the sky seeming even lower here than it had in the open country on the way from the headland.

Hecate's maidservant let me in, and conducted me directly to Hecate's boudoir, where she tended to receive me no matter what time of day it was, as a token of our intimacy and a symbolic assurance of our privacy. At least it avoided the problem of being offered tea.

I knew as soon as I stepped across the threshold that something was wrong, not so much by virtue of fact that she was pale as because of the way she looked at me.

"What's the matter?" I asked, sitting down in the armchair that she had already set out for me, facing her. Hecate poured us each a glass of some kind of cherry liqueur that she had ready to hand before answering, and when she did, she only said: "Nothing."

I judged from her tone that it wasn't a simple lie. For some reason or other, she couldn't spell out what it was that was wrong—not yet, at least. I wasn't certain how to proceed. I hesitated.

"If I asked you the same question," she said, "would I get the same answer?"

I glanced sideways into the mirror over Hecate's dressing-table, and saw that I looked as pale as she did, and just as anxious. I realized that if I were to answer the question honestly, the explanation would be long and complicated, and I wasn't quite ready to embark upon it yet.

"I'm worried," I confessed. "I feel that I'm out of my depth, and I don't know what to do. While I was finishing the triptych, I was able to distract myself, and even crating it up kept my attention busy. Now it's gone…I'm trying to evaluate my situation, and not making much headway,"

"Ah," she said, in a slightly cryptic tone. "Me too—trying to evaluate my situation, that is, and not making much headway."

I still didn't know how to proceed. "You sent Elise Parenot to see me, looking for answers to her anxieties," I said, in a neutral one. "Are yours similar?"

"I didn't send her," she replied. "I merely assured the child, when she asked me the question, that she could trust your judgment and your honesty. I wasn't mistaken in that, was I?"

"About the honesty, no. The judgment…I wish I could be certain."

"Are you ill, then?" she queried, trying to sound flippant and failing. "I never thought the day would come when I would hear Axel Rathenius doubting his judgment. Are you not the most intelligent man on the island, at least in your own estimation?"

"Perhaps—but there are circumstances in which anyone might be found wanting."

"But you did manage to reassure her, I hope? I couldn't, understandably."

"Why understandably? I would have thought you were ideally placed to give her sound advice?

"Because she classifies me with herself, as someone in need of protection and reassurance. How could she not, when she saw you race forward with her father to rescue both of us, during the mayhem at the Mesmay manse. Had you been content to shout a warning to me, so that I could rescue her, it might have been different."

That surprised me. "Are you really resentful that I came to fetch you?" I asked. "I told you at the time that it was a reflex action."

"And I told you at the time that I was grateful to the reflex. I admit that, as a frail woman, I couldn't have picked up the child and run with her, as Charles Parenot did—but even so, it diminished me in her eyes. That hasn't been entirely unfortunate, mind; it probably assists the ease of our collaboration, such as it is."

"I'm glad about that. I'm certain that it will be good for her, to work with you. I really didn't mean any insult, you know, when I tried to snatch you from the line of fire. Would you really have preferred if I'd seized the child and left you to follow me of your own accord?"

"I suppose not. Until that moment, I had never realized how deeply you cared about me. I suppose that I ought to be grateful to know."

My surprise must have shown, as I made no attempt to hide it. "Why would you not be glad to know," I asked her, letting my bewilderment show, "if, indeed, you were in any doubt about it?"

"How could I not be in doubt?" she countered. "I had always assumed that your attitude to me was casual—has it not always had that appearance?" Her tone was not bitter, but I couldn't make out precisely what it was, any more than I could decipher the expression on her face—which surprised me, given that I knew Hecate so well, and prided myself on the infallibility of my artist's eyes. There was sorrow in it, but also a hunt of resentment, of accusation. Of what, I wondered, did she think me culpable?

It was true I supposed, that I had never previously been in a situation where the revelatory reflex had been required to manifest itself in heroic action, so I had never demonstrated the reflex in question, but I could not believe that she really thought that my attitude toward her had been "casual."

"Is your attitude to me, then, as casual as you always strive to make it seem, superficially, in our banter?" I asked, warily.

"Of course," she said, with blatant insincerity. "I'm an essentially fickle and light-minded individual, as you know—and I had always assumed you to be the same, incapable of any deep-seated or long-lasting affection."

I suddenly felt the hook of a probe, but I wasn't sure what it was that she was fishing for. She was frequently provocative, of course, but usually in a spirit of artistic wit. This time, she actually seemed to be searching for something…but not something she wanted to find out; perhaps for confirmation of something she had already concluded.

I felt a sinking sensation in my abdomen, as I guessed what it probably was that that she wanted me to spell out, and why she was disappointed that I had never told her before.

"I don't consider myself to be fickle," I told her, defensively, trying to gain time while I orientated myself anew. "My sexual passions are not long-lasting, it's true, but that's because they're so closely tied to my art. I hate to be a cliché, but the simple fact is that I often become passionate about my models, and could not be as good a portraitist as I am if I did not. You know full well, however, that I don't act indiscriminately on such feelings, even when I suspect them to be reciprocated. Even when the passion dwindles, after a painting is finished, I'm perfectly capable of maintaining deep-seated and long-lasting affections, as you also know full well, or should."

"Other people might consider that the very definition of fickle," Hecate suggested. "What about Mariette? Will you act on that impulse, if you think it reciprocated when you paint her?"

I was startled by the change of subject, but I went with it, feeling momentarily incapable of resistance. "Mariette loves Charles," I said, in order to dismiss the issue, "and he loves her."

"Mariette has become dependent on Charles," Hecate corrected, "and Charles on Mariette, and they both prefer, naturally, to construe the fear that arises from that dependency as love. Doubtless it helps to maintain the edge of a passion that would otherwise have dwindled long ago. Did Elise not tell you that they have fallen out?"

"She did, and Mariette confirmed it—but I told Mariette..." I stopped, although I could not be breaking any confidence simply by repeating to Hecate what I had said to Mariette.

"What did you tell Mariette?" Hecate asked, a trifle sharply.

"I told her that she needn't worry, because she was certain to get her way in the end, precisely because he really does love her."

"Sometimes, Axel," she said, with a sigh, "the fact that you're the most intelligent man on the island doesn't prevent you from being a perfect fool. Parenot doesn't and cannot love her. He's addicted to her, in a way, and jealous of her, but he doesn't love her in the way she would like to be loved, and never has. It's more difficult to judge, but I think she's clearer in her own mind about the nature of her dependency on him. If you were of a mind to seduce her—as you surely would be if you ever did paint her—it would probably be akin to spearing fish in a barrel."

"And then there'd be one more man on the island lying in wait for me in order to stick a knife in my back," I said, trying desperately to make a joke of it. "Unless, of course, you'd like to even the score, in order to console him. He's a handsome man, after all."

Ordinarily, she would have gone along with that, but we were not living in ordinary times, and I regretted having said it, striking the wrong note in every possible way.

"I don't think I could," she said, softly. "Once, perhaps…but I'm too old now."

"Nonsense," I said, gallantly, but also sincerely. She was still beautiful. The sinking feeling in the pit of my stomach was, however, getting worse.

"When I first met you," she said, "I was young, and you seemed almost old enough to be my father, although that only made you more attractive, at the time. Now, we're the same age, more or less…and in another five years, I'll definitely be older."

She wasn't staring at me as she said it. There was no challenge or accusation in her tone. She didn't even look up in order to meet my eyes. But it was confirmation of what I'd suspected. I knew that she knew. Obviously, she'd given hints of suspicion before, but it had only been a suspicion, of something she couldn't really believe. Now, something had tipped the balance. She believed it. She was convinced. *She knew.* She wasn't going to say it out loud, perhaps because she wanted to reassure me that she intended to be discreet—so discreet that she wasn't even going to mention it to me—or perhaps she was simply disappointed that I'd kept the secret from her through all these years.

I realized, abruptly, why she could not be entirely grateful to discover how deep-seated my affection for her was.

I had not been looking forward to telling her that I had mentioned to Elise the possibility of leaving the island. In the event, I didn't have to. She brought it up herself. It was a natural consequence of the admission that she'd finally made to herself that her suspicions were true, and her realization of the corollaries of the fact.

"Have you come to say goodbye, Axel?" she asked, colorlessly

I hedged. Obviously, I should simply have said: "Not yet," but I wasn't quite ready to do that. In my confusion, I said: "What makes you think that?"

"Among other things, the fact that you think that Charles Parenot would only be *one more* man lying in wait to stab you in the back if you slept with his mistress. Without meaning to, Dellacrusca has compromised you both with the people who killed him and the people who want to avenge him. Wouldn't he be amused, if he knew?"

I tried to laugh, but couldn't. "No," I said, "he'd be angry with me too, because he would somehow talk himself into believing that I was somehow responsible for his mistake."

"Poor Axel," she said, with less sarcasm in her voice than she probably intended to inject. "misunderstood by everyone. Anyway, as you were evidently planning to leave the island soon in any case, I imagine that the present threat must have hastened your decision. That's why, when you came in with such a serious expression, weighed down by anxieties, I concluded that you had probably come to say goodbye."

"I didn't," I told her. "I'm not sure that it's come to that...yet."

"You mustn't worry about me," she said. "I understand why you can't offer to take me with you, and why I would have had to refuse if you had somehow been so foolish as to do so. It's probably better for me if you go sooner rather than later, in fact."

"Elise thinks that you're going to talk me out of it," I mentioned, unthinkingly.

She was startled. "You've told Elise you're leaving?" she said. "When?"

"I told her this morning that I'd been thinking about it," I said. "Then she told Mariette, who didn't seem to like the idea either."

"I told you so. If you had had the chance to paint her, you might have ended up being the fish in the barrel rather than the wielder of the spear...but it's not going to come to that, is it? Even if you didn't come here with the intention of saying goodbye today, the decision can't be long delayed."

"I don't know," I said. "I was almost ready to stay a while longer and take my chances with the Orpheans...until you weighed in on the side of those urging me to leave."

"There are sides, then?" she queried. "I'm the last person to know, apparently—it's perhaps as well I'd reasoned it out. You've taught me a great deal, you know, in the time we've known one another. I'll never be as clever as you, but at least I know your methods now."

"Is this the woman who was calling me a perfect fool only a few minutes ago?" I asked.

"Don't be silly, Axel," she said. "You know that no one's perfect; I was exaggerating. Does my opinion really count so heavily in the balance of your decision that it might actually tip it?"

"To tell the truth," I said, "I'm so confused now that I have no idea how the balance is going to tip. I need to think, carefully."

"Don't hesitate too long," she advised, "or you really might end up with a knife in your back. Did you know that Constable Clovis has doubled the night-guard and is trying to persuade the council to let him recruit extra deputies? He's expecting trouble, and soon. The poor fellow would like to stop it if he can, but he can't, of course."

"Clovis is a good man," I said, distractedly. "I like him. I hope he doesn't get caught in the crossfire."

"He might be an Orphean himself."

"Clovis? Never. An islander through and through."

"There were a number of men in the audience at that concert that I'd never have suspected until I saw them pull guns and started blazing away at those poor women, so I'm not making any further judgments."

"Poor women?" I queried. "You mean the machete-wielding bacchantes who nearly got you killed because you were standing between them and Dellacrusca?"

"I saw their eyes while you were carrying me off, in a very undignified posture. They were automata,

59

drugged and hypnotized. Whoever did that to them, and sent them to their deaths...I wouldn't have believed even a man like Dellacrusca capable of that. I certainly shan't be shedding any tears over *them* if they get killed in some impending bloodbath. Not that I'll ever find out who they were, though, or whether they've been killed or not. I suppose the likelier possibility is that most of the people mown down will be innocents like you...and me."

"You can't think that you're in any danger?" I said, uncertainly.

"I was there," she said. "It might not need anything more than that. Not that I said that to Elise, of course. I knew it was safe sending her to you, because I knew that you weren't even going to think it, let alone say it. You have a tendency to judge people by yourself, and think them more rational than they are. You've always made that mistake with me—for which I'm grateful, because it's helped me to become a little more rational than I was. As I say, I've learned your methods, even though I'm still as fickle as ever."

"I don't consider you to be fickle, either," I told her.

"Only because you have a self-serving definition of the term."

"I don't accept that. You're steadfast in your art, and in accepting the frequent brevity of your sexual passions you're merely honest. You're as capable of abiding love as I am." The moment I'd said it, I realized what a horrible mistake it was, given that she knew what I was. All I'd meant to imply was that I knew that she loved me, just as I loved her.

"If only," she said, wistfully.

There was no way I could make up for it. "I'll miss you terribly whenever I do go," I said, simply.

"You already do," she murmured. Then she pulled herself together. "Will you ever come back do you think?" she asked.

"I haven't even made a firm decision to go, yet," I retorted. "There'll be time for questions like that when I really do come to say goodbye."

"It might not be kind to drag it out, Axel," she said, softly. "God knows, I don't want you to go—but the reasoning that you taught me to do tells me that you really do need to go sooner than later. Don't let Mariette keep you hanging on too long—or Elise, come to that."

"I can assure you that I have no intention of seducing a twelve-year-old girl," I told her, deliberately misunderstanding her.

"I never thought you had," she replied, "but she's capable of making you hang on regardless. There's magic in that girl, whether you believe in magicians or not. If she puts a spell on you, you'll stay, whatever your reason tells you. Fortunately, she doesn't know that she has that power."

"People can't cast spells," I told her, stubbornly.

"Perhaps not consciously," she agreed, "but unconsciously…you can do that, Axel, although you'll never admit it to yourself."

I couldn't help shivering as I remembered what Myrica Mavor had said about my casting a spell, albeit unconsciously, that had brought about Dellacrusca's death. It was nonsense, of course…but sometimes, knowing that an accusation is nonsense isn't enough to get rid of every hint of suspicion.

"What spell have you ever seen me cast?" I asked, riskily.

"I've known you for a long time, Axel," she said. "I could cite more than one, but you'd just deny that it was you, or that the spells were spells at all. The apparition at Vashti's séance at the Mesmay manse for instance…was that really Vashti? Not her style at all, in my experience. I thought it was you at the time, and I still do. If it wasn't you, who was it?"

I had my own ideas about that, but I hadn't voiced them to Mariette and I was reluctant to voice them even to Hecate. I shrugged my shoulders.

"You think she's appeased, don't you?" Hecate followed up. "Eurydice, that is. Egotist as you are, you think that it was all about your painting, and that once you'd worked out, to your own satisfaction, what her complaint was, so that you could encode it in your vision, it was over. It's not. Ask any old witch on the island, and she'll tell you that the sky's dripping omens that have nothing to do with Hekla…except in the sense that the eruption was merely one more omen."

"Since when have you started listening to the old witches?" I asked her. "Didn't you think you'd performed your own ritual appeasement, when you recited your poem in the language of sighs? Do the old witches actually say that Eurydice is still making herself felt? Is Vashti still dreaming about her?"

I saw, when I made the latter remark, that I'd hit a nail of some sort on the head, if not quite the one at which I had been aiming. "That's it, isn't it?" I queried. "Vashti has said something to you. That's partly why you brought all this up. What does she think she's seen this time?"

"She doesn't know," admitted Hecate, defensively. "Not Eurydice, though. Violent nightmares about someone being torn to pieces and devoured, by ogres or ghouls, and his heart being taken away, and embedded in some poor woman's womb. She's frightened. She thinks that she's in danger—and that I am as well."

"It sounds like standard nightmare fare to me," I said. It was true—but I knew that even "standard nightmare fare" could have meaning, and artistry.

It was Hecate's turn to shrug.

"Well, for what it's worth, I'll take it into account in weighing up my decision," I told her, doing my best to assure her that Vashti Savage's nightmares weighed for very little in the balance pans of my intellect.

"Let's not quarrel, Axel," she said, once again harking back to her suspicion that this might be the last time that would see one another—that whether I was consciously aware of it or not, I had come to say goodbye. Perhaps she didn't believe it, and surely didn't want to believe it, but she couldn't shake the suspicion. If the skies really were dripping omens, she'd apparently caught a glimpse of one that scared her—or, more rationally, now that she had finally convinced herself of the suspicion she had been brooding for a long time, and understood why I had to leave the island, and why it might be kinder to her if I did, she was frightened by the simple fact of my impending absence, and the loneliness that she would feel in consequence.

"No," I said, "we shouldn't quarrel. We're old friends, after all—lovers still, in spite of…our fickle nature."

"Yes," she said, quietly. "We are."

"You're seeing Elise tomorrow, at the Toustain house?"

"Yes," she said.

"Then come over to my house afterwards," I said. "I might have made a decision, by then, and if I haven't…well, one way or another, we can be certain that this isn't goodbye, I don't want this to be goodbye. I don't know whether we have things to say to one another that we haven't said before, or at least understood between us, but we need a proper farewell, when the time comes, whether it's next week, next month or…whenever. You'll come, won't you?"

"Yes, of course," she said. "Always." She hesitated almost saying something else.

"What is it?" I asked gently.

"Nothing," she said. "I was wondering whether you could…explain it to me. But I know full well that you can't even explain it to yourself. There is no secret, no answer. It's just an enigma, isn't it?"

"Yes," I said. There wasn't anything to add.

The end of the conversation had saddened her further. She had lost her usual flippancy already, but her self-control had held her back from plunging too deeply into the morass of depression...

It saddened me, too, that she felt bad. She had been bound, I supposed, to accept the conclusion one day, no matter how absurd it seemed, but I hadn't wanted her to do it yet. I had wanted her to go on looking at me as she always had, with affection and amused tolerance, as a mere monster of arrogance, and not as an actual monster.

Now...well, obviously she didn't consider me a monster in any horrible or loathsome sense, but she knew now what I was not. She knew that I was not like her. She knew that she was not like me. I felt deeply sorry for her, and regretted the effect that knowledge would have...was already having.

If only, I thought, I really did have the power to cast spells and work magic. If only I really did have a secret, of which I could make strategic use.

I reached out and took her hand, and kissed it.

"I'm truly sorry," I said

"It's not your fault," she said.

"I kept it from you."

"I understand why you did that, too," she said. "You weren't being unkind. Quite the reverse. I have no right to feel disappointed that you didn't tell me. Please don't worry about me. I'm a little distressed for the moment, but I just need to think about it...with the aid of the reason that you've taught me. I'll be all right, really. Please don't worry...not about me, at any rate."

Perhaps there was some way I could have helped her feel better, but I didn't know what it was...and I needed to think. I thought that I would be better placed to settle things with her the following day. Or perhaps I was just a coward, who wanted to run away. How can I tell?

At any rate, I said: "Perhaps I'd better go now, my love; it's getting dark, and Jean-Jacques will worry if I'm late back, so I'll say *au revoir*, and I'll see you tomorrow."

She looked up at me, her pale face quite serene, with nothing in her gaze but a sorrow that I thought, egotistic fool that I was, perfectly understandable.

"*Adieu*, Axel," she replied, in a semi-automatic fashion that sent a slight chill down my spine, although it ought to have sent a far more powerful one.

IV. Attempted Assassination

I had been optimistic in saying that it was "nearly dark," although the sun was only just setting, and had the sky been clear there would still have been a gloriously colored brightness in the sky. The cloud was so dense, though, that it would have been almost pitch dark had the street-lamps not been lit.

I stood outside the house for several minutes, underneath one of the gas-lamps, trying to make a start on sorting out my confusion.

How many times, I wondered, had I said to Hecate, as if it were a joke: "I'm older than I look," deliberately making light of it, so that she would make light of it too, and think it a trivial matter. Tomorrow, I decided, I would tell her the whole truth: only the facts, of course, because I didn't have an explanation, but I would give her the details that I'd never told anyone else. I would tell her how I felt about it, and what difference it had made, for more than half a century, to how I had been able to feel about her, and everyone else.

That was preying on my mind to such an extent that it was quite difficult to pull my thoughts back to more immediate matters, to the present rather than the long past and the imminent future.

The thought of trying to walk back to the headland in the dark was not attractive, and even if I had had a lantern I would not have attempted it. I therefore decided, without any internal debate, to head directly for the port, intending to pick up a cab in the town square, where there were always two or three queued up.

At least, I would have headed there directly, had the layout of the streets permitted it; in fact, I had to cut through part of the quarter in which Hecate's house stood in order to reach the main thoroughfare.

The gaslight was not poor—not poor enough, at any rate, to give rise to any real cause for concern. It illuminated both the causeway and the sidewalk with a yellow radiance only slightly blurred by mist. What the street-lamps did not illuminate, however, were various coverts along the way, where there were gaps between the houses, coaching entrances and gates in garden fences.

I not only walked rapidly, therefore, but stepped off the sidewalk into the causeway, which was virtually free of traffic. I also kept my hand on the butt of my gun, ready to pull it out of my pocket in case of alarm. I couldn't help feeling slightly ridiculous as I did so, though. Despite my precautions, I had absolutely no expectation of trouble. In spite of all the mention made of the possibility during the day, I did not actually expect that there might be assassins lurking in any of the coverts, lying in wait for me.

I was on Mnemosyne, after all, where such things simply did not happen—although, of course, it was also a place where such things as the massacre at the Mesmay manse simply did not happen either…except that it had.

When a man suddenly stepped out of the shadows in front of me, therefore, holding a long knife, my first reaction was utter and complete shock—all the more so because the fact that I was walking in the roadway forced him to step out of the shadows completely, to show himself in the glare of the lamplight.

He was not wearing a mask; I could see his face quite clearly. There was nothing odd about his costume, which was that of a dock laborer, but I didn't recognize him. I had never seen him before. He was a stranger.

Perhaps the shock made me a fraction slow in pulling the revolver out of my pocket. Perhaps, too, I was maladroit, and didn't free the weapon from the pocket with the smoothness that would have been desirable, but I wasn't caught entirely unprepared, and I didn't freeze. As soon as I saw the assailant appear in front of me, I acted, and I kept my eyes on that long, menacing blade, ready to parry it with my free arm, if necessary, while I brought the gun to bear.

It was necessary.

The assassin moved rapidly, and purposefully, reaching out with the blade, holding it horizontally, at the level of my heart. I was struggling slightly with the gun, firstly to get it free of the pocket, then to cock the hammer, and then to bring it to bear, already thinking to myself that I might only get off one shot, and had better not miss.

It was not until the blade lashed out, and I tried to fend it away with my left arm, parrying it as if with a walking-stick—which I now regretted deeply not carrying—that I heard the sudden footsteps behind me, and realized that the man with the knife was not alone: that I was caught in a scissor-movement, and that even if I contrived to shoot the man in front of me, the man behind me would stab me in the back before I could turn to fire again.

I heard Hecate's regretful *adieu* ringing in my ears, ironically now, and knew that, in spite of all my skepticism, she had read the omens right.

I had no alternative. I had no viable course of action.

I did what any sane man would do, and screamed for help at the top of my voice, in order to raise the alarm, to tell all the people in the neighboring houses—all the islanders that, according to Jean-Jacques, would leap to my defense—that murder was being committed in their street, in the full glare of the gaslight. Even as I screamed, though, I knew that I was doomed, that I could not escape the trap.

I felt no pain as the knife glanced off my forearm, although I was aware of the blade slicing through my coat and the shirt beneath, and could not believe that it had not sliced the flesh too.

I aimed the revolver, as best I could in all possible haste, and fired

The gunshot seemed incredibly loud, and the recoil of the weapon was unexpectedly fierce, even though I had fired the gun before, and also larger ones, with a much more violent kick. I expected, at the next fraction of every interminable second, to feel the other knife plunging into my back, because I knew, and knew that the assassins knew, that there was nothing I could do to stop it.

The naked face of the man in front of me suddenly seemed very close, although he had lashed out at arm's length with the weapon—and not only did it seem very close, but it seemed hideously twisted, with amazement. And I thought: *I've hit him! He's shot!*

But he didn't fall, and he wasn't thrown backwards by the impact of the bullet, and I knew, instantly, that if I'd hit him at all, it was a glancing shot, and that, although every atom of my attention was focused on cocking the gun again, so that I could fire a second bullet, I knew in my heart that it was futile, that the knife would be plunging into my back at any moment, and that even if I managed to get off a second shot with the revolver, in either direction, the man in front of me would be able to plunge his own bloody knife again, fatally, before he could be hit for a second time.

I knew, in fact, that I was as good as dead. The scream had ended; I was out of breath. I would die in silence, even if I could get off that second shot...

Except that none of that happened.

The man in front of me had already turned to run away, as fast as his legs could carry him. He was dripping blood, as I seemed to be; my bullet had hit him somewhere, perhaps in the arm—which at least evened things up, since he really had raked my left forearm with his blade, and I could feel the dampness even though the pain was still delayed by shock.

Windows and doors were beginning to bang on either side of the street. Whistles were blowing to summon the night watch. People were shouting.

I turned round slowly, still half-expecting to feel a knife in my back at any second, and wondering whether perhaps the knife was already fatally embedded, but that shock had prevented me from feeling that pain too.

But I hadn't been stabbed, and I realized that I wasn't going to be.

The attacker that had come up behind me still had the blade in his hand, unbloodied, but he was lying on his back, bleeding copiously from a terrible head-wound. While he had been coming up behind me, swiftly, some-one had come up behind him, even more swiftly, and had smashed him over the head with a cudgel or a hammer, perhaps fracturing his skull, but at the very least knocking him out cold.

As for my rescuer, he had fled. I only caught the barest glimpse of him disappearing into a dark alleyway between two houses.

Then I felt weak, and sat down on the sidewalk. People began to surround me, but they seemed blurred, uncertain. They didn't know what to say or do. Eventually, a night-watchman grabbed my shoulder and shouted at me: "Which way did he go?"

I didn't answer, but one of the bystanders did, pointing in the direction which the first knifeman had fled. The night-watchman ran off, blowing his whistle stridently.

I had been recognized; I heard my name being repeated from mouth to mouth. The running night-watchman shouted at the bystanders as he ran, several of whom ran off with him. I wasn't tempted to join them.

Another night-watchman arrived, and Constable Clovis himself soon appeared in his wake, cursing volubly—which was most unusual for him, as he was normally very controlled and scrupulously polite. He crouched down beside me. He pointed to the man lying on his back. "Is he one of the attackers?" he demanded, in a sharp tone he'd never used to address me before.

"Yes," I told him.

"How many others were there?"

"Just one. I fired at him. I think I hit him, but he ran off. The watchman ran after him, with half a dozen others."

"Who hit that one?"

"I don't know, but whoever it was saved my life."

"Is he alive?" The last question was addressed to a group of people standing over the man bleeding from the head.

"I think so," one of them said.

"Pick him up, then, carefully, and carry him to the lock-up. Put him in the cell. Fetch Doctor Commonal, urgently—and don't take no for an answer. Tell him that Master Rathenius needs him." He turned back to me, and peered at my bloody forearm, anxiously.

The wound was beginning to sting now, and I could feel its length. "I don't think the cut is very deep," I told the worried constable, moving the hand to demonstrate that it was still fully functional.

"Can you walk?" he demanded

"Oh yes," I said, perhaps a little ambitiously. The arm didn't seem too bad, but I was still numb with residual shock

I tried to stand up. Clovis had to help me to my feet, but once I was upright, I found that I could, indeed, walk. We set off, a trifle unsteadily; I went with the constable meekly, assuming that he knew where he was going. He wanted to walk quickly, but I couldn't. He allowed me to slow him down, recovering his customary courtesy.

We were half way to the watch-station before I had pulled myself together sufficiently to ask, in a more plaintive tone than I intended: "What's happening, Clovis?"

He was walking close beside me, as if anxious that I might stumble and that he might have to catch me. "Not here, sir," he muttered. His eyes were restless, probing the residual shadows left by the gaslight, manifestly afraid of what they might conceal. He was exceedingly tense.

But of what did he have to be afraid? I wondered, somehow overlooking the fact that he might be anxious on my behalf.

I still couldn't believe for a moment that Clovis might an Orphean—but neither was I; I reflected that he probably had no reason to feel safe himself, if we were on the verge of a sly war.

When we finally got to the watch-post, the second attacker was already in the cell, apparently still unconscious. Fion Commonal was there, apparently about to examine the man. He looked up as I came in, and couldn't possibly have failed to recognize me, but he refused to meet my eye.

Unlike Clovis, I know that Fion *was* an Orphean; I realized that neither Clovis nor I could be certain that he wasn't an enemy, but for the moment, he certainly didn't look like someone to be feared. Quite the reverse; whereas the stolid Clovis was anxious but self-controlled, Fion looked terrified…like a man who feared to step out of doors lest he be attacked, as I had been. I remember Clovis' instruction to the men sent to fetch him not to take no for an answer.

Like me, Fion was an outsider, in terms of island reckoning, but he had been on Mnemosyne for more than ten years. He was part of its respectful society, a valuable man by virtue of his medical and surgical skill, and a well-liked man. I had long considered him a friend, and knew that he had long considered me in the same light. And now, I was looking at him, and wondering whether he was allied with the person or people who had commissioned my murder.

Even though he would not meet my eye, the doctor immediately left the unconscious man and came to tend to me. He and I had some difficulty getting my blood-stained coat and shirt off, because his right hand seemed almost as unsteady as mine, but once we had, and the wound was exposed, Fion's professional habit took over.

He cleaned the wound with cotton wool soaked in a stinging liquid, which set my teeth on edge, but was somehow reassuring in its abrasiveness.

"It's not deep," he pronounced, and I was glad to hear that he seemed genuinely relieved. "Be thankful that the fabric of your coat was thick, Axel."

With the ice broken, and Clovis standing at a respectful distance—although he was watching Commonal with a keen eye—I felt free to mutter: "What's going on, Fion? Who ordered me killed?"

In a whisper—although I was certain that Clovis wouldn't miss a word—he said: "I swear, Axel, that I don't know. Nobody knows…none of *us* is involved."

That was either a blatant lie, or gross self-deception. Perhaps the plot to kill Dellacrusca had been hatched in Lutèce, but its details and its execution had been wrought on the island, and whoever Fion Commonal meant by "us," some of them had to be in on it, in some capacity. I was, however, prepared to believe that he genuinely didn't know who—and that it was because he didn't know who that he was terrified.

"Alectryon?" I suggested, naming the most highly-placed aristocrat among the island's regular visitors. I wouldn't have identified him as a likely political conspirator, but I had once got on the wrong side of him, and he did seem to be the kind of man who would bear a grudge.

Fion went white. "Don't even think about it," he advised, faintly but urgently. He was obviously following his own advice; he literally did not even want to think about it. Plainly, Fion was an initiate in the Cult of Orpheus, but nothing more than that, even though he was the leader of the municipal council. He was not a political conspirator, not one of Dellacrusca's secret police. He was a local physician, caught up in something beyond his understanding.

Working rapidly, but with practiced method, the doctor put an antiseptic dressing on the cut, and wrapped the arm in a bandage, which he sealed with care.

"It will heal in a few days," he said. "You'll have a scar, but you'll be fine."

"Can you really guarantee that, Dr. Commonal?" Clovis put in, with a heavy irony that was as atypical of him as his earlier cursing and his continued anxiety.

Commonal wouldn't meet his eye, either. "The wound isn't serious," he insisted. "I'll call on you in two days, Axel, if I can, to change the dressing and make sure that all's well."

"And in the meantime," Clovis insisted, "would you advise Master Rathenius to stay indoors...or should he leave the island, perhaps, in the interests of his health?"

Fion looked agonized. "It might, perhaps, be advisable not to go out," he contrived, effortfully, "but beyond that, Constable, I really don't know."

"Perhaps you might advise him as to any company he might prefer to avoid, if his friends come to call, Dr. Commonal?" Clovis suggested, his voice replete with sarcastic challenge. He didn't expect an answer. He'd heard as clearly as I had that Fion genuinely did not want to think about it. A secret civil war between aristocrats might mean lucrative business for him...but only if he dared step outside his house himself, and provided that the wrong kind of friends didn't call on him there.

The Constable switched tack. "What can you tell me about the man in the cell, Doctor?"

"I've never seen him before," the physician said. "Whoever hit him definitely didn't want him getting up in a hurry. He's not dead yet, but I certainly can't guarantee that he'll ever wake up."

"I don't suppose he'll be in a talkative mood if he does," said Clovis. His tone implied that he was very conscious of the fact that, apart from the insatiable gossips who knew nothing reliably, no one on the island at present was in a talkative mood. "Don't you think, Dr. Communal, as leader of the town council, that it would be a good idea to declare a curfew, until further notice, and allow me to deputize a further twenty watchmen? You can safely leave the choice to me."

Fion licked his lips, perhaps regretting the decision to stand for the position he now occupied, which had always been a virtual sinecure in the past, associated with a very moderate hint of status. He didn't answer. He didn't want to make decisions at present, let alone take responsibility for them

"Unless, of course," Clovis put in, "you'd simply care to give me the authority here and now, so that I can do what seems necessary to keep what order I can?"

Clearly, Clovis, anxious as he might be, was prepared to step up and take the initiative. I didn't doubt that he could find twenty reliable men to deputize among the fishermen and harbor workers. There were no skilled and practiced assassins among them, but if Clovis decided that the island needed twenty burly fellows capable of defending themselves and others in a fight, he would find them.

"Yes," croaked Commonal. "Do it, Constable. Do what you think necessary. The council will back you— I'll sort that out…afterwards."

The last word, I supposed, was an instruction, or a plea, not to fail in the attempt to keep the peace. I didn't suppose for a moment that Clovis could guarantee that, but I trusted him to try.

"You'd best go home, then, Doctor," said the Constable, in a softer voice. "I'm sorry that I can't spare one of my men to escort you, but I'm a little overstretched until I can recruit those extra deputies tomorrow."

As it happened, one of the regular watchman came in at that moment, but Clovis simply took him to one side, turning his back on the doctor.

"I'm truly sorry, Axel." Fion said, as he packed his medical bag.

"I know, Fion," I said. "Take care of yourself."

With a rapid glance at Clovis, who was deep in whispered conversation with his watchman and no longer paying any attention to us, Fion leaned close to my ear and whispered: "Get off the island, if you can, Axel. Don't put your trust in the Constable to protect you. Otherwise, keep Jean-Jacques with you at all times, and go armed."

Then he went back to the cell momentarily, to check on the unconscious man. He looked at me, and shook his head—which I took to be a death sentence. Then he left.

The watchman disappeared into the night again, and Clovis returned his attention to me. He looked anxious again. I hadn't been able to grasp any of the report that the watchman had given him, but I had to suppose that the news wasn't good.

"What on earth are you doing wandering around in the dark, Master Rathenius?" he said, not quite succeeding in putting more compassion than anger into his tone.

There was no point in taking offense at the implication that it was partly my own fault that I'd been attacked. He was right.

"I was on my way to the square to get a cab home," I told him. "I'd been visiting Hecate Rain."

"You didn't bring your own carriage and your man-servant?"

"No," I said, ashamedly. "I walked. But it wasn't dark then."

"And you doubtless nodded a greeting to everyone you met," said the Constable. "Why didn't you simply carry a banner with the legend: *Easy prey*?" He normally spoke to me in a very respectful tone, and I couldn't help wondering whether that respect was now gone forever: whether he would never again think of me as anything but a fool.

I didn't say anything in reply. There didn't seem to be anything I could say. It wasn't as if I hadn't been warned, by Jean-Jacques and Luzon as well as by my own logical calculations. I simply hadn't taken the warnings seriously enough. I was a fool. I had known perfectly well that I was in danger, and yet, somehow I hadn't quite been able to believe it.

But someone had saved my life. I had no idea who, but someone had. While the assassins had been lying in wait for me, someone had been lying in wait for them—only one man, in fact, but, as it had turned out, one had been enough. Only just, but enough. I looked at the cell, where the unsuccessful assassin lay on the floor, unmoving.

"What's happening, Clovis?" I asked him. "Who's trying to kill me, and why?"

The constable sighed. "You're probably in a better position to answer that than I am, sir," he said, reverting to this normal respect, which apparently hadn't been banished forever. "In fact, I'd be very grateful for what you can tell me. You know the people better than I do, and you were at the Mesmay house when the murder I'm not supposed to know about happened. I really would like the benefit of your insight—it's been very valuable to me in the past, and the mere fact that someone just tried to kill you implies that someone's afraid of what you might say."

"I don't know anything for sure," I told him. "Dellacrusca came to see me shortly before he was killed, and he collected the document that his son had tricked me into finding for him, among the books Toustain bequeathed to me—a real poisoned chalice, alas. He bullied me into doing something else for him, but it was a purely personal matter, to do with his grand-daughter."

"The young musician—Elise?"

"Yes. I had nothing whatsoever to do with his polit-ical machinations, and I know nothing about the docu-ment except that I made copies of it to send to various people who might have been able to decipher it, since I couldn't. I had no more suspicion than Dellacrusca had that someone might be plotting to kill him. For what it may be worth, though, I don't believe that it was the Dionysians, in spite of the ludicrously theatrical way they went about it...do you know what happened at the Mesmays?"

Clovis shook his dead. "I've tried to find out, but can't catch more than the faintest hints. All the dead bodies have been spirited away, so I don't even know how many people died.

"Tommaso Dellacrusca told me that the nine at-tackers, all women, were all dead, and five men, pre-sumably all Dellacrusca's men, although one or two of them might simply have caught in the crossfire. Hecate Rain and the little girl nearly got caught that way, but

Parenot I pulled them out and ran like panicked rabbits. I didn't see any of the action, so there's not much I can add, I'm afraid. For what it's worth, though, the only way I can make sense of it is to interpret it as an internecine matter within the Orphean Cult."

"Others are saying the same, sir" said Clovis, uneasily. "You think the Dionysians aren't involved, then, even though rumor has it that Toustain was one of theirs?"

"It probably doesn't matter whether they were involved or not," I admitted. "The way the assassination was dressed up, and the fact that the document turned up when it did, must have dragged the Dionysians into it now, however reluctantly. It's possible that they might be looking to strike back at the Orpheans, if only to make a point."

Clovis nodded, uneasily. "Do you think the Sisters of Shalimar were involved, sir?" he asked.

I was genuinely surprised. Dellacrusca's killers had masqueraded as Sisters of Shalimar, after invading the convent, and I had sent the Mother Superior one of the copies of the document, thinking that she was one of the few scholars on the island likely to know what it might be, but I couldn't believe that she or any of her flock had been party to the murder.

"I really don't think so," I said.

"You know that the Superior is the Marquise de Mesmay's sister, though?"

I did. She had told me to herself. "Yes," I admitted, "but I really don't think…" I hesitated. "You don't think the *Marquise de Mesmay* was behind the plot do you…rather than her husband?"

"I really don't know what to think, sir," Clovis admitted. "That's why I'm asking you. You know the people involved, and you have a remarkably sharp eye."

"I don't know them very well," I murmured, "and the acuity of my vision might be more limited than you or I suppose."

"The rumors, sir," Clovis said, tentatively, "say that there was magic involved." He phrased the question delicately because he'd heard me discourse more than once on the theme of everything that happened being natural.

"Not in the murder," I told him. "That was brutally physical in every respect."

"But there was a séance, I've heard, at which Lord Dellacrusca was present, when Madame Savage conjured up some kind of malevolent spirit."

"There was an odd manifestation," I agreed, "but any significance it might have had was deeply enigmatic. Dellacrusca certainly didn't take it seriously—he accused me of contriving it by trickery. I didn't."

"Did Madame Savage?"

"No. She's not a charlatan. The voices she channels are her own, not those of ghosts, but she believes in her own art." I didn't mention that it hadn't been Vashti Savage's voice that had produced the sounds in question. I couldn't see that it was relevant. As I'd told Clovis, I didn't think that magic was in any way connected with Dellacrusca's murder.

Clovis didn't mention the discord produced by Elise's viola immediately before the maenads struck. Either he didn't know about it, or didn't consider it relevant. His thinking was, in any case, following a different and probably more relevant track.

"I agree with you, sir," he said, "that there was probably no magic involved in the actual violence, but some people *think* it was…and you know, of course, that some people on the island call you a sorcerer?"

"I'm not," I said.

"I know that, sir—but the point is that the belief that you are might support someone's belief that you had something to do with the murder, and thus provide a motive for what happened to you tonight. The Duc de Dellacrusca certainly didn't believe in magic, but…"

He left it for me to finish. "But the Marquise de Mesmay certainly does," I said. "And although the Cult, from Dellacrusca's viewpoint, was just a convenient mask for his covert machinations, there are doubtless people in it who take its mystical and magical affectations much more seriously…and might have resented Dellacrusca using it simply as a shield for his secret police."

"Yes, sir," the constable confirmed. Like Hecate, he might have been someone who had taken certain lessons from my method. He was not an educated man, in a formal sense, but he was intelligent, and he took his job as constable far more seriously than many of those who regarded him as a simple dolt paid to organize the watch and pick up drunks from the quays.

"There are times," I said, only a trifle hypocritically, "when I almost wish that I were a sorcerer. I wouldn't feel so helpless then. Unfortunately, we don't know, do we, what kind of magical beliefs the Orpheans might have, given that they're a mystery cult, and how those beliefs might lead them to act."

"No, sir," admitted Clovis ruefully. He seemed to be waiting for me to say something more. He had more faith in my powers of logic, at that moment, than I had, I was simply confessing helplessness, but he thought I was following a train of thought.

"But we do have some clues," I realized, thinking on my feet. "There was no magic in the murder, but there *was* ritual: the *pretence* of magic. I've been assuming that the use of a series of knife-wielding maenads was just an absurd attempt to put the blame for the killing on the Dionysians, or at least to create an apparent possibility that they were behind it—but perhaps it wasn't. The Dionysian cult, apparently, was once fused with the Orphean cult, and the rivalry between the two arose as a violent schism. Perhaps their most ancient rituals, and the beliefs connected with them, are still fundamentally similar. Perhaps Dellacrusca's murder really was a ritual slaughter of sorts—a holocaust. And just because Dellacrusca laughed off the apparent manifestation of Eurydice at Vashti's séance, it doesn't necessarily mean that someone who was present didn't take it perfectly seriously..."

I stopped there, but my mind kept going. *And if Dellacrusca thought that I was responsible for the manifestation, perhaps he wasn't the only one...except that the other might not have thought of it as trickery, but as genuine sorcery...*

Myrica Mavor had accused me, at least semiseriously, of contributing to Dellacrusca's death by means of the triptych. She was an idiot, and no one else had heard the casual remark that had encouraged her to make that suggestion, but it wasn't impossible that someone else, possessed of a different kind of idiocy, had reached a similar conclusion by a different route.

But what could I possibly do about it?

Everyone else had given me their opinion, and I had reason to believe that Clovis might be in a position to give me better advice than anyone else.

"Fion advised me before he left to get off the island," I told him. "He's not the only one to have given me that advice, some even more urgently—but Jean-Jacques thinks I'd be even less safe elsewhere than I am here. What do you think, Constable?"

"I don't know enough about what's happening to offer you good advice, sir," Clovis said scrupulously. "You know more than I do, and are a great deal more intelligent, so I'd be more inclined to trust your judgment than my own. But I will say that I'd appreciate it if you'd give me the chance to do everything I can to protect you. You're known here, and regarded as part of the community, even though you're not technically an islander. Here, I can try to make some provision for your defense. I don't have the men to do it at this moment, and even though I have Dr. Commonal's approval to recruit extra police, I can hardly organize an army—much as I'd like to get rid of the plague of outsiders that's threatening to turn Mnemosyne upside-down. I can't get rid of the rats in our walls, but it will help me greatly to do what I can if the honest people among the leisured class support me, and consent to my restrictions, starting with the curfew I intend to declare tomorrow. If you could use your influence to help me with that, sir, I'd be very grateful."

"Which means that you'd rather I stayed—and didn't even stay at home and kept me doors firmly bolted?" I said.

"I can only tell you what seems to be convenient for me, sir," he insisted. "You must make your own decisions about your own wellbeing. But if you wouldn't mind me offering one suggestion, I'd rather you didn't go home until the morning. The other man who attacked you got away. If he's wounded, it can't be serious. He undoubtedly has contacts on the island, and probably associates. The town is policed, after a fashion, but precisely because I need all my men to do that, I can't send you back to your own house with an armed escort. For myself, sir, I'd prefer it if you stayed here until daybreak, and I think you might be wise to do so."

"Here?" I queried, incredulously, my eyes automatically flicking to the cell.

There was the ghost of a smile on Clovis' face. "We can throw him in the harbor if necessary," he said, "but not necessarily *here*, specifically. Mademoiselle Rain's house is too far out, in my opinion, and I think you'd be reluctant to expose her to any danger your presence might cause. You have other friends, I know, who live nearby...although you might have to be careful in the selection. I do, however, have a watchman permanently on duty at the door of the Sprite, and I have absolute confidence, not only in Madame Auger but in the taproom regulars, who include half a dozen of the men I hope to recruit as deputies. Auger's not here, alas, because he's buying stock on the mainland, but his wife has two of her staff resident in the inn at present, Jacinth and Helen. I think you know both of them, although Helen has only recently returned to the island. You remember her, I suppose?"

I did, and quite well. I had known Helen for more than five years as a waitress in the Sprite, and had had vague plans at one time to ask her to pose for me, which had not come to fruition because she had run off to the mainland with a man—a fate by no means uncommon among the Sprite's younger waitresses. Apparently, the escapade hadn't worked out—as such escapades usually did not. Poor Helen was far from the first amorous runaway to come back to the island by way of retreat from disappointment, with or without a child in tow. Jacinth, I had also known for years, and although I had never been inspired to think of her as a subject for a portrait, she was a woman who inspired confidence.

"You want me to stay overnight at the Sprite?" I parried, uncertainly.

"It's not for me to give you instructions, sir," he said. "But I would feel more confident in my own mind if I knew that you had my watchman close at hand, and a company of sturdy dock-laborers, and also Madame Auger. She's a fearsome woman, as you know."

I did. I could understand he constable's thinking. He was no longer sure that he could trust Fion Commonal, or anyone else who might be an initiate of the Orphean cult, but the dock-workers he's known since childhood and the proprietress of the Sprite were a different matter.

"I can send for Jean-Jacques, if you wish," the constable offered. "I think I can send a messenger out to the headland safely, even though I can't be sure that you could follow the route securely, even in a cab."

"There's no need to drag him into town," I said, "but I'd be grateful if you'd send someone to let him know where I am, and that I'm safe. Ask him to make sure that the house is secure, and tell him that I'll be back first thing in the morning, once it's light."

"Very well, sir. I'll accompany you to the Sprite, if I may. It's only a few strides, I know, but I need to give instructions to the watchman, and have a word with Madame Auger."

"Of course," I said.

As I stood up, he looked me in the eyes, as man to man, and said: "I shall do my very best to keep the peace here, Master Rathenius. I don't know how many sides we're fighting against, or who they're fighting against among themselves, but I want to protect the islanders. I'd dearly like to show any and all incomers from the mainland, whatever their rank, that Mnemosyne is only a playground by our consent, to the limit we allow. I can't do that, alas, because I'm only a commoner, and can only call on commoners for assistance, but I intend to do my best to make sure that our women and children don't get hurt in the turmoil…or any of our resident artists."

He was not in a position to make any promises, I knew, but I certainly admired his determination. I had always known that he had steel in him, but I was glad to see it so evident now.

"Thank you, Clovis," I said, sincerely.

He locked the cell before we left, before checking to check to see whether its occupant still had a pulse. The would-be murderer was showing no sign of life, though, and I suspected that he was already dead. I'm not a vindictive person, but I admit that the thought gladdened my heart a little.

V. A Night in the Sprite

Madame Auger was in her most belligerent mood—
a mood that had more than once quelled potential brawls
in her tap-room.

"You'll be perfectly safe here, Master Rathenius,"
she assured me, when Clovis had explained what he
wanted of her and had returned to his duties. "I don't
have much confidence in the oaf outside, even though
Clovis thinks he's one of his best men, but Jacinth, Hel-
en and I sleep in shifts anyway, so that there's always
someone to answer the door if necessary. There'll always be one of us awake to raise the alarm, if necessary.
The whole quarter's been alerted by now—but you shot
the other assassin, did you not?"

"He was bleeding as he ran away," I confirmed,
"but his wound can't have been serious."

"Even so," said the redoubtable innkeeper, "he'll
have to go to ground. It won't do him any good. He'll be
lucky if Clovis gets to him before he's strung up, once
he's spotted."

I knew that her judgment wasn't a reflection of my
personal popularity; it was a manifestation of the same
patriotic pride that Clovis had voiced with such unusual
insistence. The inn was still crowded, as it was not yet
ten o'clock, but she had closed the upper room. When I
had arrived with Clovis, the rumor had already reached
the drinkers that I'd been attacked, and they seemed
genuinely indignant about it, especially old Nicodemus
Rham, the former lighthouse-keeper, who regarded me
as a special friend. He was far from the only one however, to assure me that no outsiders would be served in the

tap-room that night and that no one would come upstairs, even if they turned up at the door in numbers and heavily armed. Nor was Nicodemus the only one who volunteered to stand guard all night.

I thanked them all sincerely, and assured them that there was no need for anyone to lose sleep on my account.

Madame Auger offered me a similar assurance that no one would be able to use the wrought-iron spiral staircase that served as a service stair either. "I've locked the steel door giving that stairway access to the cellar, sir," she told me. And I'll lock the door at the end of your corridor too."

She escorted me up to the bedroom, although I knew the way very well. I'd been in it many times before, most recently because it was the one in which Myrica often stayed during her briefer visits to the island, and occasionally, in times past, for amorous purposes.

"Can you send up some supper, please?" I asked her. "Bread and a little cold meat, and a carafe of wine, perhaps?"

"I can do better than that," she said. "You shall have some hot soup, as well as the bread and meat, good red wine and a glass of brandy, to restore the blood you've lost."

Madame Auger had always had an abundant faith in the curative and salutary properties of alcohol, as befit an innkeeper's wife. If asked, she would always point out that Fion Commonal was one of her most regular clients, whereas she had never had occasion to call on his services.

Helen brought up the tray bearing all the promised comestibles. I hadn't seen her for a long time, and when she looked at me questioningly before turning to go, I told her to stay.

I studied her by the lamplight, with my expert eye. She was tall, slightly buxom, with dark hair, dark eyes and a sun-tanned complexion. It seemed to me more likely that her amorous adventure had taken her to the Midi than the misty Nord. "Yes," I said, "you certainly haven't suffered as a result of your absence. I was going to ask you pose for me, you know, before you disappeared."

She was startled. "Really, sir?" she said "Why?"

"I had been waiting patiently for years for your youthful beauty to reach full flower," I said. "And then, just as it did, you were gone. Evidently, I was not the only person taking an interest in its progress."

She blushed. "You're flattering me, sir," she said.

"I'm telling you the truth," I assured her. "I've painted many island girls over the years, you know—it might be the aristocratic summer visitors who pay me exorbitant sums to depict their wives and daughters, and sometimes even their sons and themselves, but when I paint for myself...or, at least, for work to send to my agent to put in her gallery and hawk to collectors in the capital, I look for beauty everywhere that it can be found. I'm truly glad to see you again—I only wish it were in calmer times, when I could safely make my long-delayed request."

She didn't know what to say to that, and simply stood there, in confusion.

"Madame Auger says that she'll force you to stand sentry duty for part of the night," I remarked. "I'm sorry about that—it's not my wish."

"Oh, I don't mind, sir," she said, as she was bound to do. "She always wants one of us to be awake, in case of late callers—and old Nicodemus is insisting that there ought to be at least three men sleeping in the tap-room. It's terrible, what happened to you. I'll be more than happy to stay up all night, if necessary."

I wasn't sure whether or not that was an offer to keep me company, or, if it was, whether or not the order had come from her employer, but I had no intention of taking advantage of her.

"You seem to have come home at an unfortunate time," I observed. "I'm sorry that your…adventure didn't work out."

The lamplight illuminated a hint of a wry smile. "Home is home," she remarked. "The trouble will blow over, I dare say. I was fortunate to get my old job back, given the season, but Madame always had a soft spot for me. All things considered, I'm lucky."

"So am I," I conceded. "Lucky to be alive, tonight. If I'd only had my wisdom to rely on, I'd be dead." I looked at her questioningly.

She understood what I meant, and why I was en-quiring. "The news is all over town. Two outsiders at-tacked you, but one of the islanders stepped in to help—no one seems to know who it was, though, or they'd be hailing him as a hero. The whole town is up in arms about it. You've been here a long time, and you're reck-oned as one of ours. If Clovis had his way, half the boats in the harbor would be gone on the night tide, warned off with the suggestion that they don't come back, but the likes of us can't tell aristocrats and their hirelings what to do. If the cultists want to settle their differences, the local folk would far rather they did it elsewhere, but what can we do?"

"You know about the cultists, then?"

"Not really. Nobody knows, or even wants to know—that's just summer visitors' games, so far as we're concerned. We like the artists, even the eccentric ones, because they're mild and peaceful, but the rest...the Dellacruscas and the Alectryons, even the ones that settle, like Mesmay...they're a different breed. We take their money, because feeding our children would be hard without it, but we've never liked them. We know that you work for them too, but...well, we've always assumed that you don't like them any better than we do."

"Some of them are pleasant enough," I said, mildly, although I didn't feel any very strong incentive to leap to their defense, "and some are very beautiful...but I can understand how you feel, and I'm truly glad that you feel slightly differently about me. If I find out who it was who saved my life, I'll be delighted to shake his hand."

She had already asserted that no one knew who the man was, and apparently had no further speculation to add. Whatever rumor was going round was probably an avid assumption, with no evidential basis. Personally, I thought that if my savior really had been an islander, he wouldn't have disappeared so promptly after doing his good deed, but would have been only too glad to claim due credit. There did not seem to be any point in debating that question with a waitress, however

Helen moved toward the door, saying: "If that's all, sir?" There was a slight wariness in her gaze, as if she half-expected that it might not be all, and that she might perhaps apprehensive about what the rest might be. I guessed that she had probably taken my comments about her beauty and my one-time intention to paint her as a clumsy amorous ploy rather than a simple statement of fact.

"Yes, that's all," I said. "Thank you—for everything."

"You're welcome, sir," she said, and disappeared.

I finished the meal, but lingered over the wine, while mulling over what had surely been one of the strangest days in my entire life...although there had, admittedly, been a lot of strange days recently. I had certainly never experienced a day on which I had received such a drastic surfeit of advice, from so many different quarters, in such dramatic conflict.

The crucial decision was, of course, still unmade, and the fact that I now knew what so many other people thought I ought to do didn't make it any easier to decide, even though the decision I had ultimately to make was a matter of when to go rather than whether to go. I had to leave, eventually...but perhaps not until I had painted Elise, and Mariette, and even Helen...and perhaps, if Hecate could be trusted, although it was not a subject on which her judgment was ever entirely reliable, had set out to seduce or to be seduced by Mariette, or even by Helen...

But that train of thought was far too self-indulgent, and I set it firmly side, instructing myself to focus on practical matters, and principally on the fact that next time someone attempted to kill me, if someone did, there might not be an obliging stranger to hand to thwart their design.

Oddly enough, though, even though I had a slashed arm to offer myself as proof, I was still having difficulty believing that someone actually did want to have me killed. It seemed so absurd, and not simply because I knew that I hadn't done anything to warrant anyone being angry with me. I really couldn't believe that anyone would want to have anyone killed for the reasons that

Constable Clovis had suggested as the possible motive for the attack on me. Sorcery? The apparition at Vashti's séance? The Marquise de Mesmay? It all seemed too ludicrous for words, and I simply could not comprehend that anyone could see it from a mind-set in which it did not seem ludicrous.

And yet, the strange manner in which Dellacrusca had been murdered might make more sense in that interpretation than it did as an attempt to cast suspicion on the Dionysians, let alone the supposition that the apparent bacchantes might really have been Dionysians, out of their minds on the drugs that the Dionysians were reputed to employ in their version of "the Mysteries"—the celebrations that had given birth to the term "bacchanal."

I wanted to think about that. Indeed, I wanted to think about it intently, because I desperately wanted to understand what might be happening around me, in order to decide what I needed to do about it, but I was tired, and it was becoming increasingly difficult to think straight, especially in the midst of such a tangle of ideas.

I stood up and went to the window, and opened it to let in a little cold nocturnal air, to enliven myself. I took the glass of bandy with me, which I hadn't touched as yet, and began to sip it, very discreetly, as I stood at the window looking out.

The room overlooked the quay and the harbor. Ordinarily, the quay would have been relatively quiet at that hour, even on evenings where there as a pre-dawn tide that some of the fishermen would want to catch, but the harbor was unusually crowded, with boats of all kinds, and beyond the harbor wall the funnels of larger ships were visible, including a handful of ocean-going vessels. The docks were correspondingly busy, taking full advantage of the recently-enhanced gaslight, which allowed boats bringing supplies and merchandise to the island to unload at any hour of the night. It seemed to me, however, that the harbor area was unusually crowded, even when that activity was taken into account. I could see one of Clovis' watchmen patrolling, but he seemed a fragile figure in the context of the extent of the waterside and the various groups strung out along it.

It was a pity, I thought, that Clovis was not only short of personnel, but that his hands were effectively tied. If the reported attack on me had triggered as much indignation as Nicodemus, Madame Auger and even Helen had implied, perhaps the constable could have mustered a ragged army of sorts, and burly islanders might have started suggesting, with varying degrees of subtlety, to many of the incomers who had flooded into the port in the last few days that it would be greatly appreciated if they went elsewhere. Alas, Helen was correct. The aristocrats and the cultists could, in effect, do as they liked, and if they wanted to use the island as a battleground, all Clovis could really do was try to make sure that no women, children or artists were caught in the middle.

For me, alas, it was too late. I was already in the middle, with no direction in which to turn.

In ordinary times, the nocturnal activity around the harbor would have seemed mildly unusual but of no consequence whatsoever; following my shock and injury, however, I could hardly help perceiving it as something sinister, as a shadowy reservoir of possible threats. Again, my reaction to that perception was a stubborn resistance to its absurdity. I was simultaneously apprehensive and ashamed of the seeming ludicrousness of my apprehension.

The island was normally such a quiet and peaceful place—but it was precisely because it was such a haven of peace, I realized, that the trouble was brewing now. It was Mnemosyne's remoteness and placidity that had lured the cultists here, as well as the artists. When the Marquis and Marquise de Mesmay had decided to move permanently to the island, I remembered, and had commissioned the building of their manse, I had thought that it was a simple case of a lover of art abandoning the hectic life of the capital. I had thought it a good thing, and I knew that I had not been the only artist who thought that Mesmay might be a useful source of commissions. We had hoped, fools that we were, that it might be the beginning of a trend.

Now, it seemed, I had to think of the Mesmay manse as a kind of fortress, an outpost of one of the Empire's deadliest factions. I did not know which one, though. Were the Mesmays among Dellacrusca's closest allies, as they must have seemed to be to him, or had they, in fact, taken advantage of his unusual visit to the island, for purposes that had caused him to let down his guard, in order to attempt a coup? And if that were really the case, what would happen now that the coup had lost its apparent organizer and leader? The Mesmay house was not an isolated example; there were half a dozen potential "fortresses" scattered over the island where incomers might set out to organize their own militias, if they were so minded. How many factions might develop within the ranks of the Cult of Orpheus, now that its former unity had been so suddenly shattered?

What a mess! I thought. *What an unholy mess!*

I hoped that Jean-Jacques and Luzon would be safe. I hoped that the Parenots would be safe too, given that, if Clovis was right in his tentative reading of the situation, then Elise might not be as immune from possible harm as I had assumed that morning. And if anyone apart from me knew, as I thought I did, that it had been Mariette, not Vashti or me, who had been the focal point of the apparition at the séance, then she too might not be secure from suspicion of sorcery and involvement of some kind in the massacre at the Mesmay manse. She had, after all, been present before it began, in close company with me, at Dellacrusca's insistence and Mesmay's invitation. That might well be more than enough to attract unwelcome attention capable of blossoming into crazy suspicion, from the kind of people who believed that Vashti Savage really could summon shades from the Underworld and that whatever secret rituals the Cult of Orpheus still practiced really did have the power to activate mysterious gods.

Perhaps, I thought, Charles Parenot and I ought to make fortresses of our neighboring houses, as best we could, and make our preparations to stand off violent enmity, if necessary.

And Hecate...

But the thought of Hecate immediately brought back a thought that promptly eclipsed all others: the manner in which she had said *adieu*. I had not thought it unduly significant at the time, even though I had known full well that Hecate believed herself to be capable of experiencing premonitions. Because I had never taken them seriously, she had stopped telling me about them...but I surely ought to have realized, should I not, that her strange insistence that I had come say goodbye must have been significant of some nightmare of her own, rather than the one she had attributed to Vashti Savage?

I wished now that I had stayed with her, that I had questioned her more closely, that I had brought out into the open the subject of my longevity, which she had so carefully refused to spell out. I wished that I had tried to explain, to the extent that I could explain. I wished that I had attempt a more earnest discussion of all kinds of matters that we had always covered, even in the most intimate circumstances, with a contrived gloss of flippancy and wit, as befit the artists that we were, the poseurs that we were...

Tomorrow, I told myself. *When you see her tomorrow, you can repair the fault...*

But she had said *adieu*, as if she could not believe that tomorrow would come, even if she could not believe either—or could not confess that she believed—that whatever dream or nightmare she had had was anything but a silly delusion...

Except, of course, I remained myself, sternly, that whatever she had glimpsed on the edge of consciousness really did have to be a delusion. Her premonitions were not real premonitions. The spirits with whom Vashti Savage conversed were not real spirits. The gods of the Cult of Orpheus were not real gods. Whatever had been strangely manifest as Eurydice at Madame Mesmay's séance had not really been the Eurydice that the musician Orpheus had loved, and had gone to the unreal realm of the unreal Hades to redeem...

Whatever the manifestation had really been, though, it *had* been real.

One way or another, there was magic in this business—and what that magic might yet do was, at least so far as I was concerned, impossible to guess.

The brandy, perhaps surprisingly, did not seem to be Auger's best, and I had been sipping it unusually slowly, but when I decided to turn away from the window and close it I drank the remainder in a single draught, in order to be rid of it, and to add an emphatic punctuation mark to the entire day. It was only then that I noticed its slightly peculiar aftertaste. I didn't recognize it, but my mind might well have jumped to the conclusion I eventually reached, much later, if it had not been so tired and befuddled.

As things were, I merely registered that something was wrong: something that might perhaps be alarming.

Then I lay down on the bed, fully dressed, set my head on the pillow, and went gratefully to sleep.

VI. At Sea

I have no real memory of what I now know to have been the next three days. I think that I was aware of them at the time, in a fragmentary fashion, but that my mind erased the fragments of real perception along with the hallucinatory visions, treating them all, by default, as if they were dreams that ought not to be preserved. A few residual impressions survive, but they remain vague and fugitive. I do have the distinct impression, however, that I returned to semi-consciousness wanting to die, because I felt so horribly ill.

How difficult and arduous it was to get past that desire simply not to be suffering, I cannot tell, but I can't imagine that it went away without a fight. It presumably ebbed away slowly, confused by all kinds of perceptions and ideas that reemerged, in direly disordered fashion, by slow and tortuous degrees. There was a long period, which might well have seemed interminable while I was actually living through it, when I was suspended in a strange dream-state in which the desire to die, to get away from the atrocious headache I was suffering, and, above all the gut-wrenching nausea, overrode any possibility of arranging other thoughts in any kind of consequential train.

Alongside those very real physical feelings, there must have been all kinds of hallucinations and nightmares that seemed terrible in their own right, but which I refused as best I could to entertain.

Somewhere along the way, I must have become aware of seeing Helen's face, and feeling the touch of her hand, which must initially have given me the idea

100

that I was still in bed in the upper room of the Sprite, and that the primitive décor of which I continually caught glimpses had to be a product of dreaming. One way or another, however, the realization that I was not in the Sprite must have formed more definitely, and stuck, because, by the time that something resembling normal consciousness did return, and regain some coherency and the faculty of memory, I already knew that I was a long way from the Sprite, and a long way for Mnemosyne. I already had it firmly established in my mind that the bizarre décor was as real as Helen was, and that I actually was lying in a bunk in a tiny cabin aboard a ship...

I knew all that in my nightmare before I became rationally conscious of it, and had doubtless tried, unavailingly, to grapple with it in my fragmentary delirium.

It was only when I began to think more clearly, however, already being in possession of those and a handful of other facts, that the corollary realization occurred to me that I wasn't vomiting continually because of the after-effects of the drug with which the treacherous Helen must have dosed my brandy, but because I was seasick.

Seasick!

The ignominy was almost as unbearable as the agony. Perhaps, in retrospect, the fact that I was able to feel that ignominy should have reassured me of my returned sanity, and the proper organization of my feelings, but at the time, it just seemed to be an extension of my misery. It is one thing to be seasick on a pleasure cruise, but quite another to be seasick when you are in the process of being kidnapped, when you really need your wits about you. A circumstance like that can really make a person feel disappointed with themselves.

But no matter: once I had realized that I was sea-sick, and had no proper excuse for thinking that I wanted to die, I began to concentrate my efforts on trying to get a grip on my situation, on trying to evaluate it properly, on at least making preparation for a time when I might be able to act positively and constructively again.

At first, when Helen persistently tried to feed me with a spoon, my foolish assumption must have been that she might be trying to poison me again, and I vaguely remember resisting, as best I could, more forcefully than might have been warranted by the mere conviction that if I ate something I might start vomiting again. Eventually, however, I accepted that she really was trying to feed me in order to nourish me, and that she had also been trying to induce me to swallow medicine of some sort, in order to calm my nausea.

Unfortunately, as she subsequently explained to me, the cocktail with which she had been trying to calm the nausea was sailors' laudanum—rum and opium—mixed with powdered clay, which was supposed to line my stomach. Perhaps it had—but the laudanum she had actually forced into me, more successfully than any food, had certainly prolonged and intensified my nightmares as well as supposedly numbing my pain.

The clay had, however, eventually collaborated with the passage of time to stop the vomiting, and also stop the perceived agony in my arm, which must surely have been delusory, given that the cut really was not serious. When I was finally capable of checking the bandage, I found that the dressing had been changed—presumably by Helen herself rather than some matelot barber-surgeon—but merely for the sake of hygiene, not because any complication had set in.

Had I dreamed about being torn apart and being devoured, in memory of the nightmare Hecate had reported to me, and had I connected that with the wound in my arm? Perhaps—I later found reasons to think that I might have done so, but I cannot lay claim to any memory of it. All I remember is having been convinced that my arm had hurt, but that the pain had eased, and been obliterated.

Presumably, I had moderately extensive verbal exchanges with Helen long before the conversations that I can actually remember, which might have included a good deal of incoherent rambling on my part, as well as a certain amount of accusative abuse, but she presumably restricted herself, during the missing three days of my life to trying to calm me down, and to assuring me that I would eventually recover my sense of wellbeing and ability to think. She cannot have attempted any kind of explanation while I was still in no state to understand it. Eventually, though, when my head did clear sufficiently for me to maintain continuity of consciousness and the capacity for coherent thought, she was immediately anxious to offer me an explanation of sorts, if only to excuse her treachery.

In the first conversation of which I have a coherent memory, she was beside the bunk, sitting on the floor of the cabin, and she seemed seriously anxious about the manner in which I was looking at her, presumably because she could read something of the anger in my gaze.

"You poisoned me," I croaked, accusingly. "I wanted to paint you"—somehow that seemed at the time to make what she had done to me far worse—"and you poisoned me."

"I'm sorry," she said.

"And you've kidnapped me."

"I'm truly sorry," she said, again. She really did sound sorry, but I remember that I didn't believe her. I thought it was further treachery

"Did Madame Auger put you up to it?" I asked, while I tried to get all the questions I wanted to ask into some kind of rational order."

"No, no!" she said. "Don't think that. I'm the only one who betrayed you—the only one. I betrayed her too. She'll never forgive me."

After a long pause, I said: "Why did you do it, then?"

"I'm under orders," she told me. "I'm truly sorry, but I do sincerely believe that the orders were given in order to save your life. We didn't have time, you see, and Clovis was interfering, not wanting you to go home...we had modify the plan and move fast. We were fortunate that he chose the Sprite, rather than some other lodging—but please don't blame him either, or the men standing sentry with Nicodemus Rham. I had the key to the doors on the service stairs; they never saw anything. Clovis, Madame Auger and Nicodemus had no idea that I was...well, not what I was pretending to be."

There was too much there for me yet to be able to take in all at once. I began at the beginning.

"Orders? What orders?"

Her answer was evasive, and lacking in clarity. "I can't pretend to know the thinking behind the orders," she said, "but if there had been another way...if it had been practicable simply to tell you what danger you were in and ask you to come away...but we thought...I thought...that you wouldn't agree to leave the island."

"Whose orders?" I persisted—but she was following her own train of thought.

"It seemed safer as well as simpler just to take you. There are things I have to tell you. Firstly, at the risk of annoying you further, you're not going to be able to leave this cabin during the journey..."

I looked around. The cabin seemed strangely familiar. I say "strangely" because I didn't know at that moment that I'd already been in it for three days. It also seemed odd, perhaps because it looked antique, like a cabin on some ancient sailing ship although one of the elements of my atrocious headache—which had not disappeared complexly, although it was more an ache than a pulverization—was the monotonous throb of a team engine whose vibrations were shaking all the timbers. It was a very narrow cabin, ill-lit by dull daylight coming through a round porthole above the bed, and it reeked of some kind of disinfectant fluid. Evidently, my illness had necessitated a good deal of cleaning up—but I thought, unkindly, that the five years she had spent as a skivvy in the Sprite before her mysterious disappearance must have accustomed Helen to that kind of labor. It was, however, a cabin of sorts, and I knew that common sailors generally had much worse accommodation. It was an officer's cabin.

"I'm a prisoner," I judged, baldly.

"In a manner of speaking—but your confinement is purely because we don't want you to be able to recognize the ship you're on, or any of its crew. That's a testament to our good faith—our intention of doing you no harm and giving you the option to return to the Empire if you wish, when...well, when you can. It's a precaution, so that you can't reveal the identity of our agents or means of transport. Except me, obviously—I'm compromised now. I can never go back to Mnemosyne again."

I took time to reflect, as best I could, on that torrent of information. Eventually, I said: "And the only reason you came back this time was to kidnap me?"

She hesitated, but eventually said: "Among other things, yes."

It was obvious that there was a great deal that she wasn't telling me, and had no intention of telling me.

"You were sent because I knew you...because I would trust you."

"It wasn't supposed to work out as it did," she said, weakly. "But yes. I was supposed to make the approach, to facilitate the removal. When Clovis threw you into my lap...I'd just been placed in the Sprite as a matter of convenience...we couldn't know it would turn out to be as convenient as it did...although operating under Madame Auger's nose, and getting you out through the cellar to evade the watchman...believe me, it would have been easier if things had gone to plan."

"Were you always a...spy? Even before?"

She was close enough to touch, and she had been leaning forward slightly, watching me anxiously, but she recoiled slightly, and couldn't meet my eye, when I asked that question.

"Yes," she admitted.

I put two and two together, and hoped that it was the correct four. "For the Cult of Dionysus?"

After a long hesitation, she simply said: "Yes."

"You were placed in the Sprite for all those years to monitor the island's summer visitors," I deduced, "or at least the Orpheans among them."

"Yes."

My mind seemed to be working effectively again, in spite of the residual headache and the fact that I felt so weak, physically, that I would not have dared attempt to get out of the bunk.

"And you didn't run away with some man three years ago," I continued. "You were transferred to some other location by the Cult?"

"Yes."

"And were sent back in a hurry after the Dellacrusca massacre, because you knew the territory?"

"Yes."

For the time being, she seemed to have decided that monosyllabic answers were all that was required, and seemed quite glad that I was able to frame the questions that elicited them, saving her the burden of constructing an elaborate narrative of her own.

"With orders to kidnap me?" I concluded, checking to make sure that I was working toward the correct conclusions. "Allegedly for my own safety? That's what you were told?"

"Yes."

I was sick of the string of simple affirmatives by then, for reasons that had nothing to do with the after-effects of my seasickness. "For the sake of all the gods," I said, "*why?* And don't just say because you thought I was in danger: I want to know why."

She must have tired of the pattern herself, because she suddenly became voluble.

"Because Mesmay thought you were a Dionysian. He probably thought so even before Toustain left you his books. That may be partly why he gave you the commission for the triptych…in order to have the opportunity to investigate you more closely—but once that stupid notary broadcast the news that Toustain was a Dionysian renegade, Mesmay became convinced of your involvement, and probably anxious, in case it affected his plans.

The fact that Dellacrusca visited you to recover the piece of parchment must have increased his anxieties. If Dellacrusca hadn't killed him..."

"What!" I interrupted. "*Dellacrusca* killed Mesmay? Not the fake bacchantes?"

She seemed momentarily surprised that I didn't know. "Yes. I suppose you must have run away by then. That last gasp on the Duc's part seems to have thrown terrible disarray into the rebel ranks..."

"Just a second," I said, as my head began to reel again. I had to pull myself together, to insist, sternly, that I needed to think clearly and hard. "So Mesmay really was behind the plot to kill Dellacrusca?"

"It seems so. We didn't know beforehand, obviously, but...well, anyway, when the bacchantes appeared, it only took Dellacrusca a matter of seconds to guess who had betrayed him, and to get his last gesture in. Had he not done that, of course, Mesmay would have continued to play the ally, and his wife presumably tried to do that anyway, trying to pass off what Dellacrusca had done as a result of accident, confusion or error."

"Tommaso Dellacrusca didn't say anything about that when he came to see me," I put in, more in an attempt to organize my own ideas than to communicate the information to her.

"He wouldn't. We don't know for sure, obviously, but we assume that the twins couldn't take Mesmay's people on there and then, having no way of knowing how many they'd have against them if they tried, or who they might be able to trust, so they beat a retreat— swiftly. Frankly, I'm surprised he paid you a visit before taking ship."

Tommaso and Lorenzo, I supposed, must have wanted to make sure that I'd got Elise out safely, and that she'd be out of harm's way for the time being, while their own faction regrouped and tried to weigh up who might be for them and who was against.

"From our viewpoint," Helen went on, "it might have been better if they'd started an all-out battle there and then, and at least killed the Marquise, but they probably didn't even know for sure whether she was involved."

"But she was?" I remembered her visit to my studio, and the peculiarity of her behavior, which I'd put down to grief at the loss of her husband. Now, I wondered if it ought to have interpreted it, even at the time, in another fashion.

"Definitely," Helen confirmed. "And she, unlike Dellacrusca—perhaps even unlike Mesmay—is a believer."

"In what?"

"In the warped dogmas of her cult. In her ability to work magic, or at least to provoke magic. Mesmay probably secured his co-conspirators with the aid of purely materialistic incentives, but now he's gone, and the revolt needs a new leader…her notion of the importance of the impending celebration of the Mysteries surely extends far beyond using it as a cover for vulgar plotting. If she intends to rally support for her own leadership, she'll appeal to the other believers."

The Duc d'Alectryon, I remembered, was a believer of sorts, albeit a reluctant one. Family tragedies had sent him to consult Vashti Savage, just as they had sent the Marquise de Mesmay. If she were in desperate need of support for her husband's foundering cause, Alectryon had the status and the influence to secure it. If she could persuade him to join forces with her…

It was all too vague and far too complicated.

"And you?" I queried. "Are you a *believer?*"

She didn't answer the question. Instead, she said: "We knew we had to move fast, and hope that we could arrive in time to get you away before Mesmay's faction figured out a new pecking-order and got their own troops in order. We were very nearly too late, as you know."

"It was one of your men who pole-axed the fellow who was trying to stab me in the back?"

"One of ours, yes. He's on the ship, but I can't allow you to shake his hand."

"But I'm not a Dionysian," I said, a trifle plaintively. "Why do you care? Why, for that matter, would Mesmay think I was, even before Toustain handed me the poisoned chalice?"

"Toustain probably did that because he'd drawn the same conclusion. It wasn't your fault...you weren't to know."

I was becoming seriously confused, and not yet feeling up to the challenge of sorting it out by means of logic.

"But I have nothing to do with the Dionysians," I said. "I never have."

"I know," Helen admitted.

"So why have you tried to save me? Why bother?"

"I can't tell you that."

"Because you don't know, or because of your orders? *Whose* orders?

"I can't tell you that. She'll tell you herself, when the time comes. She'll explain everything, and then you'll understand."

"*She?*"

"I can't tell you anymore."

"Where are we going?"

"I can't tell you that, either." Her expression seemed genuinely distraught, as if the orders she'd been given were proving distinctly uncomfortable, now that I had caught up with my situation sufficiently to ask probing question that were digging into delicate issues. She made as if to rise to her feet and leave, but she changed her mind. She decided to stick it out and get it over with, at least settling what she could and needed to tell me. She did seem genuinely concerned about me. She had known me for a long time, albeit in a purely casual fashion.

"What's going to happen to me when I get to wherever it is we're going?" I asked. "At least tell me that."

"It will be explained," she repeated. "I'm sorry, Master Rathenius, I truly am."

"I believe you," I said, deciding that a change of strategy was in order. "If you're telling the truth, I suppose I ought to thank you—you and your companions. I hope you'll understand why, for the moment, I'm unable to feel as grateful as you probably think I ought to be...and why I don't feel that I can take everything you've told me on trust."

"Yes, I do," she said, seemingly relieved at the admission. After a pause, she added: "Did you really intend to ask me to pose for you?"

"Yes."

"And that was why you sometimes looked at me...strangely?"

"There wasn't anything in the least strange about it," I assured her. "I was studying you, committing you to memory. If I'd had a sketch pad..." I stopped, realizing that there was a certain chagrin in her expression.

She saw that I'd seen her reaction, and muttered a muffled curse. "I thought you might have realized that I was spying on you," she explained. "That's not the only reason I left...but it was part of it. If I'd realized that you were just making mental sketches..."

I was puzzled. "I thought you were spying on the Orpheans, not on me?"

"I was, but I was also instructed to report on other interesting incidents and people. Sometimes, orders came back adding further names to the list of people of interest. Yours was added...almost certainly on the basis of mentions I made of you in my reports."

"You suspected me of being a Orphean?"

"No, certainly not."

"So why were you interested in me?"

"It wasn't me who was interested."

"*Her*, then?"

"I assume so."

"Why?"

Her expression was positively agonized. "I can't tell you that."

"But it's the same reason why the Marquis of Mesmay thought I might be a member of your cult, since he knew full well that I wasn't a member of his?"

"Probably," she conceded.

It was my turn to suppress a curse. Again, putting two and two together, there was one four that stood out more than the other possibilities. I'd stayed on the island too long. Hecate had worked it out because she knew me so well, but she'd been slow to convert the suspicion into a certainty, precisely because she knew me so well. If Mesmay, and other people, had had a different spectrum of possibilities from which to work, they might have jumped to the conclusion much sooner. And the Marquise believed in magic, or at least in mysteries. It might have seemed to make more sense to them, once they suspected my mysterious longevity, than it ever had to me. I wasn't at all convinced that any sense that the Marquis and Marquise de Mesmay thought they'd made of it really would be sense, rather than nonsense, but nevertheless...

Helen was watching me. She knew that I'd dawn a conclusion, and she probably had some inkling of what it was, but she wasn't supposed to talk about it. *She*—the other she—would explain. I was looking forward to meeting *her*. I could hardly wait, in fact.

"How long is this accursed sea voyage going to last?" I asked the waitress-cum-spy. "In fact, come to that, how long as it lasted already?"

"We're three days out," she told me.

"*Three days!*"

"You've been ill," she reminded me.

I looked around the tiny cabin again, and took another sniff of the disinfectant atmosphere. The lavatorial facilities left a great deal to be desired, but Helen had obviously gone to a great deal of trouble to keep the effects of my illness under control. I lifted up the blanket that was covering me to check my clothing. I was wearing what looked like a sailor's jersey and trousers, and nothing else. Fortunately, it wasn't cold. I deduced that we hadn't been sailing north since leaving Mnemosyne. In fact, when I glanced again at the daylight creeping rather than streaming through the small porthole above the bunk, I got the impression that the weather was clear, although I couldn't actually see blue sky.

"What time is it?" I asked.

"Late afternoon," she said.

I tried to estimate the direction of the sunbeams shining obliquely through the porthole. Soon, I supposed, they would be red-tinted, as the sun began to set.

I worked out that we were probably traveling south-eastwards. The throbbing engines definitely confirmed that we were aboard a steamer, but the wooden walls of the cabin were also definitely old, rotting in places and splintering in others. The evidence suggested that the vessel was far too old actually to have been built as a steamer. She was a converted sailing ship, which undoubtedly still had her masts and rigging as well as a funnel.

I couldn't be certain, but my guess, even then, was that if we weren't going all the way to the New World, we were probably making for the mid-Oceanic archipelago. That wasn't a lot of help, as what I knew about the mid-Oceanic archipelago was negligible. The islands had never been colonized. They were marked on world-maps I'd seen as "uninhabited," but world maps were not always accurate in regard to their legends, especially when they contented themselves with the modern equivalents of such traditional commentaries as "Here be Dragons."

"How much longer will it be before we get there?" I asked.

"Another three days."

Without being able to estimate our speed and to be more precise about our direction, it was impossible to be sure, but that seemed to fit reasonably will with the assumption about the mid-Oceanic archipelago. I was glad to find that I was reasoning with apparent cogency, even though my head hurt and I felt as weak as a kitten.

"How long have the Cult of Dionysus had a base in the mid-Oceanic archipelago?" I asked the lovely spy.

"I'm not sure," she said, evidently feeling no need to contradict or challenge my assumption. "About two thousand years, I think."

"*Two thousand years?*" I exclaimed, in much the same tone of amazement with which I had earlier said "three days," and probably with far more reason. "Founded by Dionysus himself, then?" I asked skeptically.

"I don't believe so. I think he was long dead by then."

"Like Orpheus?"

"Like Orpheus."

"But not torn apart by bacchantes, presumably?"

"I can't tell you anything touching on the Mysteries. You'll be initiated, with your consent."

"You've been initiated?"

"Yes."

"Before you became a spy in the Sprite?"

"Yes."

"But you're an islander. How on earth did you get involved with the cult?"

"I was born to parents who were members."

"Are there many islanders in the cult?"

"I can't tell you that."

"Of course not." I furrowed my brow. "But if this mysterious *She* is six days' journey from Mnemosyne by steamer, how do orders get back and forth between here and the empire? There wasn't time for next of Dellacrusca's death to get there, and for any kind of message to get back."

"We have a telegraph cable," she announced, serenely.

I almost repeated that in the same tone as the two implausible durations. The Empire was parsimonious with its telegraph cables; they were invaluable to the administration of the political leviathan, and precisely for that reason, carefully controlled. Dellacrusca must have had an entire network at his back and call, though, probably carefully built-up under his own direction. I had to suppose, therefore, that it was only reasonable that the members of the rival cult to the one that had been his instrument would have a network of their own.

"I'm glad you're feeling better," Helen said, apparently feeling free to get to her feet now, although she must have known that I hadn't run out of questions, and was only pausing for thought. "I was afraid for a little while yesterday that I'd given you too much laudanum. I'm responsible for you. If anything happened to you…well, I'm glad it hasn't. I'll bring you some food, and fresh water, hot and cold. Your own clothes might be fit to wear again, now. I can't make things any more comfortable for you than they are, alas, but you'll find it much more comfortable on the island, I promise you. It's very pleasant there…quite lovely. I really am truly sorry, about everything, but I really do believe that you'll end up thanking me, for everything."

She left. I heard a bolt click into place after she shut the door.

I was dubious about her assurance that I'd end up thanking her for everything, given that she'd exposed me to a nasty bout of seasickness, but the fact remained that whoever had given her the orders she'd received had already saved my life once. There didn't seem, in any case, to be anything I could do, except accept my fate meekly. There was no point trying to escape from imprisonment in my cabin, given that I couldn't get off the ship.

I was still a little queasy, but I managed to eat and drink, when Helen brought the promised food, and to wash myself with the aid of the water she supplied.

Afterwards, I managed to stand up, stretch my limbs and even perform a few exercises. Then I stood on the bunk and studied the sea through the porthole for a while. I watched the sun go down ahead and to starboard of our course.

The night that fell thereafter was replete with stars, which seemed oddly comforting, given that I hadn't seen so many for quite a while, living in the dust-shadow of Hekla's violent eruption.

The only lamp I had was a simple stout candle secured in a cracked glass frame whose small panes were held in a network of lead, and I was almost tempted not to light it, given that I had nothing I particularly needed to see. I made a metal note to ask Helen whether she could at least let me have a book or two to read, assuming that there were some on board. I did light it in the end, though, in order not to be alone in the dark, and to help me think while I sat on the end of the bunk, with my chin balanced in the palms of my hands and my elbows on my knees.

"All in all," I said to myself—speaking aloud but softly, although I couldn't hear my voice very well above the annoying throb of the ship's engines—"it could be worse. I would have had to leave the island soon in any case, having already stayed far too long, it seems, and I had nowhere in particular to go, so where I'm going might well be as good as a place as any. Jean-Jacques and Luzon will be left somewhat at a loss, but since the island to which I'm going has a telegraph link to someone on Mnemosyne, I might be able to get a message to them, and to make some provision for their resources. Hecate was already reconciled to my leaving, and we've said our farewell, even though I wasn't quite conscious of doing so. If my disappearance seems mysterious to all my other acquaintances…well, I suppose it will add to my reputation, in a way. Clovis, Nicodemus and Madame Auger will be cursing, but they might simply think that I've run away with Helen, because I did mention that I wanted to paint her before she disappeared, and that might save her from a certain amount of wrath. As long as what she's told me is all true, things *might* be working out for the best…as long as there are no more strange surprises to come."

But there were.

Almost on cue, I heard a mysterious voice speaking to me from the wall beyond the foot of my bed, saying, with seemingly desperate urgency: "Master Rathenius! Master Rathenius!"

VII. Company in Misery

It is surprising how even the most skeptical mind, faced with surprising but perfectly natural circumstances, will initially reach for a supernatural explanation, before sanity and reason take over. My first thought was that the voice really was coming out of nowhere, from some space beyond our world. But the wall from which it was coming was sufficiently shadowed from the meager light of my lantern for me to be able to make out a chink of light coming through a fissure, and it dawned on me belatedly that the voice was coming from a cabin next door, situated flush with the side of the ship, exactly like the one that I was in.

It was not until I had realized that it was the voice of a real person, however, and someone who knew my name, that I recognized the voice, and deduced that I was not the only prisoner that the Dionysian mission of which Helen was a member had kidnapped from Mnemosyne.

I suppressed a groan.

I bounded to the chink, although the sudden movement made my head spin again, and I nearly fell over before I reached the partition. Presumably, there had already been a natural crack there, but I guessed immediately that the person on the other side of the wall must have been working to enlarge it for some time—perhaps three whole days, while I lay on my bunk, a miserable retching wreck—probably with the aid of a fragment of glass detached from the lantern she had, similar to mine but equally dilapidated.

At least, I thought, she hadn't been able to see me clearly or fully while I was in the disgusting state from which I was only just beginning to recover—at least I hoped not. I hoped that she had only just contrived to make the crack large enough to see through with any range or clarity.

I put my mouth close to the crack.

"Mariette?" I queried. "Is that really you?"

"Yes," said the voice. "It really is you, then?" The voice was faint, but distinct, as if she were deliberately keeping it low while trying to make certain that what she was saying could be heard and understood.

I had to bend down to put my eye to the crack, and when I did I could see very little. There was a lamp like mine lit in a cabin like mine, but it was behind Mariette, just as mine was now behind me, and I could see nothing but a vague silhouette, with just a hint of facial features. When I had been sitting on the bunk, she must have been able to see a great deal more of me, and of the cabin, but it was understandable that she had been unsure when she recognized me, not just because of the poor light and my peculiar costume, but because it must have been difficult for her to believe her eyes—difficult to be sure that I was not some kind of illusion or apparition.

Indeed, I couldn't help wondering whether she might be an illusion, and whether I really had woken up from my three-day lapse of continuity…or whether I ever would.

"It's me," I assured her. "I can't say that I feel quite myself, at the moment, but…" My voice trailed off as my mind lost track of what I was saying. My head was reeling again. Standing up so abruptly, in the wake of my surprise, had renewed the feelings of distress in my

120

head and my body to such an extent that I seemed to be hovering on the brink of nausea and incapacity.

I had to lean on the wall in order to prop myself up, but my mind continued working stubbornly against the tide of confusion and oblivion that seemed to be trying to drown it, trying to grapple with the knowledge that I was not alone on the mysterious steamship, and the awareness that Helen had not mentioned that item of information to me, evidently by design.

"Are you alone?" I managed to croak. I had already guessed the answer, but I needed confirmation. I didn't know whether I ought to hope to be right or wrong.

"No—Elise is with me. You sound terrible, Axel. What have they done to you?" She sounded frightened. She was undoubtedly frightened on her own account, I knew, and doubly frightened for Elise, but the discovery of my presence must, I thought, have given her a surge of relief—false relief, in a sense, since it did not make her own situation any better, but relief nevertheless. Now, the thought that my presence might only be a sign of further threat...

"They haven't done anything to me," I hastened to say. "I'm feeling ill, but it's not serious. They haven't mistreated you?"

"You don't call being drugged, kidnapped and locked in a tiny cabin mistreatment? But no. The woman—the only person I've seen—keeps pleading with us to believe that they don't mean us any harm, that it's all for our own good. But she didn't tell us that you were next door, which might have done us more good than all the rest of her babbling put together...except that that's selfish of me, isn't it, to hope that someone else...anyone else...might be sharing our captivity..."

121

The support of the wall was enabling my head to stabilize, allowing my train of thought to become steadier, but I hardly dared change position, even to make my stance a little more comfortable, once I had straightened up. I could no longer peer through the crack, but as long as we could hear one another's voices, I thought, we had what was necessary: the communication that was akin to a lifeline, the guarantee that we had company in our misery.

As she had said, it was selfish, but how could either us help grasping that thought desperately, as a consolation of sorts?

"Is there anyone else, do you think?" Mariette's voice asked.

"I don't know." I said, and tried to keep my voice firm, to sound like my normal self—and, behind it, to think like my normal self. I went on, because I thought it was necessary to go on, if only to try to recover more of my normal self, by degrees. "I'll ask Helen, but she's annoyingly sparing with information. If she didn't mention you because she wasn't supposed to tell me, she's not going to tell me about anyone else."

"The woman who brings us our food and water and takes our bucket away is named Helen?"

"Yes." I had to pause after the single syllable.

"And you know her?"

I took several deep breaths. I told myself, sternly, that I had to make an effort, for my own sake, and for hers. I had a responsibility now, not just to myself. "Yes," I said. "She was a waitress in the Sprite for several years...and, it seems, a Dionysian spy." I paused, and then added: "Is Elise all right?"

"She's been ill, but she seems to be getting better. She's asleep now—which is why I'm whispering. She'll be glad to know that you're here too, but she'll be ashamed of being glad, as I am...even if she's able to believe that these people really are saving us from people who meant to harm us."

"She told you that?"

"Yes, but she wouldn't explain who they're supposed to be or why they wanted to hurt us. She keeps saying that someone else will explain, when we arrive...except that she won't tell us where we're going. It's Dionysians who've kidnapped us, then? She wouldn't even tell us that."

"Apparently. It might be unwise to believe everything she tells us, but yes, I can't see any plausible alternative." After a pause, I added: "She drugged my brandy in the Sprite, and presumably let her friends in, to spirit me away through the cellar in spite of the watchman at the door and the belated customers in the tap-room. She knew the layout of the place well, of course."

"And she told you, as she told us, that she did it to save your life?"

"Yes."

"Is it true, do you think?"

"Quite possibly. They've certainly saved my life once, when Orphean agents ambushed me. The frustratingly partial explanation she's given me does suggest reasons why the Orpheans wanted me dead, and why the Dionysians had to move quickly to get me out of harm's way."

"And what about us?"

Pulling myself together seemed to be working. My sense of responsibility seemed to be taking hold. I thought I could keep talking with a reasonable fluency and a reasonable clarity.

"I don't know. What she's said so far doesn't explain why you might have been at risk, and in urgent need of rescue, but I can glimpse vague possibilities. I was hasty a few days ago when I tried to reassure you and Elise that you weren't in danger. I might have underestimated the craziness of our enemies." I paused. I didn't want to lie to her, even by omission. If it was my fault that she and Elise were there, she had a right to know it. "On the other hand," I added, regretfully, "it might be my fault you were at risk, and your association with me, brief as it was, that made you suspect."

Mariette didn't seem unduly concerned about that. She was focused on more immediate concerns. "But when the woman told us that she was saving our lives, she meant it?"

"I think so."

There was a pause while Mariette thought about that. "It doesn't excuse their method," she said, accurately enough.

I wasn't about to start pleading elaborately on Helen's behalf shat she and her associates—especially the mysterious other *She*—really had been very pressed for time, and not at all sure what our reaction might be if they had contented themselves with a warning, an explanation and an invitation to go with them. I did put in one suggestion, though: "They didn't want our presumed enemies to be able to follow us. They didn't want anyone to know where we'd gone."

I thought, but didn't add: *Or anyone else*. I was thinking, on her behalf, about Charles, but I realized that there were other interested parties, as well as our would-be murderers and our loved ones. If Mariette had enemies within the troubled ranks of the Orpheans, Elise, at least, might have friends there too. Tommaso and Lorenzo Dellacrusca were presumably going to be annoyed when they discovered that their niece and her adoptive mother had disappeared, and might easily jump to an erroneous conclusion as to who was responsible and why.

"I don't know they managed to take us," Mariette said, her voice sounding hoarse now, as if the effort of whispering were putting a strain on it. "They must have drugged our food somehow. I hope Charles is all right. If they left him behind, he'll be in danger, won't he?"

"I don't know. I'll ask Helen. Now that I know that you're here, I hope that she'll be prepared to tell me whether Charles is here too…and why they left him behind, if he isn't."

"Do you have any idea where we're going?" Mariette asked.

"An island in mid-Ocean, I think, half way to the New World. There's an archipelago shown as uninhabited on the Empire's maps. Apparently it was actually settled two thousand years ago by the Dionysians."

"Two thousand years? By Dionysus himself?"

"That was my immediate reaction, although I realized instantly that it must be foolish. Helen said that he was long dead by then."

I knew that I was thinking more clearly and constructively because my train of thought ran on. Now that regular trans-Oceanic trade with the Iroquois Federation had been established, the Oceanic archipelagoes would become potentially significant as ports of call for long-rang merchant ships. Anything hidden there wouldn't remain hidden long. It was by no means implausible that a Dionysian colony in mid-Ocean might have remained secret until recently, for reasons of simple lack of interest, but times were changing, as evidenced by the spread of clandestine telegraph cables as well as trans-Oceanic trade. A new era was beginning.

"If they really are trying to save our lives, why?" Mariette asked. "What interest do they have in us?"

"I don't know," I said, reflexively, before remembering that I owed it to her, in our present situation, not to lie, or conceal anything...but then I hesitated, and the habit of long decades kicked in, and I hedged, awkwardly. "That is, I can guess why they're interested in me, but why they're interested in you..."

The awkward moment didn't arise. She didn't pick up on the first part of the statement, but only the second. "It's Elise, isn't it?" she said, cutting me off. "They want Elise."

"Probably," I admitted.

"Because she's Dellacrusca's granddaughter?"

I hesitated. If Helen was lying, or even if she wasn't telling me the whole truth, as she clearly wasn't, there was a possibility that Elise might be a pawn in the game by virtue of being Tommaso and Lorenzo's niece. I remembered that Tommaso had taken the trouble, after his father's murder, to make sure that she was out of harm's way.

"Possibly," I said—but I had delayed too long.

"But you don't think so?" she was quick to conclude.

"I don't know what to think," I told her, honestly enough.

"That's not good enough, Axel," she told me, her whisper taking on a sharp edge. She was right. It wasn't.

"All I know for sure," I said, "is that the Orpheans are more credulous than I thought. If Helen can be trusted, the Marquis de Mesmay jumped to the conclusion some time ago that I really am a sorcerer, and thought that I had custody of a precious secret."

Again, my train of thought ran on. Thinking back now to the questions that Mesmay was asking, and the ideas he was putting into my head the last time he had come to see the triptych, I was able to glimpse his hidden agenda. I had thought his behavior odd at the time, just as I had thought his widow's later contact odd, but I hadn't been able to find the key that would enable me to make sense of it. Now I could see that he probably had believed that I was a Dionysian, and not in the sense that I was just an agent of a political organization opposed to Dellacrusca's. He had thought that I had access to arcane knowledge, and power, and that I might have to be handled with great care.

"And Elise?" Mariette persisted. I knew that she had her own ideas about the possibility of Elise having magical powers, or at least being haunted.

"If Mesmay and his wife were convinced believers in magic and mystery," I told her, "it would have been easy enough for them to believe that Elise's talent for music was magical in nature. And..." I had to pause in order to clear my throat, for purely physical reasons, but Mariette thought that I was deliberately hesitating.

"And?" she prompted, with some slight annoyance in her tone.

"And they might have concluded at Vashti Savage's séance that you had mediumistic powers considerably greater than Vashti's."

"What! Why?" She genuinely didn't know. She didn't know that the apparition of Eurydice had usurped her voice, had issued its apparent lament from the depths of her being. She hadn't been consciously aware that it was her voice that had made manifest the language of sighs.

"It's a chain of absurdities, I know," I said, weakly, "but the Mesmays seem to have been rather vulnerable to the absurd."

There was a silence while she tried to follow the chain of logic to its conclusion.

"So you think that the Dionysians might also believe that Elise and I have magical powers?" she said, by way of summary. "*Both* of us?"

"It's possible."

"And what will happen when they find out that we don't?"

As a skeptic, I was, of course, committed to the notion that whatever had happened to them in the past was a natural phenomenon of some kind, but its manifestations nevertheless remained peculiar. Within the framework of the Dionysians' mystical beliefs, both Elise and Mariette might indeed have magical "powers," albeit powers beyond conscious control. That wasn't a discussion I was yet capable of having, though, while my head was still aching, and my thoughts were only very precariously under conscious control. I opted for a simpler answer.

"I don't know, but it's not your fault. They can't hold it against you."

Her silence suggested that she wasn't so sure.

"If Helen is telling the truth," I proffered, by way of attempted reassurance, "the fact that they're keeping us prisoner, to prevent us from identifying the ship or its crew at some indeterminate time in the future, is evidence of the fact that they do intend to set us free at some stage. I don't see why they would wish us any harm, even if their hopes are disappointed. They already

128

know that I can't work miracles, since they had to step in to save me from being killed when I foolishly walked into an Orphean ambush."

"Well," she said, after a further pause. "I suppose that should set some of my worst fears at rest...if, as you say, your Helen is telling the truth. Things could be wore—although the facilities here certainly leave a lot to be desired. And even though Elise and I are slim, that bunk really isn't big enough for two."

"Do you have some way of blocking this chink?"

"Blocking it? Why would I want to...oh...believe me, Master Rathenius, modesty is not high on my list of priorities, at the moment. And you're a gentleman, after all...not to mention that, as the crack is at my eye height, not yours, you'll get a terrible crick in your neck if you try to peep through it for any length of time. Elise can't quite reach, but I'll probably be able to see everything when you aren't blocking the view yourself, so you're the one at a disadvantage..."

I suspect that she almost added that she wasn't a lady, but I'd told her more than once that I didn't like to hear her insulting herself

A few seconds later, she said: "I'm very glad to find you here, Axel. I thought we were alone. It's selfish, as I said, but I feel a great deal better now."

"Perhaps Charles is here too," I suggested. "Perhaps we ought both to work on the opposite walls of our cabins."

"Or you could just ask your friend," she suggested. "As you said, now that the secret is out, she surely can't have any objection to telling you whether you have any more companions, can she? Except...they don't have any reason to think that Charles has magical powers too, do they?"

So far as I knew, they didn't. "I'll press Helen for answers next time I see her," I told her. "If I'm clever enough, I ought to be able to worm more out of her than she wants to reveal. If I can muster all my charm and my authority..."

"She's a pretty woman," Mariette observed, "and she obviously has access to better washing facilities than the soap and bowls she brings us. Was there something between you, when you knew her before?"

"No," I said, slightly surprised by the question.

"Did you ever paint her?"

"No." I didn't think it necessary to tell her that I had wanted to.

"She's a lovely woman, though."

"Are you suggesting that I try to seduce her in order to obtain more information from her?" I enquired, warily.

"No. It was just an observation. Has she told you how much longer this wretched voyage is going to last?"

"Three days, apparently."

She groaned faintly.

"I've been dreadfully seasick for the last three days," I told her, although that confession was perhaps unnecessary too. "I still don't feel well, even though I'm finally beginning to be able to think clearly again."

"That's probably what was wrong with Elise," Mariette told me. "At first I thought it was just the after-effects of the drug, but it's gone on too long."

"Helen hasn't tried to dose Elise with naval laudanum and potter's clay, I hope?"

"No. Is that what she gave you?"

"Apparently. Hopefully, I'll be fully recovered by the time we get to our destination...Helen says that we'll find it much more pleasant there."

"It will doubtless seem so. Our present circumstances set a very low standard for comparison. And it's half a world away from Martyr's Mount, which is another point in its favor."

I suspected that she might be thinking that Charles Parenot would be able to go back there now, with a clear conscience, assuming that he wasn't aboard. I strongly suspected that he wasn't. I was sure that Hecate Rain wasn't. She'd said *adieu*, and meant it. There wasn't anyone else I would have liked to be aboard…at least, not now.

"It's an adventure, isn't it?" Mariette added, faintly. "I've spent all my life on the Mount, dreaming of adventure. And since we've left…"

"Nothing but a nightmare."

"No! Not nothing but…by no means. As long as…" She stopped. I wasn't entirely sure how the sentence might have finished but it would have been too flattering to think that she might have added "you're here," no matter how selfishly glad she might be that I was.

It was oddly comforting for me to think that not only was my presence sufficient to take the edge off her nightmare, but that it might be a presence uniquely qualified to do so, because I was a person she thought she could trust, a person with competence.

At least that took the culpable edge of my own selfishness in being glad that I too was not alone in the adventure, and the arrogance of thinking that while Mariette and Elise were with me, they might be less vulnerable to fear and disaster than if they were not.

In the meantime, I was gradually sliding down the wall that was propping me up. My head was clearer, but my legs were giving up the struggle to support me. They had had enough.

"I'm sorry, Mariette," I said, "but I'm out of strength. I have to lie down."

"Me too," she said, although she might only have been trying to make me feel better. "I hope you won't mind too much that Elise will be very glad when she wakes up and I tell her that you're here."

"I'd be deeply offended if she weren't," I whispered—and just managed to get back to the bunk before I collapsed, and lost consciousness.

VIII. Further Explanations

I was woken up by Helen, who was bringing a tray bearing a pitcher full of water, a bowl full of some kind of porridge, and a mug of hot tea. She set it down on the floor beside the bunk, and squatted down beside it, in the same position she's assumed during our previous conversation.

"Are you feeling better?" she asked.

I was. The nausea, at least had disappeared. I had the impression of having slept normally for the first time in several days and nights. I even felt hungry, in spite of the fact that the porridge looked far more functional than appetizing, in its capacity as nourishment.

"Why didn't you tell me that Mariette Parenot and her daughter are in the cell next door?" I asked her, bluntly, as I propped myself up on my elbow.

Her eyes went to the wall. The chink was invisible in the morning daylight, but it wasn't hard for her to work out that it must be there.

"It's not a cell," she muttered, reddening with embarrassment. "It's a cabin."

"And I suppose we aren't prisoners?" I retorted.

"I'm under orders," she reminded me.

"And you were ordered not to tell me that you'd kidnapped other people as well as me? How many others? Who?"

"No," she admitted, "I wasn't ordered not to tell you. I just...didn't get around to mentioning it. It's just the woman and the little girl. Nobody else."

"You brought the girl's mother, but not her father? He must be frantic—it's hardly kind to any of them, is it?"

She flinched under the stream of accusations. "He isn't her father," she muttered, although she plainly didn't think that it was much of an excuse, because she added: "It wasn't my decision."

It probably didn't do my interrogation technique any favors, but I was hungry. I sat up and started spooning mouthfuls of the porridge into my mouth, trying to measure them out so that I could keep talking, at least now that I was sitting upright I could look down at her, and she seemed quite small now that she was sitting on the floor, in spite of the fact that she was taller than average and sturdily built.

"I trusted you," I told her. "When you brought me that meal in the Sprite, with that treacherous brandy, I talked to you as an old friend, someone I liked, someone I wanted to paint. And you're still claiming to be my friend, claiming to be saving my life, but you're still behaving treacherously. How can I believe anything you say? Can you even believe it yourself? You're following orders, you say—how do you know that the person giving you orders doesn't have motives entirely different from the ones you've been ordered to recite to me?"

"She wouldn't lie," Helen say, defensively.

"You do, on her behalf."

"I don't. I just…discretion gets to be a habit. You know that. Does Mariette know *your* secret?"

That was a palpable hit. She was quick to follow it up. "Do you want to paint her, too? Do you really care what Charles Parenot thinks, or feels?"

I swallowed a mouthful of porridge. It was salty, and I had to take a gulp of tea afterwards. That gave me time to settle upon my next move.

"Helen," I said, in a far softer tone, "I need to know what I'm involved with. Mariette and Elise are completely out of their depth. They're looking to me for help, for support. I don't know what to tell them, but I need to tell them what I can. I need you to help me do that."

Her response was to look at the wall again. "Can she see us?" Helen asked. "Can she hear what we're saying?"

"If she has her eye or her ear to the crack, yes."

Perhaps she only wanted a reason to get to her feet. She stood up and went to the bulkhead herself, found the crack that Mariette had widened easily enough, and applied her eye to it.

"They both seem to be asleep," she said. She had lowered her voice.

"Then she probably is," I said. "She's not as habitually treacherous as you are."

Helen came back to the bunk, and sat down on the floor again, deliberately setting herself at a lower level, perhaps as a gesture of appeasement. "I've said I'm sorry," she said. "We really did save your life, remember. But for us, you'd be dead. You owe her that."

"Is there really any point in keeping so many secrets, when they'll be revealed anyway in a matter of days? Are your orders really so restrictive, and are you really so much under their control that you've reduced yourself to a mere automaton? You must have needed a great deal more initiative than that when you were working for the Augers while spying for the Dionysians. That must have required a great deal of cleverness and enterprise, if even Madame Auger never suspected, and obviously liked you well enough to take you back again without an instant's hesitation when you needed to cheat and betray her again. I was only studying you back then with a view to painting you, but I do have an artist's eye, and my judgment was that you were someone worth painting, someone with character, someone whose beauty wasn't simply passive, but reflected something of your inner nature. So please don't pretend that you're just a parrot, incapable of saying anything except what you've been trained to say. Why have you taken Mariette and Elise?"

"I honestly don't know," Helen replied, "but I assume it's because of the girl's music...and because *she* thinks that the woman has something to do with that. She knows that people can't control their own magic without a great deal of training, but she knows...or believes...that it isn't usually an individual thing, that people need others to bring their magic out. I don't know, but I suspect that she believes that Mariette is necessary to the expression of the little girl's magic. You'll be able to ask her why she thinks that, when you meet her."

"I will see her, then?"

"Oh yes—she's avid to meet you. If we'd failed to stop the Marquise's hired killers, and they'd done worse than scratch you...well, she doesn't get angry, but she can certainly make her disappointment felt."

"Avid to meet me?" I queried. "Why avid?"

"Because there aren't many of you about, of course."

She was looking at me frankly, as if she expected me to understand perfectly what she meant. I watched her expression change suddenly, as she was struck by a sudden realization.

"You didn't know, did you?" she said. "You didn't know that there were others?"

I hadn't. Obviously, I had always wondered, always suspected, and always searched...but I had never been able to be sure, in spite of all the legends, and all the stories, that I wasn't unique. For a long time, I hadn't even been sure that I was what I seemed to be, and I still had no way of knowing how long I might actually live, precisely because I really didn't have a secret. I didn't have an elixir of life, and I didn't have any kind of talisman. I simply hadn't died.

I had reached a certain age, and then I had simply kept on going, without apparently getting any older. I had no idea how, and although I had always taken it for granted that it must be a natural phenomenon, albeit rare, and had always assumed that there must have been others in the past and must be others alive now, I had never been sure. I had reasoned that if there were any others like me, they must have exactly the same reasons as I had for keeping quiet about it, and that their existence therefore wouldn't be manifest, but I had never seen any solid evidence that I wasn't the only one. Nor had I any solid evidence of exactly what I was. If the Orpheans and the Dionysians knew that people like me existed, and knew enough to search for them and suspect them, they might well know far more about that than I did. On the other hand, they might only have an accumulation of misconceptions, colored and shaped by their magical and mystical beliefs.

Obviously, I had to investigate what the Orpheans and the Dionysians did know, and the fact that I might now have an opportunity to do that suddenly seemed very important indeed.

"You've met others?" I asked Helen, sharply.

"Yes," she said.

"Where?"

Her answer was slightly reluctant; I was obviously getting close once again to the things she wasn't supposed to tell me. However, she said: "On the island."

"Is *She* one of them?"

She must have realized that silence would be as good as an admission. "Yes," she conceded.

That gave me pause for thought. I was going to meet someone like me. That opened up a whole new spectrum of possibilities, even though I didn't really know what being "like me" really implied.

I knew that I wasn't immortal. I knew that I could die at any moment, from a knife in the back, or poison, or any of a thousand other commonplace causes. I simply seemed to be able to live without any further physical deterioration, so long as I avoided those commonplace causes. And as soon as I had obtained convincing evidence of that—a long time ago now—I had quickly realized that if I proclaimed the fact, if I had let it be known, then I could very easily precipitate the circumstances in which my longevity would be rudely curtailed. The fact that I had no secret that could be stolen or revealed, would not prevent people from wanting to discover one, and steal it, or force me to reveal it, by means as brutal as might be necessary.

Obviously, the fact that Hecate Rain had guessed had not been dangerous to me because she had also guessed the reasons I had for my discretion, and she wished me well—but the fact that the Marquis and Marquise de Mesmay had guessed was a different matter. It seemed, however, that once Mesmay had become half-convinced of it, on more slender evidence than Hecate had, he had decided on a much subtler approach to its investigation, because he had assumed that it was a Dionysian secret, perhaps one that the Orpheans believed that they had once possessed had but had lost, and that I had it by virtue of being a privileged initiate. He had reached the conclusion before others because it fitted in so neatly with the context of his beliefs, and perhaps his own secret magical quests...but Helen's mysterious *She*, I now understood, had guessed on even more slender evidence, not only because she not only knew that phenomenon to be real, but had known it for a long time...perhaps a *very* long time...from personal experience.

"That's why my name was added to the watch list you were given," I deduced, challenging Helen with the deduction. "Something you reported about me tipped *Her* off that I was...like her."

"Perhaps," she admitted. "I suspect, though, that it was only after I began reporting on you in more detail that she came to that realization. Initially, it was just because you were around when odd things happened."

"You mean that she drew the conclusion that I was some kind of magical catalyst? Like Mariette, with regard to Elise?"

It occurred to me that if *She* had some kind of theory of magic, which involved some kind of catalytic effect, then that too might be based on personal experience, perhaps experiments carried out over a long period of time...in which case, there might well be something to her theory, something that explained *our* nature.

"How old is she, exactly?" I added, when Helen did not reply to the vaguer question.

"I don't know—and I shouldn't even have let you guess that she's like you. Please be discreet when you meet her. Please don't give her the impression that I've given her secrets away, even if I have."

"Did she found the colony on the island?" I asked, suddenly prepared to think not in hundreds of years but in thousands. I hadn't finished the porridge, and I hadn't satisfied my renewed appetite, but I had stopped eating.

"No, I don't believe so. She talks about it as if it were founded long before she arrived there...but not necessarily long before she was born. Sometimes she talks as if she's as old as the Empire, as if she actual knew the divine Julius, but that might just be a manner of speaking. She looks young...younger than you."

I picked up on that immediately. "So not everyone stops again at the same point in their lives?"

"Far from it. It can happen at any time. Children...old people. It's the old women I feel sorry for. How they must regret that it didn't happen sooner!"

"But *She*'s young?"

"Yes. You'll probably want to paint her as soon as you see her. She's not unusually beautiful but...she's very impressive. You might forget all about painting me...and the woman in the next cabin."

The hint of double jealousy surprised me slightly, although I could imagine Hecate smiling at it. "I never forget," I told her. "I've painted a great many women, and if the gods favor me, I'll paint a great many more, but I haven't forgotten any of them. I'm a glutton for beauty as well as a true connoisseur, thankfully."

She looked at me thoughtfully—and not just because the idea that I had wanted to paint her was apparently still preying on her mind. "I think I can understand that," she said, eventually. She was evidently an intelligent woman, so she probably could, distantly. Hecate Rain, I was sure, had understood long before she had realized that I really wasn't getting any older as time went by.

"Who is *she*?" I demanded, point-blank.

"We just call her Madame," Helen replied. "That's the way she likes to be addressed. Some people call her Minerva, but that's just a name invented by the humans on the island; it's not hers. I don't suppose she's actually forgotten the name she used to have, but she's...put it behind her."

"Why did the islanders pick Minerva as a nickname?" I asked, although the obvious assumption was that they thought her exceedingly wise, as might be expected if she really had lived long enough to have been acquainted with the divine Julius. But perhaps that was just a pretence, to make herself seem "impressive."

Helen was discomfited. "There really are things I don't dare tell you," she said. "She wants you to be surprised...amazed. Please don't press me."

I raised another spoonful of porridge to my lips, thinking that chewing might help me to think. Naturally, I ignored her plea.

"How many others are there on the island?" I asked. "Others like me...and her...that is?"

She hesitated for an unreasonably long time over her answer. It was obviously a touchy subject. "I don't know," she said. "Dozens." It was painfully obvious that there was something that she wasn't saying, but I couldn't guess what it might be.

"Will I meet them?"

"Probably."

There was a great deal more that I wanted to know, but I suspected that she didn't know the answers to the questions I had, and certainly wouldn't want to give me what information she did have.

I changed the subject. "Who told Madame about Mariette and Elise?" I asked.

"I don't know."

"Not Jacinth, I assume?"

The idea made her smile. "No," she said, "not Jacinth. Someone in the capital, I assume. She must have known about them before they left for Mnemosyne."

"Did she know that Elise was Dellacrusca's granddaughter?"

"I doubt it. I doubt if anyone knew until Dellacrusca found out—and even then, he seems to have kept it to himself until he told you and Mesmay."

Perhaps in that order, I thought, wonderingly. What a strange man he was!

I remembered Mariette's anxiety. "What will happen if Madame finds that Elise can't work magic, with or without Mariette's help? They both thought that it was the viola that was haunted."

"We have the viola," Helen told me, "Although I suspect that Madame might want her to play a different instrument at the celebration."

"What celebration?"

"The celebration of the Mysteries...I really shouldn't be talking about this. Please, Master Rathenius—I feel guilty about the drugging you and assisting in your removal from the Sprite, and I don't want you to think of me as an enemy, but there really are things I mustn't tell you. I've sworn oaths. Once you're an initiate, you'll know. Until then...you can't be told."

"And will I have a choice as to whether or not to become an initiate?"

"Of course...but if you refuse, your questions will remain unanswered, including the ones that will only come to mind once you see the island, and Madame will be exceedingly disappointed."

"And Mariette and Elise? Is Elise even old enough to be initiated into your cult's secrets?"

"Ordinarily, no…but the circumstances aren't ordinary."

"So you were lying to us, at least by omission, when you told us that you're saving our lives by taking us to the island? You might sincerely believe that you're doing that, but that's not the reason your Minerva has ordered you to do it, is it? She wants something from us. She's interested in me because of what I am, and Elise and Mariette because she of what she believes them to be—and if I or they disappoint her…"

"She won't harm you, or allow you to come to harm" Helen said, quickly. "Now that she's taken responsibility for you, she won't let the Orpheans harm you, even if you decide to go back to the island before the danger is over."

"Why did the Marquise decide to have me killed?" I asked. "Her husband seemed to have very different plans in mind, from what I can see now, with the aid of hindsight."

"Your guess is as good as mine—but from what I know of the Orpheans, and their present internal disputes, Mesmay must have thought there was a possibility of using you against Dellacrusca, probably without your knowing it, and perhaps, ultimately, winning you over to his camp. Once Dellacrusca was dead, and Mesmay too, the Marquise, or her associates, probably came swiftly to the conclusion that even if you weren't deep in the enemy camp already, the possibility that you might be recruited and used by the twins and their associates made you dangerous."

143

"Do the Orpheans espouse theories of magical catalysis similar to those of your cult?"

"How could I possibly know, and how could I possibly answer the question if I did?"

"But once I'm initiated...?"

"Madame will probably tell you everything you want to know, if she knows it herself. But I have no idea what she knows about magic, and if I did, I couldn't tell you."

She stood up again and went to the crack in the wall. "The woman and the child are awake now. I need to take them food, and water, and the rest. I have other things to do than suffer the torments of your inquisition."

"You don't need my permission to go," I told her. "I'm the prisoner and you're the jailer, remember."

"Please try to understand, Master Rathenius..."

I interrupted her with a gesture. "I'm trying," I said. "Believe me, I'm trying...and thank you, for the help you've been able to give me. I know it must be difficult for you. You haven't brought my paints I suppose, as well as Elise's viola?"

She formed a wry half-smile. "No," she admitted, "but you'll find everything you need on the island. Madame will have seen to that."

And she left, leaving me with a great deal to think about.

I didn't go to the crack in the wall myself, until I was summoned by Mariette's voice, well over an hour later, if my estimate of passing time could be trusted. The situation, I thought, required direction.

"Whatever you said to your friend made her more forthcoming," Mariette told me. "She told us without being asked that we three are the only ones her companions were ordered to capture, and admitted frankly that it was because of Elise's supposed magical abilities, to which she seems to be assuming that I'm an essential presence. She was profuse with her apologies, but I didn't tell her that she was forgiven, and Elise, well..."

A second voice chimed in. "I see no reason why I should be grateful, Master Rathenius. We've all been treated very badly, whether we were in danger or not. Do you agree?"

"Yes," I told her, "but it might be as well not to voice our complaints too loudly. We need to discover what we're dealing with, and what our possibilities for further action are. We'll probably make better progress in that by being diplomatic."

There was a silence while Mariette gave the child time to digest that advice and respond. Elise eventually said; "You're right, of course, Master Rathenius."

"Axel," I said, automatically.

"Axel," she repeated, and then added, as if unable to suppress the question: "Are you really so very old?"

Apparently, Helen had been very forthcoming indeed in her explanations of why the three of us had been taken.

"Not so very old," I replied, knowing that it wouldn't be adequate. Mariette might have been discreet, but Elise saw no need to be, with regard to someone who had invited her to call him by his first name

"How old?" she demanded

There was no point in not telling her the truth.

"A hundred and twenty-seven," I said.

"No wonder you're such a good painter," she observed. "You must have had a lot of practice."

"I haven't always been a painter," I admitted, "but yes, I've had a great deal of practice. I'd like to think that I have some innate talent as well, though, even though I wasn't a child prodigy, like you."

"You didn't have an equivalent of me, apparently," Mariette's voice put in, soberly.

"Apparently not," I agreed. "People like you are probably even rarer than people like me, if you really are a magical catalyst."

"But you don't believe in magic. You don't believe there people like...whatever your friend Helen thinks I am."

"I wish you wouldn't keep referring to her as 'my friend Helen,' as if I were somehow responsible for her actions. Apparently, it's not my fault, after all, that you were taken. The Dionysians knew about you before you even left Lutèce. If Dellacrusca hadn't involved himself with your lives, you might have been spirited away to the mid-Oceanic archipelago with ever knowing that I existed, or invited to be initiated into the cult somewhere in the capital's catacombs. In time, it might have been you who were sent to the island with orders to seduce me, drug my wine and have me secretly carted aboard a steamship."

"She didn't mention that she's seduced you. She *is* your friend then?"

"That's not what I meant."

"No, I know," she said. "I obviously feel much better now, since I'm exercising my wit. I truly am very glad that you're here, Master Rathenius."

"Axel," I corrected, reflexively.

"So we're all going to be initiated into the cult of Dionysus, are we?"

"It seems so—but it's voluntary, and Helen assures me that there's no penalty for refusal except a life sentence of ignorance."

"So you're not thinking of refusing?"

"I can't see any advantage in doing so, although I'm not sure what kind of oaths I'll be required to swear."

"We're not going to refuse either," Elise put in, obviously still standing with her adoptive mother against the wall—and obviously thinking that she could speak for Mariette as well as herself.

"It might be wise not to make that decision too soon," I suggested. "You need to find out first exactly what it is they want and expect from you both. I'm not even sure what they want and expect from me, even though I can now understand why I became an object of interest. I'm just a man who happens to have lived longer than people usually do. I'd like to think that it's made me a little wiser than most, but I'm no magician, and they seem to believe that they're in possession of a far greater wisdom than I could possibly augment."

"They think you're like me," Mariette put in, presumably guessing, but probably having guessed correctly. Helen had, indeed, implied that Madame Minerva might have taken the inference from her reports of island gossip that I was some kind of magical catalyst. I didn't find that any easier to believe of myself than I did of Mariette. I even feared that Elise might be a disappointment too, no matter what instrument they wanted her to play during the celebration of their Mysteries—even if it was Orpheus' own lyre, and they possessed a readable version of the musical language of sighs.

"Do you have any idea of what the Dionysians' magical and mystical beliefs are?" Mariette asked me.

"Not really," I said. "Historians, in the days of ancient Rome, while the Empire as still in embryo, offered some record of the vague nature of the Eleusinian Mysteries and the Mysteries of Samothrace, and a vague history of the development of the Orphic cult up to that date, but everything they said might be mistaken, or the result of deliberate falsification. Modern historians and antiquarians are very suspicious of them, and far from certain about their own vague notions about the development of the cults during and after the schism that produced the contemporary secret societies. Given that they have no written scriptures to serve as an enduring reference point, like the Hebrew Torah, the Christian gospels and the Bardic hymnal, the rituals and the associated beliefs have probably undergone drastic transfigurations over time, while pretending all the while to be absolutely fixed and illimitably ancient. I can't even say for sure whether the modern Dionysians believe the original Dionysus to have been a god or a man, or both, although they do seem to believe that he died at some point in time."

"On Martyr's Mount," she said, speaking judiciously, for obvious reasons given that Elise was beside her and there was no way that she could address me privately without her hearing every word, even if she were banished to the far side of their narrow cabin, "there are...celebrations sometimes called bacchanals that are reputed to be similar in some respects to Dionysian rites. There's nothing that can happen to me in the course of a bacchanal that I haven't survived before, but I can't help being anxious for Elise. Will we be able to protect her, do you think, if circumstances require it?"

Before I had time to frame an answer, Elise intervened, saying: "Whatever has happened to you hasn't damaged you, and I'm not afraid of anything that might happen to me."

"You're wrong," said Mariette. "What happened to me, when I was only a little older than you, damaged me considerably, and the damage remains. I would do anything to preserve you from it, as my mother hoped, unavailingly, to save me. I hope that Master Rathenius will do what he can to help me, as Charles would."

"I'll do anything I possibly can to prevent harm coming to either of you," I said—but couldn't resist adding: "although I've said before that I don't believe that you've suffered any irremediable spoliation from your childhood experiences, and I'm sure that Elise can see perfectly well that you're an entirely admirable individual, in every respect."

"You don't know," snapped Mariette. "You can't possibly understand." And I heard her move away from the crack in the wall, and drag Elise with her. Discretion demanded that I withdraw again, until I was summoned back again.

Perhaps two hours went by, although it would surely have been a much shorter interval had not Helen visited both cells in the course of her daily routine, and it was not until all of that was finished that Mariette thought it politic to issue her apology.

"I'm sorry, Axel," she said. "It's a sensitive subject, but I shouldn't have overreacted."

"I'm the one who owes you an apology," I said. "You know my opinion; there was no need to repeat it, in such a stressful situation. I have no idea what faces us, and I can't promise you that there's nothing to fear, although I hope that there isn't, but I do intend to keep my promise to preserve you both from any harm, if I possibly can."

"Thank you. Once again, I'm direly glad that you're here. I don't think I could have borne three more days of this anxiety if I were alone."

Elise was presumably sitting on one the bunk, but even so, I had no difficulty hearing her say: "You're not," in a somewhat resentful tone. Elise seemed to be finding the prospect of an adventure less intimidating than her adoptive mother.

I didn't tell Mariette that I was glad that she was there, because it wouldn't have sounded like a compliment, given that she was unable to feel safe herself, and didn't feel that Elise was safe. For purely selfish reasons, however, I was far from sorry that I wasn't alone—and, given Helen's assertion that I would find everything I needed on the Oceanic island, that I might yet have the chance to paint Elise and Mariette.

In fact, I thought, I might also get the chance to paint Helen too…not to mention the challenging Madame Minerva, who was allegedly capable of outshining ordinary beauties, and who might be hundreds, if not thousands of years old. And how could I tell, as yet, what other wonders there might be in the Island of Dionysus to catch my artist's eye?

IX. The Island of Dionysus

The remaining two and a half days of the voyage passed without incident. Although the sea seemed far from calm to my admittedly inexperienced judgment, the sea-sickness, once it had retreated completely, did not recur. The food I was given was elementary fare but not disgusting, and once my own clothing had been returned, laundered where appropriate and carefully brushed when not, I felt more like my usual self. My pocket-book was intact, and my watch was in my fob-pocket, although it had stopped and I could only guess where the hands ought to be when I had wound it again. The revolver that had been in my coat pocket when I went up to the room in the Spite was no longer there, though, and my clasp-knife was also missing.

Helen offered to re-dress the wound in my arm again, but when the bandage and dressing was removed and I inspected it, it didn't seem to require further cover-age. The scar was red and ugly, but I knew that it would fade, and it was on the outer part of the forearm, so the nerves and sinews controlling the hand were unaffected. As a right-handed painter, I didn't need such perfect control in the fingers of my left hand as I demanded of the other, but it would have been annoying nevertheless to suffer any loss of function.

I spent much of the time that I didn't spend at the crack talking to Mariette and Elise staring out of the porthole, Helen having not contrived to find me any book worth perusing. Except for the few minutes when the sun was going down, however, there was nothing much to see, save for occasional clouds in the sky. I saw no other ships or boats of any other kind, and no birds or leaping dolphins.

While watching the waves, half-hypnotized, I meditated. My various exchanges with Helen as she came and went became more relaxed, as inquisitions and accusations alike faded away, and we even began to joke, to an extent that caused Mariette, at one point, to hiss through the fissure in the wall: "If you're going to screw that whore, please do it quietly." I had no such intention, although I suppose I might have formed one, at least tentatively, had the narrow slit not provided a constant reminder that everything I did, even in the dark, was potentially subject to observation.

During the night of the third day since my reacquisition of full consciousness, perhaps an hour or two after midnight, Helen came into the cabin at an unusual time, and shook me awake, before going to rap with her knuckles on the bulkhead connecting my cabin with Mariette's. When I was up and about and a glimmer of light informed her that the lantern had been lit in the next cabin too, our jailer took up a position between me and the fissure

"I need to ask for your cooperation, Master Rathenius," she said, speaking loudly and distinctly, casting a sideways glance at the wall, "and yours too, Madame Parenot. I need to request that you agree to be blindfolded while you are taken off the ship in a little while—perhaps thirty minutes. It would be no advantage to you to see the ship or any of its crew, and it would be an embarrassment to us, even though it's dark.

"With your consent, therefore, your eyes will be hooded, and you will each be carefully escorted on to the deck. There you will be enabled to climb into a launch, which will then be lowered into the water and rowed to a creek. It will take time, I fear, and the hoods will doubt-less come to seem annoying, but for what it may be worth, you will not be able to see very much even when you are given permission to take them off.

"Then there will be a brief journey overland, which will involve climbing a number of stairs. By the time you reach the top, it will be first light, and you will probably be able to watch the sun come up, over the Ocean. I shall still be with you, and will remain with you thereafter, in the guest-house, in order to see that your needs are met. Is that agreeable to you both."

She was being polite. What could we possibly have done if it had not been agreeable? I therefore allowed myself to be hooded, and then led out of the cabin for the first time—initially by Helen, although she passed me over immediately to far rougher hands. They led me gently enough through a course that was not sufficiently tortuous enough to qualify as a labyrinth, also the stair-case to the upper deck required a certain care in negotia-tion, and clambering into the launch was far more awk-ward than one might suspect while contemplating such an operation with sighted eyes.

It was not a big launch, perhaps more akin to a din-ghy, but Mariette and I were able to sit on a bench in what was presumably the middle of the boat, with Elise wedged between us. The boat was lowered slowly. Fi-nally, there was nothing else to do but listen to the plash of the oars, feel what could of the breeze through the fabric of the hoods, and catch the faint scents that made their way through the weave.

The journey to the shore seemed to take a long time. Even when the echoes informed me that we were passing between two steep walls, presumably following a creek, it continued for what seemed to be an hour more, although my sense of duration was probably exaggerated.

Helen had told the truth; when we were carefully put ashore on to some kind of stone jetty, and she removed our hoods a few minutes after we heard the boat moving away, drifting downstream with only the occasional dip of the oars, we couldn't see a thing. I stood perfectly still, afraid to take a step in case I tumbled into the water, which I could hear lapping the jetty only a few feet away.

Then she lit a lantern, and at least we were able to see one another, and the ground on which we were standing. It was a good oil lantern, not a mere candle-stub in a glass cage, and it lit our way along a narrow path that led in a zigzag fashion up a cliff. Mercifully there was a sturdy guard-rail supported on metal struts, so it was safe to negotiate, and when we came to the staircase she had mentioned, the stone steps were broad and clean-cut.

The cliff seemed to go up a long way, but by the time we reached the top, the clouded sky was indeed beginning to turn gray as the pre-dawn twilight stained the east. We reached the so-called guest-house before the sun actually came up, though, and did not linger to watch the sunrise. Helen took us inside.

The house was a two-story villa with a mansard roof, of a kind not much different from many to be found on the southern coast of Mnemosyne, not palatial or sumptuous, but well-constructed in stone and brick, with a tiled roof. The vestibule gave access to a hallway with the staircase to the left. Good-quality oil-lamps were burning in the hallway and, apparently, most of the rooms. Helen identified a drawing room without bothering to open the door, and a dining-room, a "studio" and

154

the kitchen in a similar fashion. She took us directly upstairs, where there were three bedrooms, each with its own adjacent bathroom, and a staircase that was more akin to a ladder leading to a mansard in the roof-space. She indicated the largest room to me, the smallest one to Elise and the intermediate one to Mariette. There was a tall pendulum-clock standing on the landing, which indicated six-fifteen.

"Once I return from making my report, I shall be upstairs," Helen said, pointing up at the mansard, "should you need anything. There's time for you to sleep if you so wish. No one will disturb you until ten o'clock. There are clean clothes for all of you. The cook and the maid will be here at eight, should you want food. At ten I shall make Madame's wishes known to you." She was about to go back downstairs when she turned round and said: "If you see anything...unusual, please don't be alarmed. There is absolutely nothing to fear here."

We went into our respective bedrooms. The clean clothes we had been promised bore no resemblance to the ones I had left behind in my wardrobe on Mnemosyne, consisting of loose shirts and light trousers. The only footwear consisted of light sandals, but there were broad-brimmed hats, evidently destined to provide protection from subtropical sun. The bathtub had two taps, and I was surprised to find that one of them produced hot water after being allowed to run for ten or fifteen seconds. There was also a razor and shaving soap on the sink.

I felt even more desperately in need of a bath and a shave than of sleep, and had no trouble deciding that hygiene took priority. The sound of gurgling pipes and running water suggested that my companions had made a similar decision, but the hot water didn't run out. Only when I was thoroughly clean did I permit myself the luxury of lying down on the bed, but I didn't go to sleep even then. The daylight was bright and growing brighter, and it wasn't long before I went to the window to look out over the steeply-wooded slope that led down into the cleft where a broad stream ran steam ran.

The rock-face on the other side of the stream wasn't as high as the one on which the house was perched, and it was possible to see the ocean beyond a tree-toped ridge, although the shore itself and a considerable stretch of the inland waters were hidden from view. A few sails were visible on the water, of what were presumably fishing-boats, but there didn't appear to be any human presence on the ridge. The vegetation was dense, though, and the appearance might have been deceptive.

I put on a set of the clothes that had been provided, sandals and all, and went downstairs; I took a hat with me, intending to take a stroll around the garden once I'd had a peek into the rooms downstairs.

There were sounds coming from the kitchen, so the cook had evidently arrived, but I went into the room that Helen had identified as the "studio" first. It had a broad and high north-facing window, through which I could look up the shallow slope of a mountain studded with distant fields and plantations, where numerous people were busy, dark-skinned and oddly variant in size, some being small and other exceedingly burly. Before turning my casual attention to them, however, I cast a glance around. There were easels and shelves bearing paints, canvases and various other supplies, but my eye didn't linger on them either, having been caught almost immediately by a painting hanging over the fireplace on the wall opposite the large window. My attention suddenly ceased to be casual.

It was a portrait: a portrait of a young woman. I recognized it instantly, although I hadn't seen it for more than ninety years, and had never expected to see it again. I took a couple of steps toward it in order to stare at it more intently, and then paused again, attempting to weigh up the significance of its presence.

While I was staring at the picture, with my hands nervously rotating the hat that I was still carrying, Mariette came in behind me. She followed the direction of my gaze, and then stepped in front of me in order to examine the signature in the bottom right-hand corner of the canvas.

"It's not your signature," she said, turning to look at me, curiously.

"No, it isn't," I conceded.

"And it seems to be an old picture," she remarked.

"Nearly a hundred years old," I confirmed.

"And the style is a trifle naïve."

"Very."

She stood directly in front of me, looking me up and down and appraising me as if I were a painting myself, and perhaps as if there was a certain luxury in being able to look at me freely, instead of through a thin crack in a wooden bulkhead.

"Did you love her?" she asked, curiously.

"Yes," I said, baldly

"But she's long dead now."

"Yes."

"How does the picture come to be here?"

"I have no idea. Apparently, Madame's resources in the Empire are adequate for her spies to have been able to research my past life more carefully and more cleverly than anyone else was ever prompted to do. Perhaps this is simply a way of letting me know that she has done so. Its presence can hardly be a coincidence."

"How any women have you painted, Axel?" she asked.

"I lost count long ago."

"And have you lost count of the number you have loved, as well?"

"No."

She arched an eyebrow slightly, as if she doubted me. I couldn't have blamed her. Had she demanded that I state the number, I doubt that I could have counted accurately enough, even for my own satisfaction, although I certainly wouldn't have been far out.

Helen came in then. "Breakfast is set out in the dining room," she said. She spared the painting the briefest of glances, as if it were quite indifferent to her.

Mariette looked at the painting again, then at Helen, and then at me. "This must be close to your notion of paradise, Axel," she said, with deliberate and perhaps overstated irony. "A house full of lovely women, and paintings of your old flames…and the mysterious Madame still to meet…"

I didn't comment on her immodesty, or her exaggeration with regard to the number of paintings of old flames. Instead I looked at Helen, who had promised to relay Madame's "intentions."

"Are we to be summoned?" I asked

"No," she replied. "Madame will come to see you. You're honored."

"Mounted in a howdah on the back of an elephant," I suggested, "attended by a retinue of slaves bearing fans of exotic plumes?"

"There are no slaves here," said Helen, "And no elephants either. Madame will walk." She smiled wryly, "but she will not be unaccompanied." She extended her arm to beckon us into the dining-room.

The dining room had a broad bay in its outer one wall not dissimilar to the one in the studio, but it faced eastwards, and it was fitted with glazed double doors that presently stood wide open, offering access to a garden full of flowers arranged in lush beds, with grassy pathways in between and neatly-pruned clumps of bushes, similarly in flower. I took a step toward them, in accord with my earlier intention, but thought it best to stay now that I was no longer alone.

"Breakfast" consisted of fruits, most of them unfamiliar to me, bread, with various conserves, and tea. Although a maid had been mentioned, serving at table did not appear to be among her responsibilities. Helen indicated that we should take what we wanted, and set us an example. Elise appeared shortly thereafter, and joined us.

"You look like islanders already," Helen observed, referring to the clothes we had donned. Mariette and Elise were both dressed in loose dresses made of light fabric, the former in pale blue and the latter in lemon yellow. Helen was wearing a similar garment in pale green. My shirt was white and my trousers brown.

"When in Rome," I quoted, ironically. We were obviously a very long way, in time and space, from the ancient nucleus of the Empire, to which all roads were sometimes still proverbially said to lead, although they plainly did not any longer.

"I told you, did I not, that the island is a pleasant spot? The ocean current guarantees a fresh breeze, which cools the climate in a marvelously even fashion. It's an earthly paradise of sorts…or at least a New Arcadia. I'm glad to be back, I must confess. It was interesting to see

Mnemosyne again, and to catch a glimpse of many old friends…but it's not a place where I would care to live again."

"But you're not an artist," I suggested, "sensitive to the finer aspects of Mnemosynian society."

"Am I not?" she said. "I suppose must bow to your judgment—but we have artists here too."

"Artists as fine as Master Rathenius?" asked Mariette, mischievously.

"I would not dare make that claim in present company," replied Helen, silkily. She seemed far more confident now that she was on her home ground.

"What instruments do your musicians play?" Elie enquired.

"Many kinds," Helen told her. "We call the most commonplace ones lyres, in honor of the immortal Orpheus, but they're quite various. Your viola da gamba will be returned to you before the end of the day, but Madame will send you some other instruments too, with which to amuse yourself…and a teacher too, one of our finest."

"And do you have a fiddle for Mariette?" asked the girl. "It would be pleasant to be able to play together again, as we used to do in Charles's studio while he was painting. Perhaps Axel would allow us to play in his, if our scraping wouldn't be too annoying."

"We may certainly try the experiment," I said, gallantly, carefully making no promise beyond that.

"I'm sure that I can locate a violin," said Helen, turning to Mariette. "I'm sorry—I didn't realize that you were a musician too."

"I'm not," said Mariette, blushing. "Charles taught me to pick out a few tunes, crudely, but he was a far better player than I am, and it was exceedingly tolerant of him and Elise to let me pretend to accompany her on his instrument while he painted, in order that we might attempt a kind of harmony."

"Mariette draws very well too," Elise insisted. "You should ask Axel to give you lessons, Mariette, as Charles used to do." There seemed to be more malice than mere mischief in that remark, but Elise smiled, before adding: "And of course, we must all attempt to work magic, as that that is why we are here."

"What magic do you suggest we try to work?" asked Mariette, a trifle gruffly.

"We summoned Eurydice for Master Rathenius on Mnemosyne, in order for him to interpret the myth of Orpheus to his artistic satisfaction," Elise said. "Here, surely, we must try to summon the shade of Dionysus, so that he might preside in person over our bacchanal."

"Well said, child!" said a new voice.

Of the four of us, only Helen was sitting facing the open window-doors but she was taken as much by surprise as the rest of us although she bounded to her feet as soon as soon as the voice broke her concentration, and bowed deeply.

Mariette and Elise were sitting sideways on to the garden entrance and only had to turn their heads, and I had time to notice the look of utter amazement on Mariette's face before I rose to my feet politely in my turn and turned to face the newcomer—or, as it turned out, newcomers.

As Helen had promised, Madame had come on foot, but she had not come unaccompanied. She was standing in the center of the open portal, deliberately posing on the threshold, with her companions behind her.

In herself, Madame was not particularly imposing. She was not as tall as Helen, and only a fraction of an inch taller than Mariette, although she was considerably fuller in her figure, with large breasts and well-rounded hips. Her hair was jet black and her eyes dark brown, but her skin, although suntanned, was not very dark, causing her eyebrows to stand out clearly. She was not especially beautiful. She was not as beautiful as Mariette, or as beautiful as Hecate Rain as Hecate had been twenty years before, and arguably not even as pretty as Helen. Nor did she seem imperious or commanding, and her gaze, though hypnotic, did not seem equipped to strike terror—at least, not while she was smiling as benignly as she was at present.

Even so, there was something about her that I had never seen in a woman's face before: something unique. She had every textural appearance of youth, a complexion that gave the impression of being no more than twenty years old—but that was just texture. In her gaze, in her smile, and in her attitude, there was something else entirely: an impression not merely of maturity but, literally, of antiquity. I thought at first glance that it might be purely subjective, a delusory impression created in by mind simply by the knowledge that she was much older than she seemed, but it was not. When I looked back at her again, I saw that it was real, and that there was something about her that I was not sure even I could capture on canvas, so uncanny was it.

I say "when I looked back at her" because I could not help but look away from her and beyond her. It was doubtless impolite, but there was simply no avoiding it. I knew she would forgive me, because she had obviously contrived the effect of her appearance deliberately.

The companions standing behind her, one to the right and one to the left, were tall figures made to seem even taller by her own relatively petite stature. They must have been several inches over six feet tall, but they looked even bigger, because their heads were so large and broad—and they were also horned, albeit discreetly. Their heads were shaggy and they appeared to have virtual manes running down their backs. They were naked to the waist, clad only in bulky loincloths, and their legs were equally shaggy, and slightly oddly formed. I actually glanced down to see whether they had cloven hooves instead of feet but they didn't. Their sandaled feet were hairy, but human...or at least humanoid.

Each of them was armed with a long staff, clutched in a powerful right hand, held like a guardsman's pike, although it had no blade. Their noses were squashed and their lips thick. Their eyes were large and wide-set, and their brows emphatic, with bushy hair. Their gaze, however, was peculiarly soft, neither aggressive nor bovine, but seemingly possessed of the same kind of antiquity as Madame's gaze. They were old, I guessed, perhaps very old. They gave the impression of belonging to some near-human race that ought to be extinct—and presumably was extinct, throughout what I thought of as the "known world."

Having scanned them both, with my artist's eye, and measured them with my customary rapidity, I returned the focus of my attention to Madame, and bowed.

"Master Rathenius," she said, in a warm tone. "It's a great pleasure to receive you on the Island of Dionysus, and I owe you a thousand apologies for the fact that my invitation nearly came too late, and had to be delivered with such rudeness. A thousand apologies to you too, Mariette, and you, Elise. The situation was very confused, I fear, and not conducive to formalities. Be welcome, though, as the most honored of guests. Is there anything you lack?"

Perhaps feeling that she had already been caught out in a mocking indiscretion, it was Elise who found her tongue sufficiently to say: "Only my father, who seems to have been left behind when your hirelings drugged us and kidnapped us."

Madame smiled. "Charles Parenot was not included in my orders," she admitted. "As for your father—while you are raising shades, perhaps you might attempt to contact his. He doubtless has a sigh or two to impart, since your grandfather had him killed. But he is avenged now, if you believe revenge to be possible or desirable, and in suitably Dionysian style."

"Were they Dionysian bacchantes after all, then, Madame," I enquired, "and not Mesmay's?"

"All bacchantes are the instruments of Dionysus," said Madame, "whoever fabricates them. When mimicry is slavish, it serves the functions of the original, apishly at least—and what is the Cult of Orpheus but a mimic of the true religion, and its quest a travesty of the true quest?"

"I don't know," I said. "All such things are secret, it appears, carefully hidden from honestly enquiring minds." Perhaps I was simply taking up Elise's cue, or perhaps I was reacting to the discovery that she was not as awesome as she had been made out to be, in spite of her escort of ogres.

Madame nodded, serenely, and I remembered what Helen said about her not getting angry. She didn't seem disappointed either. Indeed, although her expression wasn't giving a great deal away, she seemed to me to be exceedingly pleased with herself, almost smug: like someone with a plan nearing its end, becoming gradually more confident of anticipated success—or an artist nearing the completion of a difficult picture, who finally feels, after much groping and reexamination of his evolving brushwork, that he has grasped the essence of his subject, and the prospect of esthetic completion.

"You have every right to be annoyed with me," she said, "and every right to your sarcasm. As you say, such things are secret, and understanding only comes at a price—but once you have looked into the Mirror of Dionysus, you will understand. I want you to understand, and although you do not know it yet, you need to understand…all three of you."

She stepped fully into the room then, and veered to the right, away from me and toward Elise.

Elise hadn't even stood up, as the rest of us had. She had remained stubbornly seated, deliberately refusing to be impressed by the newcomer, or even by her monstrous bodyguards, who remained beyond the threshold outside the room. After her one bold remark, however, she had remembered the advice she had been given to be diplomatic, and was now limiting the expression of her resentment to a mere matter of attitude.

Madame did not offer the child her hand, perhaps because she sensed that the Elise would remain mutinously rigid, but she leaned forward slightly to address her, s if in a confidential manner.

"I'm truly sorry for your loss, Elise," she said. "Your grandfather did not know it, and would probably have been horrified by the suggestion, but there is a sense in which he and I were on the same side, working toward the same end. I'm truly sorry that his betrayers came to believe that he had to be sacrificed. You might not believe me when I tell you that I have heard you play, but I have, and I believe that I have understood your music better than anyone else. There is no destiny, so I can make you no promises, but I believe that you will have the opportunity here to make finer music than you could ever make in Lutèce or Mnemosyne, and I hope with all my heart that you will."

Elise had no idea how to react to that. She simply continued staring at the amazing, alarming woman, who passed on, continuing around the table. When she reached Helen she reached out and touched her on the shoulder, gently, as if approvingly, as if bidding her to relax. Helen didn't say a word either, but she did seem to take reassurance from the touch.

Madame kept going, until she reached Mariette. Mariette had stood up, but her stance was uncertain; she didn't know whether she ought to match Elise's mutiny, Helen's respect or my attempted casualness. She did, however, look the mysterious director of our capture in the eyes, as if searching there for understanding, while Madame met her gaze, not searching, but considering. It was as if she already believed that she knew Mariette, and had no reason to strive to read her secret thoughts.

""I hope you'll be happy here, eventually, Mariette," she said. "When you have discovered yourself, as the Mysteries will hopefully allow you to do, you can begin to understand, and might be able to forgive me for my interference in your life."

Unlike Elise, Mariette felt obliged to say something, to respond to the bizarre situation.

"It's a privilege to meet you, Madame Minerva," she said. "And if you really have saved our lives, then I owe you gratitude for that—although, like Elise, I would find that easier if you had saved my husband's too."

"No one can foresee the future, alas," Madame replied, "So I can offer no guarantees of Charles Parenot's safety, but I can tell you that he is alive at present, and still on the island. The Marquise has no reason to order his death, as she might perhaps have ordered yours if she concluded that she could not make a bacchante of you. She knows, as I do, that Parenot is superfluous—to her plan, to mine, and to you. You know that he isn't your husband, and that your love for him was...well, you may discuss that with me in private if you wish. This is not the time or place, and for now, I need to have a long conversation with Master Rathenius. There will be time for questions and answers, but you will not be able to understand very much until the Mysteries are celebrated. I would rather, by the way, that you simply thought of me and addressed me as Madame. Minerva is not and never has been my name, and its occasional use is merely an irreverent jest on the part of my human associates."

Madame was already turning away to continue her tour of the table, but Mariette was still staring to her.

"Wait, Madame, if you please," she said. "One question, if I may. You say that you've heard Elise play. When and what have you heard her play?"

"I heard her play on the night that her grandfather died. I heard her play the music of sighs—by strange means, I admit, but I did hear her, and, as I said, felt that understood her music better than anyone who was physically present."

"And that's why we're here?" Mariette demanded, taking a liberal interpretation of what might constitute a single question.

"Partly."

"But you haven't brought Hecate Rain, who planned and performed the piece with Elise."

Madame glanced sideways at me. "No," she said mildly. "That presented too many difficulties. But she too is alive at present."

I didn't like the sound of that "at present," which seemed to imply more than the identical phrase she had used in connection with Charles Parenot.

"What difficulties?" I asked her.

"I had to keep my instructions to a minimum," Madame replied. "I do not judge Madame Rain superfluous, as I judged Charles Parenot, nor do I think that she is free of danger, but…you will understand, I hope, in time, why I thought it best to leave her on Mnemosyne."

She was looking at me in a strange fashion; her expression seemed slightly compassionate—but the compassion was not for me; it was for Hecate. That made me anxious. If Hecate really was in danger, the implications of her final *adieu* might be even more sinister than I had so far concluded.

Mariette didn't attempt to extrapolate her one question any further, even though she plainly didn't know what to make of the answer she had been given.

Madame had already passed on, and didn't pause again. "Walk with me, Master Rathenius," she said, simply, as she headed back toward the open window-doors. She didn't even seem to look to see whether I was following the instruction; she simply expected me to follow her.

It never occurred to me to imitate Elise's tokenistic mutiny. I was avid to hear whatever it was that she wanted to say to me—and, indeed, everything that she might condescend to tell me.

I put the hat on my head, glad to free my hands, and followed her.

X. A Walk with Madame

I followed Madame through the garden, along a winding pathway that took her to the left, and then out through a small gate on the northern side of the enclosure, facing the mountain. I looked once again at the sprawling patchwork of upwardly-inclined fields, and this time realized easily enough that the smaller laborers at work there were adult humans, and the larger ones kin to the individuals making up Madame's escort. The latter seemed to be in a small but noticeably majority. The two enigmatic individuals were not rare freaks of nature; there were evidently thousands of them on the island.

Once we were some distance away from the house, moving between flowering bushes, Madame allowed me to draw level with her. Her two silent attendants walked three paces behind, slightly displaced to either side of the path. I didn't know whether their purpose was to protect Madame from any possible threat from me, to protect both of us from some mysterious threat from elsewhere, or simply to mount a symbolic presence, purely for show. The last seemed most likely.

"They're Sileni," said Madame, answering the question that I hadn't voiced.

I recognized the word. Silenus, or the Sileni—the legend seemed uncertain as to whether to employ the singular or the plural—had been companions of the mythical Dionysus, along with the original bacchantes.

"I've always confused Sileni with satyrs," I said.

"You're by no means the only one," she told me. "It's difficult for me to be sure, since the satyrs were extinct long before I was born, but it's possible that they were different variants of the same species rather than two different species. By the time I began to investigate, it was impossible to determine exactly how many semi-human species there had been before our own kind exterminated them, with their typical genocidal ruthlessness. There were certainly more than the two who have survived here."

"Two?" I queried.

"I'll introduce you to the Nymphs when the opportunity arises. Of the rest, we only have mythical and legendary reports, which become terribly distorted over time—although there's one legend relating to the Sileni that has proved extraordinarily resilient, perhaps because of its symbolic importance. I doubt that even a tiny fraction of today's initiates, let alone those who merely read it in books on ancient Greece, have any inkling of what that importance is."

That was a definite challenge, or inquisition.

"I know the story you mean," I said. "Silenus—or a silenus—was captured by humans, and tortured by them, because they believed that he knew a precious secret. He resisted for a time, but yielded in the end, and told them the secret of human existence: that the best thing of all is not to be born, and after that to die young. But I don't know what its hidden meaning is, if it has one. It seems transparent enough to me, albeit somewhat ironic, in my…situation."

"How old were you when you realized that you weren't following the common path of aging and deterioration?" she asked, seemingly out of pure curiosity.

"I was very slow to accept the reality of it," I admitted. "The people around me became aware of it while I was still convinced that I was simply…not showing my age. I had plenty of opportunity to judge their reaction,

170

while I was still denying it to all and sundry, including myself. I was over sixty when I finally realized that I had to abandon my first life, and start again elsewhere, pretending to be much younger than I was. I bungled the whole process, of course...I was a painfully slow learner, I fear. It wasn't until I went to Mnemosyne that I finally had a reasonable grasp of what it was necessary to do, and how, in order to build and protect a new identity. Even then, I seem to have made a mess of it in the end, by staying too long...but I was happy there, and although I knew that I'd have to go eventually, it was so difficult to give it all up. I was still able to fool myself that nobody knew until last week. It came as a terrible shock to realize that your people had known for years, and Mesmay's too, and that the covert attention I'd attracted had already drawn me into the jaws of exactly the kind of trap I'd always feared."

"Don't be too harsh in your judgment," Madame said. "My corporeal clock stopped much sooner than yours—which is rare, for both women and men—and I faced far worse difficulties in the superstitious days of yore than I would have today, with no intellectual equipment whatsoever with which to begin to cope with the problems that arose as a consequence of being deemed a witch, an analogue of Circe or Medea. I was extremely fortunate to survive all the perils that afflicted the world in my real youth, given my awful incompetence. You've had a lot of advantages I didn't, but even so, to have reached the situation you have in a mere hundred years—a mere sixty, counting from your initial realization—is a real accomplishment."

"When you say *the days of yore...*?"

"I was born a less than a hundred years before the reign of the divine Julius began. I'm very nearly two thousand years old. It's been an exceedingly long process of maturation, and I certainly don't think it's complete yet. I might need another two thousand...although there's no guarantee that, even if I were to live that long, I wouldn't suffer some form of catastrophic deterioration. I've seen worse things than death overtake Macrobians much younger than I am. We don't seem to have the adaptive gifts—if they can really be reckoned gifts—that the Sileni have."

"Macrobians?" I queried.

"It's what Herodotus called the long-lived. He represented them as a tribe living in Ethiopia, but if there really were whole tribes in the days about which he was writing, our fellow humans would have wiped them out, in accordance with their genocidal custom. Only the rare isolates, like us, who developed the skills necessary to concealment, survived for long."

"But the Sileni are long-lived?"

"Typically, yes. It's rare for them to live longer than a few centuries, but there are some on the island who might be as old or older than I am—they have no written records and don't place much value on counting. These two, of course, are much younger. The tradition of the so-called Cult of Orpheus represents the Sileni as vile monsters, but you can see perfectly well that they're not. They're fearsome when angry, but they're very slow to anger, and usually very gentle."

"*So-called* Cult of Orpheus?" I queried.

"Yes. Ours is the true cult of Orpheus *and* Dionysus. Theirs is a mimic, formed by dissident initiates—long before I was born, alas, so I only have a vague and uncertain notion of how and why the schism occurred. They, of course, have done their best to demonize us over the ages, but as I told Elise, there's a sense in which

Dellacrusca and Mesmay were working toward the same goal as us, even if they had a mistaken sense of how to reach it. I shouldn't be too harsh in my judgments. It took me a long time to realize that the methods that the Dellacruscas of the world try to employ are the wrong ones, and that the ends don't justify means of that sort. I've got far more blood on my hands, alas, than he had the chance to accumulate in his brief career, and, although most of it stained them a long time ago, it never really washes off. It still weighs on my conscience."

"You really did know the divine Julius, then?" I said. "Did you become the power behind the Imperial throne?"

She permitted herself a wry laugh. "No, Master Rathenius," he said, "although there was in time in my foolish youth when I had that dream. Yes, I did meet the divine Julius, although I knew some of his successors more intimately. As vulnerable to myth as anyone else, I really did imagine then that I might be able to play the role of Egeria to the ultimate descendants of Numa, and it required several common lifetimes of continual frustration to realize the impossibility.

"The Duc de Dellacrusca, unfortunately, seems to have made the same mistake, encouraged by the advantages that the telegraph gave him, and those that he expected to stem from its use in future. He was able to increase and expand the degree of his own control, over decades, but that only led, in the end, to a parallel increase in the determination of others to usurp the power he had gained.

"No one person can determine the course of an Empire, and in the ultimate balance, the Emperor, or anyone lurking behind his throne, has only a little more power than many of his generals or aristocrats. The maintenance and stability of an Empire depends on countless factors, many of them beyond any human control. Even the contribution of a scheming Macrobian much cleverer than I was—and there must have been many whose existence I didn't suspect, as well as those I know—could only have been a slightly larger drop in the ocean of circumstance. Looking back, regretfully, I can see opportunities I missed that might have allowed me to make a bigger and better difference, but I did make a small difference, while I was endeavoring to be a mastermind and using my whorish assets…as well as accumulating a good deal of blood on my dainty hands.

"Perhaps I might have done more if I'd been more beautiful…but then, what did the legendary Helen accomplish, for Achaea or for Troy, except for generations of senseless slaughter? I saw your slight disappointment when you first caught sight of me—there's no need to hide it politely. I'm not a goddess…just a human woman who happened not to die. I know that I'm not as beautiful as many women that you've painted, or will paint, and not even as beautiful as my own dear Helen, who never looked out of place as a waitress in a harbor-side inn on an out-of-the way island off the Gaulish coast."

We were now walking between hedgerows, with fields to either side, but I was too intent on following the conversation to pay much attention to the crops or the laborers. I was glad I had brought the hat, though; there was a breeze that prevented the heat from seeming too oppressive, but the sun was very bright, and subtly harsh.

"I should like to paint you anyway, Madame," I remarked—and not for the sake of politeness.

"Of course you would, given the artist that you are. You do realize, do you not, how very special that makes you...perhaps unique? Most Macrobians are, alas, perfectly ordinary individuals, who require many decades, or centuries, simply to begin to make themselves exceptional with the aid of education. A talent like yours is rare...but even so, you ought to avoid overweening arrogance, and it might be better to regard yourself as an instrument rather than a player, accursed as well as gifted. Your Orpheus is a triumph of sorts, I believe, but you can't be sure how much credit for that triumph is really due to you."

"Elise certainly played a role," I admitted, "but unwittingly, I think."

I knew that she wasn't really talking about Elise, or about Mesmay, or herself, when she spoke of the credit for the triptych not being entirely mine. She was talking about something supernatural, something magical, perhaps something literally Dionysian. She knew that I had deduced that, and didn't bother to press the point. She had her own roundabout way of doing things, and she obviously had some reason for doing things in that way, and for deliberately postponing at least some explanations until whatever crucial celebration of her Mysteries she had planned...at which point, apparently, we would all have an opportunity to make some kind of spectacular leap to understanding.

"May I see your arm?" she asked, abruptly.

The loose sleeve of the shirt with which I'd been supplied was very easy to push back, exposing the scar. She looked at it, saw that it was healing, and nodded, in apparent satisfaction.

"I owe you an apology for that," she said. "My emissaries certainly had the opportunity to warn you, but we had no idea that the Marquise would act so rapidly or so foolishly. I'm extremely glad, though, that our intervention came in time. And who can tell? Perhaps Diony-sus thought it necessary, for purely symbolic purposes, that you take a scratch. If you are to play the role of Zagreus, perhaps a token gesture in the direction of mutilation was necessary."

"It was the Marquise, then, who gave the order to have me killed?"

"I believe so. My conviction is that she needed you to finish the painting, because she knew that there was magic in it, but she wanted to be the one to exploit that magic and, for safety's sake, she wanted you out of the way, completely and permanently, once you had delivered it."

"And she'd have done the same to Elise and Mariette?"

"Not immediately, and quite possibly not at all. They were undoubtedly part of her plan—but if they had refused to cooperate, and even if they had agreed, they might well have been in danger."

"Just as Hecate might still be in danger?"

"Yes, and Vashti Savage. The Marquise undoubtedly intends to make bacchantes of them both if she can—but we might be able to ease that situation, as well as alleviating a great deal of other harm."

"From here?"

"Yes."

"By means of magic, I assume, not the telegraph?"

"Yes—provided that the three of you are willing and able to play your part, and Dionysus is able to play his."

"Do you really believe in the active power of a personalized Dionysus," I asked, "or are you only speaking figuratively?"

"The latter, if it makes you feel more comfortable," she said. "The actual Dionysus, god or man, died a long time ago, but the myth survives, and the idea that initiates have of him, especially when guided by the ceremonies, still has a power of action in the world—but he does require initiates, because the images retained by myth and legend are transformed by the dilution of time and number. In order for Dionysus to remain powerful as an aspect of mystery and magic, the mystery and the magic have to be maintained by ritual, and its artistry. In order to retain an effective aspect of personalization, a god needs the active collaboration of the human mind, in whose Underworld he dwells, but while the true cult survives, Dionysus is not devoid of personality or the power of action. We bacchantes and the Sileni are merely his servants, but his survival and power of action need our loyalty, our conviction and, above all, our art. That's the essence of the cult."

"So you see yourself as an instrument of Dionysus rather than the actual instigator of whatever plan you've made for us?" I said, a trifle incredulously, trying hard to weigh up exactly how crazy she and her adversaries might be.

"I suspect that we are all mere instruments, and that all of us, including Mesmay and his wife, in submitting themselves so completely to the inspiration and the dictates of their warped version of the Mysteries, are unwittingly serving a higher purpose," she replied, serenely, although her smile suggested that she was disdainfully aware of my suspicion of her insanity.

I was uncomfortably aware myself that if she really was two thousand years old, and had long outgrown Dellacruscan fantasies of Imperial domination, she might know vastly more about the mysterious workings of magic and mystery than I did, and might have every justification for her disdain for my naivety.

"The higher purpose to which you refer being that of Dionysus?" I asked, unable to suppress my skepticism completely, even though I suspected it to be out of its depth.

"Or the forces that are sometimes manifest by way of that concept, if you prefer that way of expressing it."

"You mean that we're all simply pawns of destiny?"

"Certainly not. There is no destiny, nothing is fixed in advance; in spite of the tyranny of causation, time is an authentic exploration, not a mere unfolding. But we are, nevertheless, parts of a greater pattern. We are not merely passive instruments, but we are very tiny, and the scope we have to intervene in the great empire of causation is limited, even when we can combine our forces, not in vulgar armies but in genuine associations of feeling and desire. We do strive toward our ends, whatever they might be, in circumstances partly of our own choosing. We have to use our physical instruments in accordance with their capacities, and our magical instruments too, to the limited extent that we can. To the extent that we are instruments of a magic far beyond our power, however, we need to be as careful as we can be in cooperating with it and furthering its ends."

My mind seemed to be spinning slightly as I tried to maintain my equilibrium on the swell of ideas, Strangely enough, watching a small group Sileni working in a nearby field with hoes, plying the seemingly crude instruments with a remarkable measured dexterity, seemed to help. They were not even fully human, and were doing a kind of work quite alien to my personal experience, and yet I felt a sense of fellow feeling with them.

"That's why you brought us here?" I said to Madame. "You believe that you're...cooperating with the dictates, or the whims, of the gods?"

I had turned to look at her face, and was examining her with my artist's eye, trying to fathom her, even though I had every reason to believe that it would require long and expert contemplation even to scratch the surface of her inner being. She smiled again, but there was no mockery in the smile; she was trying to be patient.

"Like you, Master Rathenius," she said, "I now believe that characterizing the forces of magic as personalized gods is crude and somewhat misleading. It was helpful once, as a necessary crutch for thought, and it still is, in a symbolic sense, but the guidance it provides can sometimes lead us astray."

"So you're not actually taking orders from Dionysus?"

"It's equally misleading to treat such ideas as utter absurdities. Were you not following the guidance of Eurydice when you produced your Orpheus triptych? And were not Elise and Mariette participants in that guidance, albeit unwittingly?"

I had no answer to that.

"I'm still being *guided*, then?" I said, with a hint of bitterness. "Rather more brutally, it seems...and by Dionysus rather than Eurydice

"The brutality is mine, I admit," she said. "Nor can I claim to be acting to the specific dictates of whatever it is we conceive as the gods. I can't even guarantee, Master Rathenius, that in bringing you here, I've saved you from anything but the immediate danger that threatened you on Mnemosyne...which, I admit, I might even have unintentionally played some part in provoking, given that the Mesmays might have obtained some inkling of my interest in you. Nor can I guarantee that if you agree to do as I ask, you will be safe; it is not impossible that you might face dangers of a different kind, but no less deadly."

I was beginning to feel that I was going round in circles, lost in confusion.

"But what is it that you're asking, exactly—not just of me but if Mariette and Elise?"

"I want you, with their help, to complete the Orpheus."

"The triptych? I already have."

"You've completed the brushwork, but not the depiction. You've infused it with what you and I both consider to be the correct meaning, although the Marquise and her associates don't know what that meaning is, or the true purpose of the depiction. They believe that they're magicians, as many of those who have intercourse with magic tend to do, and they hope to use the image, one way or another, in an invocation, when they celebrate the Mysteries in six days' time. I shall celebrate a version of the Mysteries here at the same time—not something resembling the elaborate Great Mysteries of Eleusis, which were mostly theatricality, or even the Petty Mysteries, but an authentic bacchanal nevertheless."

"With what end?"

"I hope to cooperate—or, to be strictly accurate, to enable you, Elise and Mariette to cooperate—in enabling the painting to perform its true purpose."

"Which is?"

"I can't be sure, but I suspect, and hope, that it might be the redemption of Orpheus."

"Speaking symbolically, that is?"

"There isn't any other way to speak, given that we have no other effective language."

"It's a rather vague way of speaking."

"True. Perhaps you'll be able to help me develop a better one, if you decide to stay on the island."

"Provided that I survive the supernatural danger I might still be in?"

"That too. But magic's reputation for direct destruction is overstated. The gods have always been blamed for a great deal of evil that is accidental, or purely human."

"You say that Mesmay's co-conspirators believe themselves to be magicians, as many people fortunate or unfortunate enough to have intercourse with magic do...but you believe that you really *are* a magician?"

"Yes, but not in quite the same way," she said. "Do you believe that you're a magician?"

"I'm an artist."

"And you've always claimed that other magicians, whether self-described or accused, are artists too?"

"I've often used that argument," I admitted.

"But you don't claim to be in complete conscious control of your creative process. At the very least, you're responsible to esthetic principles that determine, independently of you, the value of your work. And you believe that there's an element of *discovery* in your work—in all true art work?"

"Yes."

"I agree. Magicians are not artisans, following repetitive methods to produce standardized results. Magicians are, or ought to be, artists engaged in a process of discovery, and responsible to esthetic principles. Magic isn't amenable to conscious and deterministic control, and no amount of wishing will make it so. Wanting to live indefinitely, no matter how avid the desire might be, isn't sufficient to make a Macrobian, nor is there any potion, talisman or spell that will do the trick. It might well be the case, too, that the Sileni are correct in the assertion that humans are simply not equipped for Macrobian existence, and that for the ultimate purposes of magic, the best thing really is for humans not to be born at all, and after that to die young—which could mean, given the vagueness of Silenian calculation, after three-score-years-and-ten, or thereabouts. For humans to live longer than that, given their innately self-abusive tendencies, might be reckoned an inevitable road to frustration and madness. You might yet become the closest thing to an exception I've seen, apart from myself, but you're still relatively young, and only time will tell. Given what you know of yourself, and what little you can see of me, thus far, can you be sure that the Sileni wisdom is wrong?"

I had long believed, sincerely if somewhat arrogantly, that I was the sanest person I knew, and that I owed that sanity even more to my longevity than to my artistry, but Madame had more information on which to draw than I had—and as for my observation of her, thus far...

The more important point seemed to be the degree to which would-be magicians could or could not obtain control over whatever forces were involved.

"If you were really able to hear Elise accompany Hecate's version of Eurydice's Lament over half the breadth of the Ocean," I observed, "then you really do have some...artisanal facility in magic."

"That was visionary magic," Madame agreed, "but I did not produce the vision deliberately or control it. It was gifted to me...or foisted upon me. You know something about how such things work. If Helen's reports are accurate, you have been party to numerous magical manifestations in the past, but you know full well that it was not you, or anyone else, that produced them deliberately. Even where there was deliberate effort involved, as in the séance when Eurydice was manifest, the role of the medium was not what she intended. I know that you have a better understanding of magic than that of common superstition, Master Rathenius. You seem to have guessed more in little more than a hundred years than I guessed in a thousand, but you have a rare artistic talent, and I required an extremely laborious education. Now, though, I think we have a broadly similar understanding of what art is, and what magic is, and why they're similar in certain crucial respects, if not identical. Even the child, who has very little education and has hardly begun to practice her art, has a fundamental grasp of the matter that you probably envy, just as I envy you."

Magician or not, she certainly seemed to know me a good deal better than she had any right to do, even if her agents had been spying on me for years.

"Go on," I said, when she paused.

"When you paint portraits," she said, "you believe that you have a special insight into the people you're painting—your artist's eye. What you are doing is not mere depiction, akin to a mirror or a photographic apparatus. And the process of producing the painting is not merely something that you are doing mechanically, with the brush. While reproducing the image, you are also *seeking*. Am I right?"

"Yes."

"And in the same way—even more so, given that music is a purer art than painting—when Elise improvises music, or even when she simply plays, as well as inventing the series of notes, she feels that there is a sense in which she is discovering them, while answering to some kind of esthetic standard that exists outside of her, independent of her?"

"True." I recalled, quite vividly, having tried to give Elise a similar explanation.

"And for all your skepticism, you admit that there is a magic in Elise's music, albeit not entirely of her making, and that there is also a magic in your painting, not entirely of your making?"

I hesitated. It was obvious given that Elise was a child, that any magic there might be in her music was not of her making—but I was an adult...

In fact, I realized, wryly, that in one sense, at least, I was a magical adult, no matter how much I tried to deny it, and I had no control over that particular magic. I was a Macrobian. It seemed oddly comforting to have a label for what I was, instead of simply being something other than mere human, something that I *was not*. But there was a sense in which even I, by Macrobian and magical standards, was still a child, only slightly older that Elise, and certainly no more of an artist than she was—perhaps less. I was, however, an artist, and if art was essentially magical, then I was a magician in that sense too."

"All right," I admitted. "The magic in my art and my life isn't of my making, even though I...cooperate with it. If there's some kind of magic in the Orpheus triptych, as you and the Marquise de Mesmay believe, I certainly helped to incorporate it, and to make it come out right, artistically, but that doesn't mean that I was entirely responsible for it—quite the opposite, in fact. I see what you mean, and I concede the point."

That was a conclusion of sorts, but she wasn't content simply to win the point. She had further arguments to make.

"And one of the expressions of the magic in your particular art," she said, "is the passion that sometimes binds you to your subjects?"

That took me by surprise, but I guessed immediately where she wanted to go.

"I've never thought of that aspect of my endeavor as magical," I replied, knowing how weak it sounded, given that I'd already conceded that I'd never thought of any aspect of my artistry or my longevity as "magical."

"Think about it now," she said. "It might be important. It is not just art and magic, is it, that seem to come partially from outside us, that seem to manifest themselves as external forces, something powerful—sometimes almost irresistible—which can evaporate as rapidly and mysteriously as it appears?"

I didn't bother to argue that if we followed that line of argument as far as it would go, a great deal of commonplace human experience might end up being redefined as magical. Her line of attack was more personal than that; she was asking me to think specifically about my art, and my passions.

"In matters of passion I had always considered myself to be simply...changeable," I observed, slightly uncomfortable in remembering the sophistry with which I'd tried to counter Hecate's assertion that I was fickle, and her corollary assertion that I was only able to deny it because I had my own self-serving interpretation of what the word implied. I hastened to add: "I seem to be incapable, at any rate, of maintaining the kind of durable passion that is generally held up as an ideal, and of which some people seem to be genuinely capable."

"Perhaps some are," Madame suggested, "but in my long experience many more are not, no matter how they might deny it. Many more are merely maintaining a fierce pretence, or perverting some other kind of dependency."

"That has always been my impression too," I admitted.

"Reflecting the remarkable human capacity for self-deception and denial, which even Macrobians have difficulty leaving behind..."

"Perhaps," was all that I was willing to concede for the moment, although I was aware that the reluctance of the concession was itself perilously close to a proof of the argument.

She didn't press the point any further, and didn't even recommend that I try to open my eyes a little wider and make more effort to shed the prejudices I'd inherited. Instead, she said: "Let's return to the Orpheus triptych. I deduce that you found difficulty executing the commission, until you received the appropriate inspiration, from Eurydice and Elise. Am I right?"

"Yes," I admitted, freely enough.

"But eventually, you believed that you had made the crucial discovery, the one that enabled you to complete your conceptualization of Orpheus in your mind, and hence on the canvas?"

"Yes—but I'm not foolish enough to believe that I had actually intuited an actual historical fact. Indeed, I don't believe there ever was any actual fact to intuit. If there ever was a real individual on whom the legends surrounding the name of Orpheus are based, he certainly never visited the Underworld in order to recover his lost love, whether or not he actually had slain her in a sudden burst of uncontrollable anger, and if any real individual was torn apart by maenads, his severed head didn't actually continue singing, accompanied by his floating lyre, while it drifted downriver to the sea."

"Indeed," she said. "But the painting isn't devoid of meaning in consequence, is it? Its meaning is expressed in symbols, but it is a real meaning. What you were doing, in seeking appropriate inspiration, was trying to sort the symbolism into a pattern whose esthetics seemed satisfactory to you—not your client."

That was a fair point too. I certainly hadn't intended to communicate my understanding of that symbolism to the Marquis—or to the Marquise, once Mesmay was dead. I didn't suppose for a moment, given that they were members of the Cult of Orpheus who took their Mysteries seriously, that they would approve of my interpretation of the story of Orpheus and Eurydice; nor did I think there was any danger that the Marquise or her associates might deduce it simply by looking at the painting. But Madame seemed to know it; magic had told her…just as it had told me. That was why, in her attempt to cooperate with the magic, and assist it to fulfill a purpose of which she approved, she had employed her own clumsy and brutal methods to bring me here, along with my unwitting collaborators.

In Madame's view, it seemed, the art embodied in the triptych, insofar as it was authentically magical, still had to take its effect—and it still had to be enabled to take its effect. Given that she was the one gifted, or cursed, with magical vision, I was in no position to deny it, no matter how reluctant I might be to believe it.

All I said aloud was: "I finished the painting to my own satisfaction, in the way that made esthetic sense to me."

"Much of what you say about the dearth of actuality behind the myth is probably true," Madame conceded, "although you might want to add an element of doubt to your assertion that Orpheus never actually went to an

Underworld, now you know that the Sileni, whose one-time existence you would doubtless have dismissed as pure fantasy two hours ago, not only existed in ancient Arcadia, but still exist here. The real point is that nothing you've said opposes my argument, but actually supports it."

"You argument being that the magic producing the symbolic imagery of Eurydice is real, and that those supernatural manifestations not only helped me straighten out in my own mind what I needed to see as the heart of the story, in order to complete the paining to my own satisfaction, but actually incorporated magical properties into the triptych."

"In essence, yes. Attributing a personality to the force involved with a name is a convenient artifice, a matter of symbolization. My argument doesn't rest on the supposition that Eurydice was a real person, who actually went to a real Underworld following her death, where she lamented and is still lamenting. The force that we're dealing with is more impersonal than that, and more mercurial. It does appear to have a purpose of sorts, but that purpose might not comprehensible in terms of vulgar human motives. All we really know about it—all *I* really know about it, at any rate, after more than a thousand years of intensive study—is that it has an esthetic quality...or perhaps that it's the very definition of esthetics."

"So, magic—which is to say, the mysterious force behind the natural phenomena that we call supernatural because we don't yet understand them—is fundamentally esthetic? All its operations are aspects of some vast work of art? In fact, the universe...existence itself...is fundamentally a work of art?"

"Isn't that what you've always believed?"

"Not always," I said. "In fact, it's taken me rather a long time to reach that conclusion, and I'm not sure I'm quite there yet."

"I suspected as much. That's why I'm trying to help you arrive there."

I studied the landscape again while I thought about that. It was becoming more impressive the higher up the mountain we ascended. I was surprised to observe that we had now surpassed the crop-fields and the orchards, and had come into the higher pastureland, where I now observed, in the distance to the right and the left, that sheep and goats were grazing in places as well as cattle. There were cottages distributed on the side of the mountain, built on a scale that seemed to me to be more appropriate to Sileni than humans—unlike the farmhouses whose russet roofs I could now see strung like strange beads among the crop-fields, which seemed more like human dwellings.

There was bushier uncultivated vegetation to either side of the path ahead of us, and the path, although it have never been straight, seemed more obviously winding as it followed the contours of the terrain. From the guest-house—whose mansard I could just about make out, at the limit of vision, the region in which I was now standing had seemed smooth and even, but now that we had reached it, its many folds and bumps were much more obvious.

A few hundred paces ahead, if we kept going, we would enter a dense wood, but for the moment it was possible to look back all the way to our starting-point, and over the entire panorama of the southern part of the island. From this vantage, the overwhelming impression of all the fields growing cereals, and all the orchards producing fruit was one of order and discipline, but devoid of a regularity that had been forced on the landscape by geometry. The order seemed harmonious with the contours of the gentle slope, their ridges, dales and streams. It was beautiful, and it was placid. As Helen had promised, the island was lovely.

Although the human laborers tending the fields and the herds were almost equal in numbers to the Sileni, it seemed to me that the Sileni were somehow setting the pace and the pattern of the labor. They weren't unduly slow-moving, but their bulk make their actions seem more ponderous more carefully-weighed. From our present lofty position, even the Sileni on the lower slopes seemed relatively tiny, not significantly different in dimension from their slightly smaller fellows, but there was something about the way they went about their work that seemed particularly measured and unhurried.

Just as there was a harmony in the landscape, I thought, there seemed to be a special kind of harmony in the movement and maneuvers of the Sileni, a kind of rhythm. Those working the fields were by no means children of nature; everything I could see, looking back down the mountain, was the produce of artifice and endeavor, of science—but it was not quite the same kind of artifice and science that could be seen in the fields in the heart of Mnemosyne. Nor was the difference simply a corollary of the fact that the farmers on Mnemosyne used heavy machinery and horses, whereas the implements employed on the Island of Dionysus seemed, from what I could see, to be almost all hand-held. The only plow I could see in current employment was being drawn by oxen.

The matter, I thought, needed further investigation—but not yet. I still needed further clarification about many matters that seemed far more urgent.

"So," I said to Madame, who was standing by patiently, almost as if she too were modeling her conduct on the Sileni, "what you're telling me is that, in a magical sense, the triptych hasn't yet begun to fulfill its function. The Marquise de Mesmay and her associates in the cult intend to use it in their next celebration of the Mysteries, as a symbolic aid in some kind of evocation of Orpheus?"

"Yes—but partly thanks to you, they have no idea of what possibilities are really inherent in the role that the painting might play, and they are not aware that the magical rite they intend to carry out will almost certainly misfire, even if we do not or cannot intervene."

"But you do know what possibilities are inherent in the painting's magic?"

"I hope and firmly believe that I have a better idea—but it's only fair to admit to you that I might be wrong. I'm not in control of this, even though I believe that I have a part to play that requires both effort and ingenuity."

"And you want me—us—to play a part in your theatrics?"

"I do. That's why I brought you here."

"You want Elise to play at your bacchanal?"

"Yes."

"Under the influence of some kind of drug?"

"She will not need the cyteon; she has her music."

"Mariette's afraid that you might want to involve her in some kind of orgy."

"Our rites can and do make use of erotic magic on occasion, but Elise needs to remain apart from that kind of passion. Her role requires that she concentrate fully on her music, with no distractions."

"And Mariette? What's her role?"

"Aren't you more concerned about what I expect of you?"

"Perhaps, but I've made Mariette a promise that I'll do my best to protect both her and Elise. I have a responsibility. Anything I might agree to do is dependent on what you want them to do."

"How very chivalrous. To begin with, at least, I don't want either of you to do anything that you had not already decided to do. Firstly, and principally, I'd like you to paint her portrait, before the rite."

"You want me to paint her portrait during the next six days?"

"Yes. The timescale shouldn't cause any difficulty, and you have already decided that you want to paint her, just as she has decided that she wants you to do it, so in this instance, the requirements of the magic are merely collaborating with your own desires and intentions."

She was smiling slightly, to symbolize her deliberate ingenuousness. She knew what she was really asking, and she knew that I knew it.

"And suppose it doesn't work?" I said. "Suppose that I don't feel an erotic passion—as I sometimes don't—or suppose, which happens even more frequently, that she doesn't?"

"But you already do," she countered. "And so does she."

I remembered Hecate Rain's comments about spearing fish in a barrel, and the possible difficulty of identifying the spear-wielder and the fish.

"All right," I conceded. "You want me to paint Mariette. You want to stimulate passion between us. What then?"

"I want you to invoke Orpheus...the real Orpheus, not the one that the Marquise de Mesmay will try to invoke...and Dionysus. *My* Orpheus and Dionysus, that is—and yours, as an initiate. That's why I cannot achieve anything without you. For the time being, that magic is in you, in your creative imagination. You cannot enact the redemption alone, but without you, it cannot be enacted."

"I'm just a painter. I don't understand how I can accomplish anything at all in your rite, even as a mere cooperative instrument—and I don't see how my painting Mariette is going to help, whether it not it involves my seducing her...or her seducing me."

"You will understand, I hope, once your initiation is complete, and you have looked into the Mirror of Dionysus. If you don't...well, you won't have done anything you didn't want to do anyway, and at least you didn't get stabbed to death on Mnemosyne. You won't have any reason to feel disappointed, even if I will."

Her diction and her manner had become noticeably more relaxed, less formal. I realized that she too had been apprehensive about this encounter, not certain that it would work to her satisfaction. She was beginning to feel more comfortable in my presence, perhaps more confident that I was capable of fitting into her scheme.

"And you think that I owe it to you to comply with what you want me to do?" I suggested.

"No," she said. "I abducted all three of you, by force. You don't owe me anything, even for saving your life, which I did it for my own motives. But you might feel that you owe me something—or at least, that you wouldn't like to disappoint me—because there's so much that you might obtain from a continued sojourn on the island, and so much that I might be able to teach you that you'd very much like to learn."

There didn't seem to be any point in resistance. I really might have an enormous amount to gain, judging by what I'd learned from her already, about the world and about myself.

"You'll teach me the necessary rite for the...invocation, I suppose? All I'll need to do at your celebration is recite the requisite formulae?"

"Oh no," she said. "You'll surely need to do a great deal more than that. That's only what I want—that's where my part ends. What the magic wants—what the esthetic pattern demands, if it's to be completed to the satisfaction of Dionysus, isn't for me to determine or predict. It will probably be necessary, in sense, for you to *become* Orpheus, and Dionysus Zagreus, in a symbolic sense. Exactly what that will involve, I can't tell. All I can say for sure is that if you refuse, or fail, the pattern will remain incomplete, and the work of art will be spoiled. What the consequences will be of that, in detail, I don't know...but I've seen many nascent magical patterns aborted in the past, by virtue of human reluctance and failure, and in my experience, it doesn't tend to work out well, either for the people directly involved or for others."

"Is that a threat?"

"I fear so, but it's certainly not my threat. I mean no harm to anyone. Like you, I even mourn Dellacrusca, for all his faults, and it disappoints me greatly to see innocents get hurt. I believe that if the evocation of Orpheus and Dionysus goes awry, or even if it works out to the Marquise de Mesmay's warped satisfaction, there will be bloodshed, perhaps abundantly, and uncontrollably. My hope is that if the true Orpheus can be allowed to act, through the person of Dionysus Zagreus—for symbolic purposes, you—then much, if not all, of that bloodshed might be avoided. Human history doesn't give the relevant impression, I know, but the magic of the universe has a liking for peace, and harmony. Harmony, as you know, is one of the most fundamental aspects of esthetics. If magic gets its way—as it sometimes can, with the cooperation of our limited artistry—harmony results. Tragedy has its own esthetic, but it's a plaintive esthetic. It's not the ideal. The ideal, as you know full well, is beauty, and love."

XI. Initiation

We followed the path into the outskirts of the wooded area, but instead of continuing up the mountain, Madame took a path that veered to the right and led along the flank of the hill. There were sounds audible to the left of us, which suggested the presence of large creatures, and I immediately thought of the "nymphs" that Madame had mentioned, but none put in an appearance that I could detect. If they were there, then they were being discreet—which didn't necessarily mean, I thought, that they weren't keeping watch on us.

I didn't recognize the tree species any more than I had recognized most of the fruit-trees under cultivation in the orchards, but they were just trees, and in the part of the wood where we were walking they were modestly-sized. There were birds in the branches, and animals recognizable as squirrels, although they weren't identical to species I'd seen in the trees of the Empire, as well as others I labeled as monkeys, but I didn't see any larger animals. We didn't stay in the woods long; we soon veered to the right again and came back into the open, in order to head down the mountain again by a different but equally winding path. From the vantage point at the top of the path, I could see the distant roofs of what seemed to be a coastal town, with a harbor, but it was soon hidden by rising ground.

"My house is beyond the wood," Madame told me, "I'll take you there before the ceremony, at least briefly, to show you the library, and the laboratory. I'll show you the rest of the island too, in time, and you'll be able to select your own living accommodation if you decide to stay. For the time being, though, I'd rather you remained in the guest-house. You're free to explore on your own, of course, with or without Helen's guidance."

"Helen's guidance sometimes leaves much to be desired," I observed. "All this is a great deal to take in at short notice. Helen could have told me at least some of this while I was on the ship. In fact, Helen could presumably have told me some of this years ago, when she first identified me to you as a person of interest."

"Doubtless she would have liked to do so, and would have been delighted to invite you to become an initiate then, if she had been able to reveal her affiliation. She was distinctly regretful when she told me today that she'd discovered that you wanted to paint her then, as she would have liked you to do. Perhaps I was selfish in reserving so much to tell you myself, and putting strict limits on what she could tell you, but her own knowledge of many things is limited, and the accounts she would have been able to give you might have been misleading."

"Perhaps she ought to have been better informed."

"Perhaps—but there are reasons why the Mysteries are mysterious, and why initiation precedes by stages. Magic is a form of art; for esthetic reasons, it requires mystery and suspense. It requires things to be done in particular ways, in order not to spoil the effect. I cannot cast spells or work miracles to order, but I have reason to believe that I now have a better understanding of magic than any other person now alive, and probably better than anyone in the past ever had. You know from long experience how difficult it is to respond to all the questions your clients ask about what you're doing and why, and how you simply have to ask them, much of the time, to trust your judgment.

"I'm working a lot harder than that to include you, but there's a still a line where I simply have to say: *Trust me*. Six years isn't time to take it all in, let alone six days, and it requires careful thought that takes even longer, and of which many people are incapable—for reasons I understand only too well, having long been incapable myself. You don't have the hundreds of years that it's taken me to follow my path, and even if your native intelligence and a good tutor might permit you to reach a similar stage in a tenth of that time…we don't even have a tiny fraction of that, at present."

I could see her point, although it didn't prevent me from feeling resentful about her parsimony in forbidding Helen to tell me the things that I had most dearly wanted to know.

"How many human Macrobians have you known?" I asked her, after a brief pause for reflection.

"Hundreds…but mostly in terms of distant acquaintance. Only seven or eight that I could properly call friends, or associates…and those associations proved to be disappointingly brief, for one reason or another."

I needed to know what those reasons were, given that I could hardly help thinking about the possibility of forming some sort of association with her myself, but I wanted to stick to questions with short answers, for the time being.

"How many are there on the island now?"

"Perhaps twenty, but none more than two hundred years old and all, with the possible exception of Theano…disappointing, one way or another."

"Who's Theano."

"A musicienne. You'll meet her shortly. I want her to work with Elise."

"I presume that the Macrobians you've known didn't all die violently or accidentally? Some of...us die naturally long before reaching your antiquity?"

"Indeed. Some simply start to age, as arbitrarily as they stopped, and die of belated old age, and there are other kinds of natural death that Macrobianism has no power to prevent; we're not completely immune to disease. Death isn't the only form of disappointment, though. Some Macrobians lapse into stereotyped and repetitive forms of behavior and mentality, like the semi-human Macrobians, but more exaggerated, and they lose what you and I would consider to be their humanity. Not many can preserve their artistic or intellectual verve even for as long as you've contrived to do. The kind of longevity we have is a long way from veritable immortality, alas. Perhaps some individuals coped with its problems better back in the Golden Age, if the legends of the better gods really are based on exceptional Macrobians rather than fantasies of other sorts, but I'm skeptical. That might be just an effect of my own arrogance, though: the desire to believe that I'm the most exceptional of the exceptional, the most accomplished of the accomplished."

I wasn't particularly surprised by any of what she had told me. I'd long ago concluded that my apparent privilege was probably very limited in its scope: that I was still a mortal, subject to all mortal fears and all mortal possibilities of distress, merely one who was enjoying an unusually protracted adulthood, which might turn to incipient decay or be interrupted by sudden death at any moment. I hadn't even made any particular effort to study my condition; I had simply set out to make the most of it while it lasted, as best I could...and not entirely successfully, in spite of having made steady progress.

The news of the statistical failure rate was still unwelcome, however, and ominous.

"You never managed to find a...long-term companion among the Macrobians you've known?" I asked

"No," she replied, simply. "I've had Macrobian lovers, obviously, but passion between Macrobian humans is just as perishable as it is between common mortals. We're not Sileni."

"Do you still have the capacity for temporary passion after two millennia?" I asked, curiously.

"Yes," she said, "but you'll understand that one does become gradually more blasé. If you do eventually get the opportunity to paint me, I hope you won't expect too much of any...corollaries."

"To tell the truth," I said. "I think I'm becoming a trifle blasé myself. I'm not convinced that the old reflexes will still operate...in the next six days."

I wasn't being insincere. I genuinely wasn't sure what effect painting Mariette's portrait might have on me. I had, as Madame had pointed out, wanted to do it since I first saw her—but I had also wanted to paint Elise, and had always given that project a tacit priority in my mental plans, perhaps precisely because it could not lead to anything further, and the prospect embodied no threat of disappointment.

"I'm convinced," Madame assured me. In a tone that sounded slightly wistful, she added: "You're still young." Then, she moved swiftly to change the subject. "Shall we continue with your initiation now?"

"My initiation? I thought we'd settled that. I'll do what you want, as and when you want me to. I thought that, for the moment, we're just having a conversation?"

"We are, but in the course of that conversation, your initiation has begun—although, there's a sense in which it began as soon as you accepted the commission to paint Orpheus for the Cult. Your route to the heart of the mysteries is already unconventional, but exceptional circumstances require exceptional measures. The version of the rites we'll celebrate in six days' time to coincide with the version being held on Mnemosyne will necessarily be an abbreviated version, which will skip much of the indoctrination—the educative element, that is. I've already begun the revelation simply by mentioning the name Zagreus, and you probably have certain other pieces of the puzzle in your possession, although some of them are doubtless misleading. The Marquise's sister paid you a visit, I gather, to warn you that you might be in danger, before Dellacrusca's murder."

"Yes. Clovis asked me whether she might be involved in Mesmay's scheming, but I couldn't believe that she was. Am I wrong?"

"Not as far as I know, and my spies would be very incompetent if they hadn't uncovered any misrepresentation on her part. To the best of my knowledge, she and her sister went their separate ways long ago, in ideological terms. The Marquise doubtless took sly advantage of her in order to pass off her own murderous instruments as Sisters of Shalimar, but it's extremely unlikely, in my view, that Ursule lend herself to the conspiracy willingly. The reason I mentioned her is that I know you sent her one of the copies of Toustain's document, and must have consulted her, when she came to see you, as to what she knew about the legendry of Orpheus. Any information she gave you was undoubtedly sincere, but possibly mistaken, and her notion of Dionysus and our cult is undoubtedly tainted by prejudices obtained from her sister."

201

"She didn't tell me anything about Dionysus, and was very tentative in what she told me about Orpheus and the history of the cults. But while we're on the subject, what exactly was the document, and why was Toustain hiding it?"

"He stole it from the island—from my house, in fact. He was an advanced initiate, so he should have known better, but not everyone acquires the same wisdom and the same attitude from the initiation process. He was a seaman originally, an officer on board one of our ships, and seamen have a tendency to be excessively superstitious. His understanding of magic was evidently seriously mistaken, and he probably believed that if only he could decipher the script and make use of the formula contained therein, he would be able to practice necromancy. You can understand why he hid that purpose, and the document that he hoped to use as a means."

"The document isn't really magic, then?"

"Of course it is, but not in the sense that he understood magic. It's not a formula for a spell that merely has to be deciphered and then recited in order to take effect. Elise and Hecate Rain do seem to have made something of it, enabling my vision, among other effects, but they barely scratched its surface. I have others like it, and Elise will have time to investigate them, with Theano's help, if she decides to stay on the island."

"Why on earth did Toustain bequeath it to me?"

"I can't be sure, but I don't think he meant any harm to come to you. He must have realized fairly rapidly that it was useless to him, but that doesn't seem to have decreased his determination to hide it, and himself. I've known where he was for years, although I had no idea what he had done with the document. I was content for him to retain custody of it, for the time being, and would have been content for it to remain buried in your library if I'd known that he'd passed it on to you—but once the notary had revealed Toustain's true identity, I couldn't act quickly enough to forestall Dellacrusca. Can we return to the initiation now? There's still a great deal that I need to explain."

"Indeed—for a start, who's Zagreus?"

"Dionysus. He has several names, as most of the old gods do. As well as Zagreus, Dionysus is also Iacchus the torch-bearer, and he became fused with Bacchus, the god of wine, although the intoxication he symbolizes is considerably more refined than mere drunkenness. For the purposes of the Mysteries, however, the most important identification—the heart of the Mystery—is that Dionysus is Zagreus.

"So far as I've been able to determine, because their origins were long before my time, the Eleusinian Mysteries were originally centered on the story of two children of Zeus, who were also related to Demeter, the Earth-Mother: Persephone and Zagreus.

"Persephone, as exoteric mythology also relates, was abducted by Hades, the god of the Underworld, and although Demeter eventually recovered her, Persephone had eaten a pomegranate seed while she was in the Underworld, and was obliged by that negligence to remain bound to Hades for part of the year thereafter, during which time Demeter, out of resentment or grief, stopped the earth from flourishing: hence the origin of the cycle of the seasons.

"Zagreus was, according to one version of his story, fathered by Zeus on Persephone, although other versions make his mother Demeter. Either way, Zeus is said to have planned to make Zagreus his heir."

"That seems to be at odds with his own alleged immortality," I couldn't help interjecting.

"The Greeks of ages before my own don't seem to have had any difficulty about crediting their gods with mortality—or, indeed, with the faculty of resurrection after death.

"According to the story incorporated into the Eleusinian Mysteries, Hera, who wanted one of her own children to be Zeus's heir, persuaded Titans to abduct and kill Persephone's child, which they did by beguiling him with a magic mirror, in which he saw himself, not reflected in mere appearance, but as he truly was and might yet become.

"The Titans not only killed Zagreus but devoured his flesh, except for the heart, which was recovered and returned to Zeus—accounts vary as to who was responsible for that. Zeus implanted the heart in the womb of a mortal woman, Semele, where it became an embryo, allowing Zagreus to be reborn, as Dionysus.

"Dionysus could not remember, to begin with, having previously been Zagreus, and was thus ignorant of his own identity, nature and destiny—until the day eventually came when he was able to look into the same magic mirror with which the Titans had beguiled his former self, which had been held at Eleusis and kept in a special casket called the kiste. The climactic moment of the Eleusian rite consisted of a reenactment of that moment: the opening of the kiste and presenting the mystes—candidates for initiation—each in his or her turn, after elaborate preparation and indoctrination, with a supposedly magic mirror in which they were supposed to be able to see their true selves, and their potential selves.

"Although many naïve initiates must have interpreted the phrase 'potential selves' to mean their predestined future, that was a mistake, because there is no destiny. What they were actually supposed to see, and understand, was what might become of them if they made the appropriate effort, and were sufficiently strong and clever, and received the endorsement of the gods—or the forces behind magic, in a depersonalized sense."

"Where does Orpheus come in?"

"I'm getting to that. So far as I was able to piece together the history, long after the fact, Orpheus was a human, albeit a uniquely gifted one, almost certainly a Macrobian, and definitely a musical genius. He was initially a priest of Apollo, but became a zealous convert to the worship of Dionysus Zagreus, and eventually became the effective leader of the Dionysian cult in Eleusis. That caused political disputes with the followers of Apollo, represented in symbolic terms as a conflict between the gods themselves, which became confused.

"Somehow, by virtue of a chain of causation I couldn't reconstitute, the disputes in question led to a conflict within the Cult of Dionysus itself, provoked by the Apollinians, which eventually led, long after Orpheus' death, to the formation of a splinter cult devoted to the direct worship of Orpheus. The Apollinians seem to have vanished from the scene, or at last become irrelevant to the new rivalry between the two cults whose remnants still exist today—represented in Orphean mythology as a conflict between the figureheads.

"The story was put around—long after the death of the actual individual, of course—the Orpheus had been torn apart by maenads at the behest of Dionysus and his severed head cast into the river Hebrus. The story of the excursion to the Underworld probably originated from the same period. Those eventually became the key features of the Orpheus myth, both in the esoteric dogmas of the Cult of Orpheus and the exoteric mythology featured in your triptych. Within our cult, however, both stories are denied—or, rather, regarded as pastiches of the account of Zagreus being torn apart by Titans, and Demeter traveling to the Underworld to attempt to recover Persephone from Hades.

"In our version of the Mysteries, Orpheus has been despoiled and belied, but the possibility remains of a reconciliation between Orpheus and Dionysus, who have been made into enemies by ignorant followers, if only Orpheus, symbolically resurrected or reborn, can see himself in the Mirror of Dionysus, not only as he truly is but as he might become, with the right determination and the appropriate godly, or magical assistance. That would involve a symbolic fusion of the resurrected Orpheus with Dionysus Zagreus: a fusion necessary to the completion of Zagreus' ultimate becoming, and his fulfillment of his own thwarted potential.

"I can't be certain, because it's a secret, but I have reason to believe that the Orphean version of the Mysteries retains the kiste, for symbolic reasons, but that it no longer contains a mirror. In their rite, the climactic revelation of the initiation is shifted to another container, the kalathis, which contains a musical instrument, representing Orpheus' lyre. According to the myth of his death, the original lyre was salvaged from the sea and hung up in a temple of Apollo until it was stolen. In the Orpheans' version of the rite, I suspect, initiates stroke the strings of the instrument taken from the kalathis, and the vibrations are supposed to awaken a self-awareness in them akin to the one supposed to be provided by the mirror in ours.

"The Orpheans are supposed to believe—the mystics among them at least—that the kalathis instrument is capable of evoking the spirit of Orpheus, for the purpose of issuing oracles, and instructions. I strongly suspect that Dellacrusca and his predecessors have used that belief in the past to contrive instructions to be given to their credulous followers. I also suspect that the organizers of the coup against Dellacrusca intended to turn the trick against him at the forthcoming celebration of the mysteries, and to organize a charade identical in its principal effects to the one that you saw—but that when an unexpected opportunity presented itself in the form of the concert that Dellacrusca organized for his newly-discovered granddaughter to play the alleged music of sighs, they decided that the chance was too good to miss and brought their plans forward, intending to follow up at the impending celebration of the Mysteries in order to consolidate their takeover and deflect their followers' ire against the Dionysians.

"It was a bad plan, in my opinion, and I'm not sure that Mesmay could have brought it off even if Dellacrusca hadn't caught on to what was happening at the last moment and killed him, opening the present split and confusion in the Orphean ranks. Now, the Marquise and her associates have had to improvise, rapidly. They still intend to use your triptych, as Mesmay had, to help them produce an invocation of Orpheus and an oracle of some sort, but exactly what they have in mind, I can't be entirely sure. I'm certain that the Marquise, at least, actually hopes to employ the magic of the rite and the magic of the painting, to enable her to contrive a genuine magical manifestation, but some of her supporters probably have a deceptive back-up plan ready to pronounce a supposed oracle by cruder means."

"But what does the Marquise hope to achieve by her invocation?"

"Domination. She wants the entire cult to submit to her will, and through its instrumentality, she hopes to become the effective ruler of the Empire—the power behind its throne."

"But you don't think it will work, even if you do nothing?"

"No. Like so many people who fancy themselves to be magicians, the Marquise believes that she can actually bend magic to her will, to serve her ends—but she can't. Her efforts, in my judgment, will only lead to confusion, and perhaps to disaster."

"And you think that she would have tried to involve Elise and Mariette in her rite, if you hadn't stolen them away, and that she'll still attempt to use Hecate and Vashti."

"Yes—and probably an entire company of bacchantes, drawn from the ranks of the cult. Vashti and Hecate will doubtless be presented as mystes, if they can be persuaded, or pressured, into doing so, as you and Mariette will be presented at our rite. That might well go awry too, even if we do nothing, but now that the Marquise thinks she has some expertise in the making of bacchantes, having successfully manipulated the ones she employed to kill Dellacrusca, she's probably dangerously overconfident."

"You think that in trying to obtain control over the cult, she'll actually unleash conflict—bloody conflict—but you hope that your intervention…our intervention…might prevent that?"

"Yes."

It was all inordinately complicated, but I was able to grasp the bare bones of it.

"And I'm supposed to look into your magic mirror, and make what effort I can to evoke the spirit of…Orpheus, or Zagreus, or whatever symbolic form the esthetic pattern of the forces of magic requires?"

"Precisely."

It still seemed anything but precise to me. "In order to do what? And how?"

"Hopefully prevent, to prevent the assembly at the Mesmay manse turning into a bloodbath that might spread all over the island and send repercussions through the entire Empire."

"But why? Wouldn't it work to the advantage of your Dionysian organization if the rival Cult tore itself apart?"

"No. As I said before, Dellacrusca and I were always working to the same ends by different means. We both wanted stability and order within the Empire, but he wanted to obtain it by stern authority and tyrannical oppression, whereas I want to promote peace and harmony. If the Cult of Orpheus disintegrates bloodily, it will be a disaster from my viewpoint as well as theirs. I'd rather its members returned to the true fold, but even the fervent rivalry that has subsisted for millennia has maintained a certain equilibrium, a valuable balance."

"And you think that Dionysus Zagreus, or Orpheus, can prevent the rival cult's disintegration?"

"With your help, yes—at least, I'm hopeful. I can't give you any more detail, though, of what you're role will involve, once you've looked into the mirror. As I said before, my calculated endeavor stops there. After that, it's up to the forces of magic, and the logic of esthetic completion."

"But you're certain that *something* will happen…otherwise, what can the purpose of the various manifestations of Eurydice have been? Assuming, that is that they really did have a purpose...and assuming that they were more than a collective hallucination."

"Those are the assumptions on which I have to work. You have the recourse of believing that they were produced by your own unconscious mind, simply to prompt you to make up a suitable story to tell yourself in order to help you complete the triptych, and in a sense that's true...but even so, you ought to ask yourself whether your unconscious mind might have had a purpose beyond spurring you to complete the painting."

"That's the difficult point," I admitted. "I'm not sure I can believe in that further purpose."

"Belief might not be necessary, at least in advance—just the willingness to try. If your skepticism turns out to be justified, you have nothing to lose. If it doesn't...well, then you might have something to lose, but you will surely also have something to gain. It's a gamble I would take. In effect, it's a gamble I have taken, many times."

In fact, I wasn't sure that I could continue to refuse to believe that there was more involved in what had already happened than my own unconscious mind prompting me to finish an awkward painting. Could I really think that my unconscious mind had had any authority over Elise and Mariette, to name but two? It was Mariette, not me, who had appeared to channel Eurydice at Vashti Savage's séance. And I knew, beyond a shadow of a doubt, that Elise had improvised the music of sighs, with a little promoting from Hecate Rain. I'd had nothing to do with it—except that I'd reaped the benefit, in realizing what Eurydice's lament was apparently trying to tell me.

And Madame had brought all three of us to the island of Dionysus, in order to retain the collaboration.

"Do you think that Elise and Mariette are really necessary?" I asked her. "That I can't do anything without them?"

"My hard-won knowledge of the workings of magic suggests that there's a much greater chance of success if the nexus can be sustained, and refined."

"The nexus?"

"I've been studying manifestations of magic assiduously for more than a thousand years. Although I'm convinced that no one can actually produce determined magical effects by means of incantations and apparatus, I'm equally convinced that there are combinations of objects, events and individuals—especially individuals—that are conducive to magical effects of some kind. I call a combination of that sort a nexus. The assembly of the cult is a nexus of sorts, but a broad one. A more focused manifestation of magic seems to require a more narrowly focused nexus. In respect of the phenomena associated with your triptych, I judge that the other elements, apart from the paintings and you, are Elise, in combination with her viola, and Mariette. By gathering three of those elements here, I hope to complete a kind of symbolic mirror in which the human triptych here and the artistic triptych on Mnemosyne can, in spite of the distance involved, unite the two bacchanals."

"And the Marquise of Mesmay will also be attempt to contrive a nexus of sorts, with her company of bacchantes? In fact, that's what she tried to contrive with the bacchantes who murdered Dellacrusca—the fact that there were so many of them wasn't just ludicrous overkill; it was part of some kind of rite?"

"Yes—it was a perversion of the process, of course, but she presumably sees it as a great success, as her husband would have done had he not fallen into his own trap."

"And you hope, by linking and fusing the two rites, to induce harmony where the Marquise de Mesmay wants to assert control—perhaps even bring about a reconciliation between the two cults?"

"That's one way of looking at it."

"What's the other?"

"To bring about a rebirth and reconfiguration of Orpheus and the spiritual fusion of Orpheus and Zagreus."

"Which is just a symbolic representation of what I said."

"And as I said, that's one way of looking at it."

"Which way do you look at it."

"The same way as you do, with conscientious skepticism—but I'm not sure that magic looks at it the same way."

I stared at her, and then nodded. She was a very strange woman—but she was two thousand years old. What else could I expect?

I glanced back at the silent Sileni, who were still dogging our footsteps.

"Do they ever speak?" I asked.

"Yes, of course, in their own language. They can be quite voluble, when necessary. When it isn't, they aren't."

"Do they always follow you around like this?"

"Yes. It's a tradition of theirs that two of them should always accompany me. They take turns. It was necessary once, as a protective measure, when I first came to the island. There were troubles then; the Sileni now regard me as their protector, perhaps their savior from the evil ways of our humankind. Because I'm a Macrobian, and an exceptionally long-lived one, they consider that I've transcended the curse of my human birth and nature, and become quasi-divine. They credit me with the fact that peace and harmony reign here, and they're at least partly correct, just as I once had a little to do with the fact that peace and harmony presently reign, albeit more precariously, in the Empire. The Sileni don't like change; once a tradition is in place, they tend not to let it lapse. I don't need bodyguards any longer, but their attendance helps maintain my image and status within the human population. The humans are intimidated by them—not entirely without reason. If anyone did take it unto his head to move violently against me, he'd certainly regret it. They're not as slow as they seem, and they're extremely strong and persistent."

"What about the other semi-human race you mentioned? The Nymphs?"

"They're shy and retiring, which is why you didn't catch a glimpse of one while we came past the edge of the forest. They're not unintelligent, but they're even simpler in their thinking than the Sileni…ideal bacchantes, in a way. They're long-lived, like the Sileni. They're all females, but, although they're able to conceive without male intervention, their anatomy suggests to me that there must once have been males of the species, although they obviously became extinct long ago. Physically, they're even closer to human appearance than the Sileni, but their mythological reputation for beauty is exaggerated, as you'll see at the celebration, if you don't have a chance to meet any of them beforehand. Charles Parenot's various paintings depicting Mariette as a nymph are, to judge by the descriptions I've heard of them, drastically romanticized. Their lack of pulchritude didn't stop the original human invaders of Arcadia from subjecting them to rape as well as massacre, of course, although they didn't dare subject the female Sileni to the same discourtesy. Even human bestiality has limits, when fear is involved. But that's hearsay, from long before my time."

She didn't seem to have a high opinion of human nature—but she was two thousand years old, and must have lived through a great many interesting times before settling permanently on the island. She seemed to have succeeded in maintaining peace and harmony in this small enclave, or at least collaborating with its maintenance; I wondered how much contribution she had made, in her days of empire-shaping dreams, to the stability that had permitted the consolidation of present-day quietude. It had doubtless been small, but small contributions cam sometimes make big differences as their effects accumulate over time. Perhaps, I thought, if I stayed on the island long enough, she'd be able to tell me the whole story, but it would require a long time.

We had come full circle and had returned to the garden gate. For now, the conversation was over. Although it had lasted for hours, I couldn't help feeling that it had hardly begun. I'd learned a great deal; arguably, I'd clarified my own situation, barring matters of detail—but I had only made a small beginning in the matter of understanding the bigger picture, of the Cult of Dionysus, Madame, and the world. The little I'd seen of the island, even from the edge of the forest at the top of that path, was only a fraction of its extent, and I hadn't even got half way up the mountain.

"I won't come in, if you don't mind," Madame said. "I have other things to do. I know that you must have a thousand questions, and I'll do my best to answer them, in time, but it will take time. I'll come to visit you again tomorrow. More specifically, I'll come in order to introduce Elise to Theano, and to the lyre. She needs to play her own viola da gamba at the ceremony, not so much because it's familiar as because it's a fragment of the nexus, but it will help her own magic to broaden her acquaintance before then, and in the longer term…well, who knows? Will you start your painting of Mariette tomorrow, as soon as the light is good enough?"

"If you wish," I said.

"I can't give you orders," the remarkable woman said. "You're all free agents—but it would certainly help to reassure me that my scheme is proceeding smoothly if you were to start as soon as possible."

"Tomorrow, then," I said. "As you say, I'd like to have the best of the light, at least to start with. It will be good to have a brush in my hand again, after all those frustrating days imprisoned in a tiny cabin on the ship, without so much as a book to read."

"I'll send you some books from my library," she said, instantly. "If there's anything else you need, ask Helen."

And with that, she bid me *au revoir*, and turned on her heel, setting off up the hill again, followed by her faithful Sileni.

XII. Elise and Mariette

I didn't back go into the house. I found Mariette and Elise in the garden, taking advantage of the sunlight and the scented air. They were sprawled on divans, resting, presumably having been active enough while I'd been away to tire themselves out. They seemed to be waiting for me now, avid for news. They must have been able to see the quartet I'd formed with Madame and the Sileni while we were still a long way off on the hillside

"You were gone a long time," observed Mariette.

I glanced at the sun. It was not yet close to setting, but it had passed its zenith hours before. It had been a long walk. I realized that I was tired myself, and I collapsed on a bench. Elise ran inside and came back with a mug and a carafe of cool water that must have been standing on the dining-room table, in the shade. I thanked her.

"Madame had a lot to tell me," I said, by way of response to Mariette's comment.

"But not us, apparently."

"I think she thought it would be easier to talk to one of us, at first, rather than try to field three sets of questions simultaneously."

"She obviously made an impression on you," Mariette remarked. "You're making excuses for her already. Does she want you to paint her?"

"No. She suggested strongly that I ought to paint *you*, as soon as possible."

"And Elise?"

"She wants a local musician, a woman named Theano, to work with Elise, to teach her to play the lyre, and presumably to have Elise demonstrate the viola to her. She wants Elise to play at a celebration of some sort in six days' time."

"A bacchanal?"

"She did use that term, but she assured me that Elise won't be given any intoxicants and certainly won't be subjected to any physical abuse."

"And did she make the same promises in regard to me."

"You won't be required to do anything you don't want to do."

"I'm not going to be required to join in an orgy with those ape-men, then?"

"No. The Sileni are apparently very gentle." I didn't bother to add the rider about their being fearsome when angry.

"And what about you?" Mariette persisted. "What does she expect of you, at her bacchanal?"

"She wants me to look into a magic mirror in order to discover my true self, and make psychic contact with Orpheus and Dionysus."

Mariette arched a blonde eyebrow. "Nothing too difficult, then?" she suggested.

"Probably not—it remains to be seen. You'll be offered the chance to look into the mirror too, I think."

"And me?" Elise put in.

"I don't think that's part of the plan, as yet."

"I think I'll pass," said Mariette, with a glance at Elise that clearly suggested that Elise ought not to protest at not being included in the examination of her true self. Elise did not seem convinced.

"Perhaps you should do it," I suggested to Mariette, carefully.

"Why?" she countered.

"Partly because I'd rather not be the only one to do it."

She dismissed that reason with a slight curl of the lip. "And the other part?"

"We've come a long way, albeit not by our own choice. Given that we're here, surely we ought to make use of the opportunities the location has to offer."

"Magic mirrors that will show us our true selves?" she countered, larding her tone with sarcasm.

"Why not?" I said. "What have we got to lose? "

"I think..." Elise began—but Mariette cut her off.

"I don't think we ought to play her games," she said, emphatically.

"I disagree," I said, mildly. "I think we should. As I said, I don't think we have anything to lose...although I suspect that I might have a higher opinion of your true self than you sometimes seem to have."

"That again," she said dismissively. I didn't press the point; at least the remark hadn't made her angry.

"I want to do it," said Elise. "See my true self, that is...if it's really possible. You think that it is, then?"

"I'm not sure that the mirror works automatically," I told her, "if it works at all. The initiates presumably believe that it does, but if you tell initiates to a mystery religion, after several days of indoctrination and preparation, that something important is going to happen when they look into a magic mirror, how many of them are going to admit, or even believe, that all they've actually seen is their everyday reflection?"

"Especially if they've been dosed with some illusion-inducing drug during the *preparation*," Mariette suggested.

"That would certainly help," I admitted.

"Even so...," began Elise.

"It might be better if you were to concentrate on your music," I suggested. "You might well find your true self more easily there than in any supposedly magical looking-glass."

"So you really are going along with all this meekly, and you expect us to do the same?" Mariette said—but not as if she found it hard to believe.

"That's one way of looking at it," I conceded.

"What's the other?"

"What's the alternative?" I countered.

She spent half a minute or so considering her lack of an alternative plan, and looking round at the flowers, as if reluctant to concede the beauty of the garden. She wrinkled her nose, as if the scents of the various flowers, which were actually delectable, were offensive to her. It was a kind of rebellion, but she couldn't carry it through. The simple fact was that the garden was beautiful, in both visual and olfactory terms.

Finally. she said: "At least we're in a comfortable cage now. Do you think she was telling the truth about Charles and Hecate being unharmed?"

"I think so," I said. "She has a telegraph cable to the Empire, as we already know, with a connection to the island. She should be able to keep up to date with what's happening there. War hasn't broken out yet, apparently. Getting rid of me was apparently seen as a special case, requiring urgent action as soon as the triptych was delivered. Perhaps I should have taken my time, and dragged it out—but I had no idea when their secret ceremony was scheduled, or that the paintings were going to be used there to produce, or perhaps to help fake, an invocation of Orpheus."

"Did Madame Minerva tell you that?"

"Of course. I believe her, though. It's the only way to make sense of all the things that have happened, if there's any sense to be made of it at all." I was tempted to reach out and touch her, in the hope of reassuring her, but I wasn't sure how she'd react. Her posture was relaxed, but that was an appearance. She was uncertain and afraid, and not sure how to react to her present circumstances. Elise seemed much more accepting of the situation, but that had probably only served to make Mariette warier.

"What will happen to us after this *ceremony*?" Mariette asked, after a slight pause. "Will we be members of the Cult of Dionysus then?"

"Only if we want to be," I told her. "As to what will happen next, that might depend on what happens at the ceremony. If, as I suspect, nothing much happens, in spite of Madame's carefully contrived magical nexus…well, I expect that you'll be free to go back to the island, if you want to, and if you can bear to be cooped up in one of those disgusting cabins for another six days."

"Why leave yourself out?"

"Because I don't think I can go back to the island."

"Because you're a hundred and twenty-seven years old? So what?"

"I've seen what happens before when people begin to believe, seriously, that there's a sorcerer in their midst, who might have a secret elixir of life or some similar secret. Even if it doesn't move them rapidly to violence, the manner in which you're treated…it's far better, believe me, to be able to pass for an ordinary human being, with the extra license for eccentricity and mystery that being an artist confers. And now that Hecate knows…."

"Why does that make a difference?" Elise asked. "Hecate isn't going to treat you unkindly because you're not getting any older."

"No, but the difference between us has already altered her attitude to her own aging. If you'd seen her on the evening before I was stabbed...she understood why I had to leave. While she only suspected what I am, and wouldn't permit herself to believe it, it was a mystery of sorts, more intriguing than ominous, but once she was convinced...she'd never be able to look at me the same way again."

"*We* know," Mariette pointed out, soberly.

"Yes you do—and there will come a day, if we're still acquainted then, when looking at me will begin to affect the way to look at yourself, when you'll become more conscious with every day that passes of the difference between us."

"If there is a difference between us," Elise put in. "After all, if we're like you, we wouldn't know it yet, would we? We might be."

"That's true," I conceded, readily enough. "You might."

"But it's highly unlikely," Mariette supplied. "It has to be rare. How many others are there on the island? How long do they usually live?"

"Only a few humans, apparently—and they don't necessarily live much longer than I already have, given that they can always suffer violent death. Madame's two thousand years is a striking anomaly, apparently. But Elise is right—you can't know, yet, whether you might be like me."

"I know," said Mariette.

She was barely thirty, still at the peak of her beauty, still in the full vigor of youth—but that didn't mean that she wasn't already conscious of her aging. I looked much older than her, perhaps even old enough to be her father, but since she had discovered my true age her attitude to me had already changed. I didn't know exactly how, and neither did she, but it had changed.

Elise caught my eye. I could see that she was anxious about Mariette, that she would like me to be able to reassure her, make her feel better—but I wasn't sure that I could. I didn't dare to reach out to touch her, for the moment. I thought it might be better to let the peace and harmony of the surroundings take gradual effect.

"So you're going to stay here?" Mariette concluded. "With *her*—so that you cannot grow old together."

"It's not like that," I said. "And I'll need to know a lot more about the island before I can decide whether I'd like to live here for any length of time. It's certainly intriguing, though, and there's a great deal that Madame can tell me that I'm curious to learn. I'm not in a hurry to leave."

"Nor am I," said Elise, supportively, and looked at Mariette, as if challenging her to try to issue a prohibition.

Mariette didn't dare. Among the many things of which she was afraid was losing Elise...or, more accurately, discovering that she had already lost her. Mariette loved Elise, in a far less problematic fashion that she loved Charles Parenot, and because of that Mariette was dependent on Elise. I looked at the little girl, trying to communicate to her with my gaze that now was not a good time for issuing challenges, or threats of disobedience, even of a pseudoparental authority that was purely imaginary.

Elise seemed to get the message. She did what I had not dared to do, and moved from her own divan to Mariette's, and put her arm around her.

"Axel's right," she said, although she didn't go as far as addressing Mariette as Mother. "The only thing we can do is make the best of things. It's pleasant here—and Axel's going to paint you, as you wanted."

Mariette reacted to that. "On Madame's orders, apparently," she said.

"No," I said. "I've wanted to paint you since I first saw you. This is a good opportunity. From my viewpoint, it's a very valuable opportunity. I certainly don't want to be idle, and Madame intends to claim Elise's time. I'll admit that the opportunity to paint a Silenus has intriguing aspects, and the opportunity to paint an authentic nymph has its attractions too, but my first choice, by a wide margin, would be to paint someone truly beautiful, someone I know, and someone to whom I feel close, having shared adversity."

Mariette stared at me, as if trying to read my mind. She seemed to be drawing resolution from Elise's affectionate embrace.

"What's the alternative?" she muttered, as if to herself. Then, more positively, she added: "When?"

"I'll begin tomorrow morning, if I may."

She didn't bother to signify assent. "What did you mean by *authentic nymphs*?" she queried.

"The Sileni aren't the only semi-humans here. I haven't seen one, but Madame assures me that the Nymphs are less attractive than their artistic reputation. Charles' representations of you as a nymph are apparently flattering to the real species. They'll be present at the ceremony, I believe."

"Taking part in the bacchanal? With the ape-men?"

"I think mythology probably misrepresents the relationship between nymphs and satyrs too, if the Sileni are to be regarded as satyrs of a sort. The Sileni have their own females, which doubtless set their standard of beauty for them. The Nymphs, by contrast, don't have any males of their species. They probably have no sexual inclinations at all."

"Really?" said Elise. "Not even..." She cut the remark off, presumably out of respect for her adoptive mother.

"The island is a place of peace and harmony," I said. "I don't think passion plays as large a part in life here as it does in the Empire...certainly not as much as it does on Martyr's Mount, which is extreme even by the standards of over-civilized humans."

For a moment, I thought Elise was going to begin to say something else shocking, but she suppressed the thought, whatever it had been. Instead she said, quite deliberately: "What kind of a self-portrait will you be able to paint, do you think, Axel, when you've looked into the magic mirror and seen your true self?"

"That's an interesting question," I admitted. "I'm privately convinced that I'm already thoroughly acquainted with my true self. After all, I've had a long time to get to know him inside out—but I suppose there's always scope for astonishment."

""That's true," said Elise, "and once you've painted Mariette, she won't need to look into the mirror either, will she. All she'll have to do is look at your portrait."

"It doesn't work like that," said Mariette. "Charles has painted me a hundred times over, and all I've ever seen in those pictures are fragments of Charles's true self. I don't suppose for a moment that the picture hanging in the studio tells us more about the woman it depicts than it does about the man who painted it."

I could have argued that I was a better painter than Charles Parenot, as well as a better painter than my earlier self, but I was being diplomatic, so I said: "You're probably right. Perhaps it's through my paintings that I know myself so well…or think I do. Perhaps I still have things to learn though, and painting you will have something to teach me."

Mariette stood up, nervously and awkwardly. "The sun's too bright," she said. "I'm going indoors." She looked at Elise, but Elise shook her head.

"I'll come in shortly," she said. "I want to ask Axel something."

Mariette almost sat down again, but hesitated, and then shrugged her shoulders.

Elise watched her go, and then moved closer to me, while carefully leaving a respectful distance.

"Madame doesn't just want me to play music, does she?" she said. "She expects me to make magic?"

"Yes," I said, "but she thinks much the same way I do. She doesn't expect you to be able to do it deliberately. She thinks it will come naturally. All you have to do is play. Don't worry about it."

"And she doesn't want me to make magic just for the sake of it, does she? She wants it to have an effect on you?"

"Yes," I said. "Don't worry about that either."

"The people you call Sileni," she went on, without a pause, obviously having a series of questions already queued up. "Are they like the women that killed my grandfather?"

I blinked. "In what way?" I asked, genuinely surprised.

"Drugged…hypnotized…I don't know. *Under control*?"

"No," I said. "I think they're a little like that naturally, but they're not automata." I realized why she was asking. "Maybe the cultists do have ways of doing that to people, but Madame's not going to do it to us. It doesn't seem to be her way of doing things, and it wouldn't serve her purpose. I don't think she could force you to play magical music by taking control of you. Even though you don't know how you're doing it, it has to be *you*—your mind, not just your hands."

She nodded, as if she had just been seeking confirmation.

"If we'd stayed on Mnemosyne," she continued, "Would the Marquise de Mesmay have wanted me to play at her ceremony?"

"I think so, although I don't think it would have been a good idea, even from her point of view."

"Why not?"

"Because I presume that Tommaso and Lorenzo Dellacrusca are going to be there. I don't suppose she has any idea how they feel about you, and nor do I, but you're their niece, and that gives them an obligation. I think the Marquise would have been wiser let you well alone, for diplomatic reasons, even if she thought your music might be helpful to her plan. Anyway, you're not there anymore."

"Hecate is. The Marquise might try to involve her."

I pulled a face, but I didn't want to lie to her. "That's true," I conceded.

Elise didn't press the point. She still had more questions in mind. "Why is Mariette here?" she asked.

"Because Madame thinks that you, she and I form components of what she calls a nexus. She thinks we're associated magically—but only temporarily."

"Because of something that happened at the séance I wasn't allowed to attend?"

"Partly."

"I thought so," she confirmed. She didn't demand further details, perhaps because she was being diplomatic, but probably not, as her next question was: "Is that why she wants you to…paint her?" The hesitation before the word *paint* was ostentatious rather than merely obvious.

"Yes," I said, and left it at that.

She looked at me in an arch fashion. "I'm just a child," she said, sarcastically "who's lived all her life on Martyr's Mount, so I don't understand these things at all, but I've just been watching Mariette bite her knuckles at the idea that you might screw Madame, just as I watched her bite her knuckles on the ship at the mere thought that you might screw Helen. I don't think she even knew she was doing it, let alone that I was watching, but still…if, as it seems, she wants to screw you so ardently, and you obviously have no objection to screwing her, what's the problem?"

"It's not as simple as that," I said.

"Why not?"

"For one thing, she loves Charles, and he loves her."

"Yes, but in the wrong way."

"I don't think there is a wrong way to love someone," I countered, almost reflexively.

"You promised you wouldn't lie to me, Axel. In the hundred years since you painted that picture in the studio, you must have loved a lot of women. Can you name a single one whom you loved in the ideal, exclusive and enduring way she really wanted to be loved?"

"That's not what I meant," I said. She had a point, though, and I was beginning to find the conversation uncomfortable in more ways than one

She let me off the hook. "I know it's not," she admitted. "Do you want to know what I think about it?"

"Go on," I said, uneasily—although I did want to know, because I could hardly help thinking it relevant.

She showed me her clenched fist, without saying a word. It took me a few seconds to catch on that she was showing me the unbitten knuckles. In what might or might not be a naïve fashion, she was telling me that she didn't have any anxieties, jealous or otherwise, about what Mariette and I might do. She was tacitly giving me—us—her blessing.

I nodded, not simply because I understood, but because I was grateful. Even though she knew that I was no more capable of loving Mariette than anyone else— anyone at all—in what they might consider to be the right way, she was giving me her blessing to do what I could.

I couldn't help thinking, though, that I would probably still be exactly the same age, physically, when Elise was as old as Mariette was now, by which time Mariette would be as old as Hecate was now, and Hecate would be…and so, perhaps *ad infinitum*: a long sequence, at any rate, of regretful adieux

"I'm sorry if I'm making you uncomfortable," Elise said, probably insincerely, "but please don't tell me that the sun's too bright and you want to go inside now. If we're part of a magical nexus, the least you can do is not run away from me."

"I wasn't about to run away," I said, even though I'd promised that I wouldn't lie to her, and the assertion felt uncomfortably close to the margin of untruth.

She deliberately changed the topic of conversation. "Do you really think that nothing is going to come of all this?" she asked. "That even with my music, Madame's mirror and any other tricks she has up her baggy sleeve, that nothing at all is going to happen at this bacchanal of hers?"

That was a much better question than the others she had just asked, from my point of view. That one, I wasn't averse to thinking about, even though I didn't know the answer.

"Something might well happen," I conceded. "She's been studying magic for a thousand years and more. She must know a lot more about it than I do. Of course, she might be completely out of her mind, but…what she said connects too closely with what I've always thought for me to refuse to take it seriously."

"What does she actually expect you to do?"

"I don't know, exactly, and I don't think she does. But she expects all of us to assist, unwittingly, in the invocation of Dionysus, to coincide with the Orpheans' ritual invocation or Orpheus…and she expects the two invocations to fuse somehow, so that the one on Mnemosyne will deliver Dionysus' edict to the Orphean assembly, rather than the one the Marquise plans to try to impose. Madame only offered me the incentive that it might prevent warfare and bloodshed in the Orphean ranks on Mnemosyne, but I'm certain that she has much greater ambitions than that: a reconciliation of the rival cults, perhaps a whole new era for the Empire, and the world."

"That's a lot of responsibility for you…and me."

"We're just instruments. The plan is hers…or, in fact, not even hers. We're supposedly just collaborating with the forces of magic and their drive toward esthetic completion. If it doesn't come off, we can put the blame on Dionysus Zagreus, Orpheus and Eurydice. It won't be our fault."

"But that doesn't mean that we won't suffer in consequence, does it?" she said, putting her finger on the nub of the issue. "If the gods are…disappointed, it might rebound on us, whether it's our fault or not."

"It's probably safer, as well as more diplomatic, to try to satisfy them," I agreed.

She moved along the divan, a little closer, but didn't reach out to touch me. "I'll do my best," she said, "even though I don't know what I'm doing."

"Me too," I said.

Neither of us mentioned Mariette, but I got the impression that we had a tacit agreement to try to make sure that Mariette would feel a little better about playing her part, whatever it might involve.

"I'm going to stay here," Elise told me, confidentially. "Whatever Mariette decides to do."

"She'll stay too," I predicted, confidently.

"For me or for you?"

"For the nexus. For the magic." I smiled, to emphasize that I didn't mean it literally, that it was just a manner of speaking—but I was no longer sure that it was.

"We still have to win her over, though," Elise observed.

We did. Elise couldn't see the problem, but I knew that it really wasn't as simple as she naively thought. I didn't just have to paint Mariette, or sleep with her, but to seduce her in a much more fundamental sense. Mariette had it in mind, somehow, that she was still just the

230

whore she had been forced to become after her mother died, and he hadn't thus far been able to accept my insistence that she wasn't. Reaching her heart, symbolically and metaphorically, would be a lot more difficult than reaching her literal vagina, but that was what the nexus really required. That was what the esthetics of the situation required, even in a purely unmagical sense.

It would have been difficult, even when she thought that I was only human. Given that she knew now that I wasn't, and that there could be no question of ideal, everlasting love...I wasn't at all certain that I was going to be able to achieve the capture of her heart. Spearing the fish in the barrel was the easy part; the artistry was all in the culinary dimension.

XIII. Passion

Unlike the previous six days, which had been more-or-less equally divided, for me between nightmare and frustrated tedium, the six that elapsed before the scheduled celebration of the abridged Dionysian Mysteries were part-dream and part-delight, in a complex admixture. At times, in fact, I wondered whether I had ever actually recovered from the delirium of the first three days after drinking the drugged brandy in the Spirite, and whether everything that had happened since might simply be the strange phases of a complex hallucination. At other times I rejoiced in the fact that, more successfully than ever before, I had negotiated the transition between a life that was becoming unviable because my secret was leaking out, and a new one, synthesized in its entirety.

Except, of course, that my new life on the Island of Dionysus did not have to be constructed from scratch; not only could I retain the same name, but the same identity. I no longer had to hide what I was. There were more than a dozen others on the island—although, as Madame had warned me, they were almost all disappointing; the only one who could really qualify as a good advertisement for the Macrobian condition was Madame herself.

I soon began to realize why the Sileni thought that they were far better adapted by nature for long life than humans. It was not just that they seemed to live at a slower pace, seemingly unhurried by all the stresses that afflict humans, or that they were such great lovers of routine. There was a kind of harmony in their being and their relationship with their environment—not with "nature," because, although their technology was primitive, they controlled all the aspects of their environment, indoors and outdoors, with a meticulous concern for order, but with their ambience. They seemed to be content with themselves because they were content with their placement in the world. Except, that is, when they were not; ordinarily mild in the extreme, if their environment were seriously disturbed, rudely and unnecessary, they could indeed build up a slow but insistent anger.

I only caught glimpses of that, when I visited the town, where the proximity of humans was far more intense and problematic for the Sileni than in the fields and on the hills, and it did not have a serious result on any occasion that I witnessed, but it was enough to stimulate the imagination, and assure me that the Sileni were definitely people that it was far better not to upset or annoy.

The Nymphs, when Madame eventually introduced me to a group of half a dozen in their forest home, calling them out of hiding in order to submit themselves to the examination of my artist's eye, were markedly different. They were, in fact, reminiscent of wild creatures, whose harmony really was with the placid natural environment of the forest. They were not devoid of technology; although they made no use of the first of humankind's primary arts, cooking, they did practice the other, clothing.

At first, that seemed odd to me, for, although not as hairy as the Sileni, the Nymphs did have a sleek down on their bodies reminiscent of a pelt, and the island's climate was so temperate that cold was rarely a significant oppression. Clothing seemed to them, however—as it is for most humans, of course—primarily a matter of adornment rather than protection against the elements.

They were clever spinners and weavers, and produced beautiful fabrics from various vegetable sources; they did not use wool. Their dyes were all of vegetable origin too, but they had an assortment of colors, including various shades of blue and yellow as well as the more expectable greens and browns.

As Madame had said, one could not describe them as beautiful by strict human standards, although their stature, figure and facial features were closer to the human than to the Sileni. That did not mean, however, that they were not beautiful in their own right. There seemed to me to be something slightly feline about them, although that probably had more to do with the way they moved rather than the actual cast of their features. They had an innate, sleek grace that was very attractive, and I had no sooner come close to a Nymph than I wanted to paint one—or a group of them, for they were not solitary creatures, usually congregating in groups of four or five.

The Nymphs were long-lived, as were the Sileni, but if one judged them by human standards—which might have been grossly inappropriate—they seemed to be arrested in their aging process in a much younger phase than the Sileni. What was most striking about their Macrobian properties, however, was their near uniformity. All the Nymphs seemed to reach the same stage of development and then pause, just as the Sileni did, in a seemingly later phase. In that respect, they differed greatly from human Macrobians, whose arrest phase seemed to be greatly variable, ranging from admittedly very rare "eternal children" even younger in appearance that Elise to those, relatively more numerous, condemned to perpetual antiquity, like Theano, Elise's appointed music teacher.

When I met Theano, I understood the import of Helen's remark that it was people like the old woman for whom she felt sorry. Theano might once have been pretty, perhaps beautiful, and if she had only arrested her aging process in that phase of her existence, she might have enjoyed a very different life from the one she had apparently led for the century or more that she had spent with the appearance of a geriatric, in her late seventies at least. Wizened though her face was, however, and curbed as her stature was, her fingers remained flexible and nimble. They too were wrinkled, but they were certainly not arthritic or in any way clumsy. The lyres that she played seemed gross and primitive to me, especially in comparison with Elise's viola da gamba, but the music Theano could extract from them was truly beautiful, and sometimes gave the impression of being truly divine.

The excursions we undertook to the port and the forest were replete with surprising discoveries and gave me abundant opportunity for marveling, but I must confess that for me, at least, they paled into insignificance by comparison with the visits I was privileged to pay to Madame's home. Her house was not particularly impressive, and could not qualify as a palace. Architecturally, I suppose, it was undistinguished, but its library put any collection on Mnemosyne dramatically in the shade, in terms of the range and abundance of its books and documents. The modern textbooks of physical, natural and human science were neatly classified, opposite or at right-angles to the entire tradition of the Empire's esoteric writings on magic and metaphysics, most of which were completely unknown to me. Even the library, however, paled by comparison with the laboratory in which Madame carried out chemical, optical and electrical experiments, and undertook extensive studies in anatomy and physiology.

As an artist, and an artist living in the relatively remote imperial enclave of Mnemosyne, I had never seen any of the modern laboratories of the University of Paris, and my notion of what a laboratory might look like, and what might go on there, had been largely formed by literary descriptions of alchemists' dens. I confessed to Madame my complete incomprehension of almost all the apparatus she employed, and of the kinds of projects she described to me.

"You're young," she told me, "still locked in the obsessive phase of your art. You'll never cease to be a painter, of course, but as time goes by, your endeavors and your interests will gradually broaden out. With luck, by the time you're a thousand years old or so, you'll be interested in everything—not to the same degree, of course, and highly selective in the areas to which you devote intense attention, but nevertheless, you'll have begin to grasp, approximately, the ensemble of human understanding in a way that simply isn't possible for a mere centenarian or bicentenarian."

"But that doesn't seem to be the case with any of the Macrobians to whom you've introduced me," I pointed out. "Even Theano, who seems to be more than a bicentenarian, remains obsessively confined to her single art, and none of the others seems to me to be broadening their horizons in the way you suggest—none, that is, except you."

"True," she admitted, "And there can be no guarantees. I've been optimistic before, and have been disappointed—but perhaps one of the stubborn characteristics of my character is the perennial triumph of hope over experience. If it turns out that you follow the same path of confinement or derangement that seems to afflict so many human Macrobians, as is certainly possible, I shall be...disappointed."

"So will I," I confessed, after a few moments' thought. "I'm an artist, through and through, and I've found it a long-winded process perfecting my skill even in the relatively narrow field of portraiture...but I think I'd have every reason to be disappointed if I remained imprisoned by that single activity indefinitely. My reading has always been wide, and I've always been enthusiastic to grasp the ensemble of knowledge to the extent that I can. If I really do have time; if I really can live as long as you...then I'd be very disappointed indeed if I couldn't continue to evolve and grow."

"That," she said, "is a good beginning."

Privately, I was delighted to have the possibility of studying under such a useful teacher, and for a long time, but it was a topic that I couldn't air in conversation, for fear of exciting Mariette's jealousy. That jealousy already burdened by the knowledge that she would probably continue aging while I did not, and the fear that once Madame had extracted whatever magical reward she hoped to claim from the development of a sudden and intense passion within her expertly identified "nexus," the seeming immortal might immediately begin to think in terms of equipping herself with a suitable consort for her sovereignty over the Island of Dionysus. I had no reason to think that Madame might have any such long-range plan, let alone that my feelings for her might develop to the point of being able to compete with my feelings for Mariette any time soon, but I was clearly in no position to dismiss Mariette's fears, given that they had the strong support of the logic of the situation.

I painted Mariette in the studio, with my back to the hundred-year-old portrait of the first woman for whom I formed a fervent and intense passion while painting her, which was perhaps a slightly ominous reminder in itself, but she didn't ask to have it removed even though she could see it over my shoulder as I worked. It posed no problems for me, of course, because it was behind me in a far more important sense than the merely literal one. While I was painting Mariette, and viewing her with my painter's eye, she monopolized my gaze, my fascination and my feelings.

I had warned Madame than I didn't always conceive strong lusts for my sitters, and that it had happened less frequently of late, as I became more blasé. She hadn't seemed to take the cautionary note seriously, even though she had had no opportunity to see, as Elise had, apparent signs of Mariette's own ill-repressed yearnings. Elise had, of course, been deliberately understating her observation that I "obviously had no objection" to the idea of getting closer to Mariette, although I hoped that I hadn't given any tell-tale sign as evident as biting my knuckles.

At any rate, nature or magic took its course, and Mariette and I began sleeping together after the first day's sitting—but that, as I'd already realized, was only a fraction of the true project. The fact that sexual attraction became intense on both sides, and blossomed in a familiar fashion, wasn't the crucial issue There was, as I had carelessly told Elise, a sense in which there was no "wrong way" for us to love one another, all love being good love...but I wanted more than the bare minimum, and so did Mariette. The problem was that we didn't know how to achieve that "more," or even whether it was possible to achieve it by conscious effort. It was

238

something that had to develop spontaneously, and something that could not be faked. In order that it might develop, in order that out binary nexus could fulfill its true potential and its true purpose, we had to commit ourselves, metaphorically if not literally, to the lap of the gods.

But the painting did help. It was enormously helpful to me, and I think to her too—not in the crude sense that I was able to watch its develop continuously on the canvas, and that she was able to monitor it in occasional glimpses, but in the sense that we could feel the process of discovery as it was proceeding. I was able to look at her with my artist's eye, and she was aware of my looking at her. In the beginning, what she was presenting to me, consciously at least, was an appearance, but as time went by, with every day that passed, she consented to the intensity of my stare, my probing, my discovery. She consented to the synthesis that it was making of her identity, and consented to become the image I was making of her.

She had been painted before, of course, a hundred times, and a similar process had taken place...and that was precisely the problem that she and I had to overcome. Charles Parenot had loved her—honestly, I believed, and not in a "wrong" way—but Charles had never been able to get past the consciousness that she had once been a whore, and that she had initially taken up residence in his studio in order to be useful to him, to assist him in looking after a small child for whom he was incapable of caring on his own. No matter how hard Parenot had pretended that he was painting her as a nymph, or a legendary queen, or a forlorn Eurydice, he had never been able to sustain the conviction in his heart, even though, consciously, he wanted to.

Consciously as well as unconsciously, Mariette had always been aware of that. She had slept with Charles, she had been passionate about him, she had loved him, and not in a "wrong way"—but there had been something absent from the esthetic of their nexus. She had had no good reason to think that it would be any different when I panted her. She had had no reason to think that it was even possible that it might be. Charles Parenot, on the other hand, might have thought so—and that might have been the reason, conscious or not, why he had not wanted me to paint Mariette.

But I did paint her. Had I been able to remain on Mnemosyne, I would have painted her there, and with the same result.

It took time for the wall to crumble—several days, in fact—but crumble it did. Mariette allowed me to paint her, and she allowed me to see her, and she allowed herself to be seen as I saw her, as the true self that was anything but a whore. And the passion not only blossomed but evolved, and took on its full, complete, true beauty. In spite of what she and I both knew about the essential transience of our potential relationship, we committed ourselves to it wholeheartedly, and with the wholeness of hearts that had themselves been renewed, and subtly but significantly transformed.

As Elise had shrewdly calculated, I had loved a considerable number of women between the one depicted in the portrait on the wall and the one depicted on the evolving picture on my easel, but Mariette was still unique, and so was I, and the passion we developed, in collaboration, reached a maximum of intensity that seemed, in its essence, unsurpassable.

There was a sense in which we didn't need words, but also one in which we couldn't avoid them, and had

to try to make the best of them even while we were painfully conscious of their expressive inadequacy. I didn't
tell Mariette about the conversation I had had with Elise
in which the phrase had cropped up, but I did try on one
occasion to reassure Mariette, as best I could, that what I
was offering her, and sharing with her, wasn't "the
wrong kind of love" even if it couldn't live up to her
ideal of durance.

"Don't be ridiculous," she told me. "The only
wrong kind of love is the kind a person doesn't want,
and even that's only wrong from her point of view."

I wasn't sure that I could agree with her entirely,
but I didn't tell her that either. I didn't lie to her, but I
rationed the truth discreetly. That's one of the many duties that love demands.

At any rate, we became inseparable. When went to
the port, we were together. When we saw the Nymphs in
the forest, we were together. When we visited Madame's
house, her library and her laboratory, we were together.

Elise was rarely with us in our excursions. She was
often shut away in one or other of the rooms of the house
with Madame or Theano. Even when she was not playing for Madame or receiving tuition, however, she often
sentenced herself to solitary confinement, in order to
practice and to improvise. Her playing, muffled by the
walls, was the accompaniment to our love-making, and
even when she was inexpertly plucking the strings of the
lyre—or, more accurately, the cithara—that Madame
had given her, rather than composing with the viola da
gamba, the accompaniment never seemed less than me-
lodious to us.

Madame brought her music, too, some of which, in
modern notation, sounded stylistically akin to the music
that Elise had improvised to accompany Hecate's "po-

em" composed in a language of sighs, but it was not identical to it, being less wistful and more soothing. I couldn't detect anything in it that was reminiscent of Eurydice's anger and lamentation. The music for the cithara that the old woman played so beautifully, and had begun to teach Elise to reproduce, was quite different, much of it stirring, and a good deal of it seemingly adapted for dancing

"My memory is slightly vague," I said to Madame on the penultimate day of the six, when she came into the studio briefly to watch me paint, while Elise and her tutor were playing upstairs, "but wasn't the cithara an instrument designed primarily to accompany epic and lyric poetry?"

"I believe so," Madame agreed, "but it was also used, and very significantly, in religious rituals."

"And wasn't it the instrument favored by Sappho for the accompaniment of her erotic lyrics?" Mariette interjected. She liked to show off the modest erudition that she had acquired from Charles Parenot and her other acquaintances among the unorthodox intellectuals of Martyr's Mount.

"It was before my time," Madame said, as she had an irritating habit of doing, with a smile of blissful irony, "but my understanding is that Sappho played both the cithara and the barbitos. Her music did have the legendary reputation of being intensely and uniquely erotic, in my day, but I suspect that to be an exaggeration, and I doubt, in any case, that it was an effect of the instrument, even to the extent that it was true. You'd be wrong to read too much into the music that Theano will play for the Nymphs in the ceremony. On that score, Mariette, you surely ought to have more suspicion of the viola, which is held between the legs rather than maintained in a higher stance."

That ironic commentary was not calculated to set Mariette's mind at rest, given that it was the viola that Elise would be playing at the "bacchanal"—a term that still seemed to cause Mariette some anxiety, all the more so as she had not been allocated any specific role to play herself. She had elected to accompany me through the phases of the initiation—to precede me, in fact, at Madame's demand—and to look into the magic mirror immediately before me, but she was slightly envious of Elise's more active function in the manufacture of magic.

"I ought warn you, Mariette," Madame told her, "in view of your reservations, that the preparation for the initiation involves the drinking of cyteon."

"What's cyteon?" Mariette demanded.

"A ritual beverage, although it had a more commonplace variant used in ancient times purely as nutrition and refreshment. Axel must have seen the term, as it's mentioned in Homer as being made from barley and wine—but the kind used in the ritual also contains honey, and other herbs. It has an intoxicant effect, and can induce illusions, but it does not incite the kind of wild behavior credited to bacchantes by our detractors, and it does not include raw meat or fervent spices, as scandalous rumor once alleged. Although the two of you will be the only mystes at the special ceremony, the other humans in attendance, the Sileni and the Nymphs, will all drink it, as they always do. Its consumption assists the cadence of the cycinnis—the ritual dance—to fuse the nexus of the assembly. I shall drink it myself, in my capacity as hierophant, as will my assistants, the hieroceryx and the dadoukhos, so you may be assured that it is perfectly safe."

Mariette was confused by the unfamiliar terminology, but skipped any request for an explanation of their meaning in order to say: "And Elise?"

"She and Theano will not drink cyteon. I need her to be focused as minutely as possible on her music. Her role is vital to my project."

"Unlike mine, apparently."

"On the contrary. Your presence is vital and your participation much appreciated. The nexus needs to be complete." Madame stepped back, away from the spot where Mariette was sitting, in order to inspect the painting, which was almost complete. I was adding refining strokes, to add a little extra distinction to the features. Then she glanced back at Mariette, and it was to her that she said: "It's fine work. I think you'll be delighted with it."

Mariette almost took that as an invitation, and made as if to stand up, but I gestured to her to stay where she was.

"It's almost complete," I said. "A matter of minutes. Be patient."

"I'm in the way," said Madame. "I should go."

The painting had reached a stage where her presence was not a serious disruption, else I would not have encouraged her to stay by asking her questions and allowing Mariette to do likewise, but we never had enough opportunities or time to do that, and I hastened to say: "Have you any news from Mnemosyne?"

"The best possible," she said. "All is quiet. Clovis is said to be chagrined by his inability to arrest the man who stabbed you, but he is observing himself the peace he is striving to keep. He knows that the assassin is lodged in the Mesmay manse, but cannot continue his pursuit therein. Tommaso and Lorenzo Dellacrusca have arrived on the island, with an extensive entourage of armed men, and Alectryon is by no means the only other to have brought a strong continent of his personal retinue, but the various factions seem to be perfectly calm and placid for the moment."

"That was when the twins were at their most dangerous, as boys," I said. "I always knew what I saw them looking angelically placid that there was mischief afoot."

"They are only subsidiaries within the camp of their father's old supporters," Madame said. "Alectryon is taking the lead, albeit with pressure from behind, and he is a great believer in discipline. The Marquise has persuaded him to play the role of hierophant in the ritual, and she probably intends to establish him as the titular leader of the cult if her magic works, but only on her sufferance. He is not a man easily ruled, as you now, but he is a man able to reconcile himself to what he sees as necessity."

I remembered that. Alectryon had once asked me to paint his daughter, but very grudgingly, and he had probably never forgiven me for that perceived necessity.

"There never was a man with a greater belief in discipline than Dellacrusca," I observed, "but he could never keep the twins under control. If they've planned something on their own initiative..."

"There will be hundreds of people in the hall at the ceremony," Madame said, "and a thousand more scattered about the island awaiting orders. The twins are no longer small boys playing pranks, but heirs to the Dellacrusca fortune and the family's status. They know that, and will act accordingly."

She was almost certainly correct. The last time I had seen Tommaso Dellacrusca, he seemed to have grown up very rapidly indeed, and to be steeling himself to take his father's place, along with his brother—but I was not entirely sure what Tommaso and Lorenzo thought that replacement might require of them. Alectryon's family must have been Greek originally, but had been civilized in Lutèce for generations. The Dellacruscas were still Italian at heart, and had the notion of vendetta in their blood.

"How is Charles?" asked Mariette, a flush of guilt bringing an unwelcome change of complexion.

"Safe," was Madame's dismissive comment.

"Did you manage to get money and a message to Jean-Jacques?" I asked.

"Yes. Your servants will be in no difficulty for six months and more, and have been reassured as to your safety. They will take care of the house and your possessions until further notice."

The message I had sent had mentioned that Mariette and Elise were safe too, and Jean-Jacques would doubtless inform Parenot quietly of the fact, although I suspected that the painter would not find the news that they were with me entirely reassuring. I didn't know whether he was in the habit of biting his knuckles, consciously or not, but I was still acutely aware that he had not wanted me to paint Mariette even while she was still living under his roof.

Upstairs, Elise played a false note on the cithara, and then swiped the instrument's eight strings with a gesture of annoyance before setting it aside. Theano didn't take over the instrument, and Elise took up her viola instead.

"Perhaps you shouldn't have distracted Elise by giving her the other instrument, Madame," Mariette suggested.

"Perhaps," echoed Madame, politely, and offered no excuse, although I was certain that she had a reason for providing the "distraction" in question.

"The telegraph cable must be a great convenience to you, Madame," I observed. "I must admit that I'm surprised that you don't seem to have introduced other modern technologies to the island, in spite of the sophistication of your personal laboratory. I haven't seen a single steam engine on the island itself, although your ships employ them, and your farm machinery seems distinctly primitive. The streets of the port would surely benefit from gas lighting, just as Mnemosyne's port has."

"The Sileni don't like innovation," she said. "What happens beyond the shoreline does not cause them any anxiety, and we have no need to increase agricultural production. I had no alternative but to have the cable to Europe laid, once Dellacrusca started making elaborate use of telegraphy, and to equip my ships with engines, but I would rather he had not made it necessary. The fool thought that rapid communication would facilitate his dream of centralizing control within the Empire and making domination easier."

"You don't agree?"

"No. Rapid communication spreads and sows dissent. What he did was more likely to lead to disintegration than domination. Indirectly, that is what paved the way for his loss of control in the heart of his own organization. Gaslight is a great boon to readers in Lutèce, and the bane of nocturnal thieves, but it also assists troublemaking. I am fond of the innovations of civilization myself, and certainly would not like to live as the

Nymphs live, almost as wild animals, but in spite of my sentiments of justice, I have no wish to democratize the gifts and curses of technology here any sooner than I have to. I dread the inevitable increase in trans-Oceanic shipping now that trade agreements have been signed with the Iroquois and the Maya, and trade with the Far East will surely increase too. The world is becoming too small for my liking, and the Empire too compact as well as too broad in its external relations. The increase in agricultural production has been facilitating an increase in population throughout the Empire for two generations now, and that always leads to strife. Domination cannot suppress it, and tyranny can only intensify it."

I was not sure that I agreed entirely with her judgment, but it was certainly interesting as an additional insight into her thinking. How could one expect, though, that someone two thousand years old would not find change threatening, and prefer constancy. As a Macrobian myself, however, I wondered whether I ought to share her view, especially if I were to take up residence on the Island of Dionysus for a long time, to live alongside the Sileni.

Madame's own Sileni were waiting for her patiently in the garden. They did not come into the house, but I had no doubt that they were alert for any sign of distress or disturbance. They never went to sleep while maintaining vigil. I had learned enough of their language to greet them politely, but had never obtained any more response from the bodyguards than a slight nod, and only little more from the agricultural works of that species.

Even the humans on the island spoke their own idiosyncratic dialect of the Empire's lingua franca, which made them difficult to understand, although Madame seemed fluent in the Imperial tongue, as well as the local dialect, the language of the Sileni and that of the Nymphs, and probably half a dozen dead languages as well. Her library certainly had no shortage of texts that were quite opaque to me. So far as I knew, she didn't speak any of the languages of the New World, but I suspected that she might soon feel obliged to learn to least a few. She seemed to have an awesome memory, although she could be frustratingly vague about things that had happened long after her birth as well as those "before her time," and I suspected that she had forgotten far more than she cared to admit regarding people she had known and events she had witnessed, let alone things that had only been reported to her second-hand.

Finally, I declared the painting finished, with regard to brushwork, although I knew that the texture and color would change slightly as the paint dried.

I summoned Mariette to inspect it, and Madame went upstairs to invite Elise to come down to take a look.

"Well," I said to Mariette, "is that my true self reflected, in the way that I see you?"

She glanced at the ancient picture on the wall, in order to compare the two, but made no comment as a result of the comparison.

"Thank you, Axel," was all she said aloud, "for preserving me thus. At least the image will not age." I thought she might have been a little more gracious—it was a fine portrait, and it had been painted with true passion—but I knew that the awkwardness of her comment didn't reflect the actual depth of feeling in her heart.

Elise was more complimentary. "If you can make me look as beautiful as that," she said, "I'll be very grateful indeed—all the more so knowing that you'll be able to paint me again in seven years time, and again a further seven years thereafter, so that I can monitor my own maturation. That will be a rare privilege, I think."

Mariette did not comment on her assumption that she would still be acquainted with me in fourteen years time. The question no longer arose as to whether she might return to Mnemosyne in the short term; she had no intention of leaving me so soon, even though she knew full well that we wouldn't be together forever, and perhaps not for very long, even relative to her lifespan, let alone mine..

"Are you content?" I asked Madame.

"Certainly," said Madame. "It's a fine piece of work. But I have no intention of taking possession of it. Mariette must keep it."

Mariette's "Thank you" was distinctly lukewarm, for reasons whose full depth I couldn't quite fathom. I hadn't seen her biting her knuckles, but I knew that her attitude to Madame was still fundamentally hostile and jealous, albeit somewhat confused.

Helen came in then, to compliment me in her turn, but she carefully didn't ask whether I still had an intention to paint her, after Elise.

If I really am going to stay here indefinitely, I thought, *I wonder if it will be possible to use Madame's steamships to transmit my work to Myrica in Lutèce, in order that she can display it in her gallery and sell it to her clients.*

In fact, although money seemed to be one of the numerous post-Arcadian innovations with which Madame had decided not to trouble the Sileni, the ability to make purchases from the Empire seemed to me to be a very useful convenience, which I would be loath to do without. Madame clearly had no difficulty in funding her own lavish purchases, but I assumed that in the course of two thousand years she had built up very considerable assets there, which allowed her considerable self-indulgence as well as funding the operation of an organization of informants and agents whose vastness I could only begin to estimate.

When I had had my fill of looking at the finished painting I went out into the garden, where I stayed until dusk, when Madame took her leave.

"You'll have all morning tomorrow," she said, as she went. "Given that the sun sets some two hours later here than on Mnemosyne, our own ceremony will have to begin earlier in the day in order to coincide with the other. I shall be occupied all day, but Helen, in the role of hieroceryx and torch-bearer, will fetch you to the appointed place at the necessary time in the afternoon. Your preparations will not be elaborate, but might seem tedious, and the early phases of the ceremony will probably seem long-winded and incomprehensible. Be patient, I beg you. You will not see me again until I receive you in the role of hierophant. Thank you once again for your patient collaboration. I appreciate it greatly—and so, I believe, will Orpheus and Dionysus Zagreus."

"Thank you," I said, quite sincerely, "for everything." I didn't think it necessary, as yet, to thank the gods.

XIV. The Mysteries

The morning of the next day was cloudy. Not long after noon it began to rain: a steady, heavy, relentless rain. It had rained before while we were on the island, but only during the hours of darkness; the days had all been bright.

"That's a bad omen," Mariette observed, while we waited to be summoned to the ceremony.

"I don't think so," I said. "The Sileni, at least, wouldn't see it as such. They like the rain, being fully aware of the role it plays in maintaining the life of the island. Drought is a danger here, although the mountain serves to some extent as a sponge absorbing and storing rain, in order to maintain the flow of streams and the fertility of the soil during protracted dry spells."

"We still have a long walk ahead of us in the pouring rain," Mariette pointed out. "We'll be soaked to the bone. How far up the mountain will we need to go?"

"I don't know. Not to the top, I'm assured." Helen had warned us to be prepared for a considerable hike, but had been very vague as to where it would take us, the place of the ceremonies being notionally secret, although the entire population of the island, except for us, had to know where it was.

"How is she supposed to play the torch-bearer in this?" Mariette persisted.

"I don't know," I said. "Perhaps the torch isn't lit until we're under shelter."

"Assuming that we will be under shelter."

"We will," Elise put in. "Theano told me. The ceremony takes place in the Underworld."

That was a detail that Madame hadn't mentioned to me.

"The Underworld?" I queried.

"Well, not *the* Underworld, obviously. Not the one that Orpheus went to, that is—the realm of the dead. Just a cave of some sort. The mountain is riddled with them."

That wasn't surprising, given that it was the relic of an extinct volcano. The idea that the ceremony would be taking place in near-darkness, illuminated only by the relatively primitive forms of artificial lighting that the island routinely employed might have been another opportunity for Mariette to wax doleful, but she refused the opportunity, heroically, perhaps telling herself that, one way or another, it would all be over by tomorrow, and that she would then be able to relax, free of apprehension.

While not entirely unjustified, her fears about our being soaked to the bone proved to be exaggerated. When Helen arrived, clad in white and carrying a huge and carefully-wrought torch, she was accompanied by half a dozen Sileni, four of whom were carrying the supports of an awning that served as a kind of vast umbrella. The others had bundles, from which they supplied us with waterproof capes made from the skins of some kind of marine mammals, presumably seals. The torch was lighted before we set forth, and seemed rather smoky in the damp air, but the awning protected it from being extinguished—indeed, it provided somewhat better protection for the torch than it did for us.

The walk was long, but it didn't take us to the top of the mountain, or anywhere near it; although the route sloped upwards, it did so very gently, and most of the displacement took us around the mountain to a part of its flank that I had not visited before, nor looked down upon from the viewpoints I had been able to reach in my various excursions. It wasn't an easy path, in spite of its lack of inclination, because it took us through gorges and across ravines, sometimes on suspended bridges that seemed a trifle precarious, especially in the company of the bulky Sileni. Nevertheless, after some two hours of walking, we finally came under cover again, and the protective awning was dismantled, rolled up and put away, along with the sealskins.

Initially, we followed a tunnel, illuminated solely by the torch. Then, in a more copiously-illuminated chamber, where there was a pool of water, there was a symbolic cleansing, and Mariette and I were clad in loose-fitting white robes not unlike the one worn by Helen, presently playing the role of hieroceryx and that of Iacchus. Elise, by contrast, was given a black robe, as was Theano, who joined us at that point in the proceedings. There were recitations, most of them incomprehensible, but the only ones to which we had to make ritual responses were couched in *lingua franca*, having evidently been adapted over the centuries from origins that must have been Hellenic Greek, or perhaps an older tongue than that.

There were more ill-lit tunnels, but the ventilation seemed efficient; the air wasn't stale and the torchlight flickered continually in various currents. The most remarkable thing about that part of the journey, it seemed to me, was the sound that surrounded us: a strange susurrus that ebbed and flowed, and which might almost have been taken for a peculiar kind of music—another music of sighs—had I not realized that it was actually caused by the rain-water soaked up but the volcanic mountain's multitudinous fissures, following various tortuous passages to reservoirs akin to the one that had supplied lustral water our symbolic ablutions.

The time it took to reach the cave of the ceremony gave the impression that it was deep within the heart of the mountain, but I suspected that that was an illusion, assisted by the many changes of direction that we had taken. The cavern itself was huge, its full extent difficult to estimate because of the limited lighting, almost all of which was provided by oil lamps, but often shielded by gauzes that dissipated but also filtered and softened the light.

For the same reason, it was difficult to calculate exactly how many people were assembled there, but it was at least a thousand, and perhaps more. I estimated that at least half were Sileni, and as many as half the remainder might have been Nymphs, who seemed a trifle out of place in such aggregation and away from their forest environment.

Almost all of the members of the assembly were situated lower down than the uneven shelf of rock to which we were taken. The hierophant was on the highest part of the shelf, costumed and masked, accompanied by another officiant, whom I assumed to be the dadoukhos, The hieroceryx, no longer playing the symbolic part of Iacchus, and now masked in her turn, joined them. The only other humans on the shelf, positioned on a ledge above the bulk of the assembly, were Theano and Elise. Elise's instrument was waiting for her, indicating her allotted positions, but there was no cithara there. Even so, Theano went with Elise to sit down, at least temporarily, beside her.

While Elise took up her position and her instrument, a gesture from the hierophant indicated that Mariette and I, as mystes, should kneel.

Behind the three officiants, set into the wall of the cave, were two doorways, one containing of a double-battened door seemingly made of lacquered wood, and the other a single light panel resembling wickerwork. It took me several minutes to work out in my mind that they must be the kiste and the katharis, the coffer and the basket, and I had to revise my estimate of the probably size of the magical Mirror of Dionysus. Tacitly, I had been thinking something akin to a hand-mirror, or the looking-glass attached to a dressing-table. The double doors implied something considerably larger.

As for the katharis, we did not have to wait very long to discover what it contained.

First, though, there were more recitations, presumably prayers, to which various sections of the assembled host responded, in what appeared to be a mixture of languages. Then there was the serving of the cyteon, in polished bowls. Ours were brought to us by the hieroceryx. I watched Mariette out of the corner of my eye; she did not appear to have any difficulty draining the bowl, once she had tasted the liquid, which was liberally sweetened with honey, and she finished before I did.

After the bowls had been collected and put away, the katharis was opened by the dadoukhos and the object it contained brought out, and handed ceremoniously to Theano. It was, unsurprisingly, a cithara: in symbolic terms, the lyre of Orpheus, the partner, in this version of the Mysteries, of the Mirror of Dionysus.

And Theano immediately began to play.

I had, of course heard her play many times before, in the house, on her own instrument, while teaching Elise the rudiments of her art, and I don't suppose that the symbolic instrument was much different—but what *was* different were the acoustics of the cavern. The instrument was not particularly loud, and the cavern stretched away into the gloom to such an extent that I wondered whether the notes were audible in its further extent, but where we were, close to an exceedingly uneven wall, not far beneath the curve of the roof, there were echoes. I didn't suppose that architecture of the cave could have been deliberately adapted to enhance the music, so I presumed that the music must have been adapted to make use if the echoes, perhaps intended to be played in that specific location, and nowhere else.

At any rate, the music of the lyre seemed strangely loud, strangely complex, and, all in all, simply *strange*— a strangeness greatly enhanced by the chorus that soon joined in; or, to be strictly accurate, the choruses. Sometimes, the entire assembly participated, sometimes only sections, often, but not exclusively, consisting of members of a single species. The nymphs, unsurprisingly, supplied the highest registers, the Sileni the lowest, with the human contribution intermediate, but the complexity was greater than that summary implied, and a further dimension was added to it by the dancing.

The term "bacchanal" had inevitably conjured up in my mind something wild and hectic, and the Cycinnis was certainly no pavane or saraband, but it was no tarantella either. Its rhythms varied, sometimes grave and sometimes lively, and the steps were various too, but the overall impression was one of phenomenal order, in spite of the face that there were no lines, no couples or quadrilles, nor even any separation between the species whose members were gathered there. Even the gregarious Nymphs didn't seem to cluster together, but dissolved into the shifting stirring crowd, along with the Sileni and human of both sexes.

To my naked eye, there seemed to be nothing in the way of formal organization in the dance at all. How could there be, when the area was so densely packed that there hardly seemed to be room for individuals to move? But move they did—all of them, each individual following a convoluted path between all the others. They were moving simultaneously, in different directions, following different trajectories, but somehow never colliding, never tripping, always maintaining the impression of a perfect admixture, a perfect flow, a dynamic smoothness. And while they danced they sang, albeit wordlessly, in a strange onomatopoeic language that was surely akin to the language of sighs, although it did not consist of lamentations, but expressions of other emotions: of yearning and satisfaction, and a kind of passion that seemed strangely serene by human standards, but was nevertheless definitely passion.

While the dance was in progress, Elise joined in the accompaniment, with the viola. I deduced that she was making use of the elements that Madame had shown her, which she had learned to play, but she was not playing them in fragmentary form now; she was incorporating them into a continuous flow that was partly improvised, partly discovered—and in which she not only had to seek and find her own part, but to seek and find its harmony with Theano's cithara.

I could barely make out Elise's face in the dim light, but I had the impression that she was entranced: entranced by her own music, the music of the cithara, and the combination of the two. And I felt that, under the combined influence of the music and the cyteon, I was slipping into a trance too.

All of it, I realized, was magic: pure magic, following its own esthetic course, on the one hand age-old, traditional and, to everyone except myself and Mariette, familiar, but on the other hand new, innovative and questing, bringing the past and present together, and interweaving with them the future potentialities that could not yet be specified, but were nevertheless latent, in the participants in the assembly, in the Cult of Dionysus, and in the universe, in existence itself.

The Cycinnis was, I suspect, originally and fundamentally a production of the Sileni. They were its choreographers, its designers—but the Nymphs and the humans fitted into its seamlessly, as if the extrapolated civilization of the former and the retained closeness to nature of the latter, were like wings or fins extending from the main body in equilibrium, giving it the power of controlled locomotion. It was as if the assembly had been had been accustomed to that triple alliance, the fusion of that interspecific nexus, and its innate magic, since birth—as presumably, they had, or very nearly.

I felt strangely proud of the humans of the island, who were, in essence, Ephemerae, and had not had the long lifetimes that most of the Sileni and Nymphs had had, in order to learn and absorb the technique of the dance, in order to master its magic. But they were all initiates. They had all made contact with their true selves by looking into the Mirror of Dionysus. They knew a secret that the humans of the Empire had lost a long time ago, in the course of their genocidal quests for domination, their disequilibrated passions

It struck me, as I watched and listened and felt, in frank amazement, how different this version of the Mysteries must be from that of the Cult of Orpheus, which was a purely human affair, and probably did not include a Cycinnis at all, even though it was centered on a lyre of some kind, although it evidently had its own cyteon, its specialized bacchantes, and perhaps its own perverted satyriasis.

I could not get over the fact that what I was witnessing was something lost to the world outside the island, stamped out by the genocides that humans had carried out so ruthlessly in an era that now survived in memory and legendry as an age of Golden-tinted fantasy. Plainly, as Madame had told me without my being able to judge its significance, the celebrations of the Cult of Orpheus as that cult had been preserved in the Empire could only be a hollow travesty of real thing, a feeble mimicry of a harmony that had long ago been murdered and rendered impossible.

But here, it survived.

Why, I wondered, in a sudden rush of regret, had the forces of magic not preserved the Cycinnis everywhere, if they were so fond of peace and harmony? Why had the example of Dionysus, with his retinue of Sileni and Nymphal bacchantes, vanished into the mists of forgetfulness, perverted by mythic representation? Why had the original Orpheus, the charmer of beasts, the bringer of harmony, degenerated into the resentful Orpheus, the regretful murderer of his treasured lover, leaving his ultimate followers to degenerate even further, into a company of treacherous and violent manipulators, eager to dominate their fellows and to tear one another part in completion for the privilege? How could the gods ever have permitted that to happen? Were they so very feeble?

The simple answer, I realized, under the inspiration of the cyteon, was yes.

Clearly the gods were very feeble, in spite of their reputation for omnipotence. They loved harmony, but they found it very difficult to produce, very difficult to sustain. They even found themselves very difficult to sustain, difficult to formulate and characterize. Insofar as they existed at all, they could only cling on to a marginal, liminal existence—and in order to accomplish anything at all, they needed the collaboration of material beings, conscious beings...among whom, it was easy enough to appreciate, simply by studying the Cycinnis, the Sileni and the Nymphs, humans were the least well-equipped to maintain the harmony on which the forces beyond our understanding apparently thrived.

Humans were not merely ruthlessly genocidal, I realized, but ruthlessly deicidal, in spite of their relentless fervor for inventing new gods, each more violent and virulent than the last, for all their relentless prating about the necessity and the ideal of love. Nevertheless, I was quick to add, by way of apology for my own species, that they did have art, and art in some abundance. Humans had not lost touch with the esthetics of magic, the esthetics of life, and the esthetics of the universe. Some of them, at least, had the gifts of music, painting, sculpture, poetry and rhetoric, the avenues through which the forces of harmony could still reach them, albeit marginally and liminally, in mysterious ways.

I don't know how long the cithara and the viola played and the Cycinnis went on. Probably not as long as it seemed at the time, or at least some of its participants would have been exhausted—but while it lasted, time seemed to be almost suspended. Doubtless the effects of the cyteon collaborated with that sensation. It was, as Madame had advertised, an intoxicant, but the intoxication it produced was more refined that that produced by alcohol or various other drugs in which I had indulged in the past. If it produced illusions and hallucinations, it did so discreetly. I assume that it did, but so

261

subtly that my sense of reality was merely massaged, not twisted out of shape or rudely crushed.

The precise effects of the novel combination of the viola and the cithara were impossible for me to judge, since I had never participated in the ceremony before. The quality of the sound produced by the bow drawn over the viola's four strings seemed to me to be very different from that of the sounds produced by Theano's plectrum plucking the cithara's eight, but there was no clash; the music of the two instruments fused. In the same way, it seemed to me, there was no clash between the high-pitched voices of the Nymphs and the deep baritone of the Sileni. Everything fused, everything united.

As time went by, however, the viola took over. Little by little, the cithara faded away, and as it did so, the Cyncinnis began to peter out, and the participants in the ceremony gradually returned to immobility. It was not the same immobility as before, however; the entire ambience had changed, and it was the music of the viola that expressed that changed ambience.

The piece that Elise had improvised to accompany Hecate's poem in a language of sighs had been an expression of complaint, of Eurydice's lament: a voice from the Underworld that was coming from a wilderness after death, a world of shades. The music that she was playing now was quite different. Doubtless she had been improvising it mentally all week, or at least preparing its elements and practicing its phases, but hearing its fragments within the guest-house, muffled by the walls and confined by the limited architecture of the edifice of brick and stone, had not allowed me any clear perception of its true nature. Now, in the cavern, collaborating with the echoes, taking proper shape, it sounded completely different.

It was, I thought, once again a lament of sorts, but it was not the lament of a lonely shade, betrayed by the interruption of a life already doomed to brevity, and by a love that, however passionate, was doomed to a brevity fare more restricted. It was the lament of a god: specifically, it was the lament of Dionysus, the lament of an individual not cursed with brevity, but cursed with an ignorance of his true nature, his true identity. It was the lament of Dionysus born of Semele, of an embryo that had had previously been a heart, who had not yet looked into the magical mirror that had beguiled his former self, and had not yet discovered that he was Zagreus, the child of Zeus and Persephone, once destined to be the heir to the legacy of the gods, to become the personality and the shaper of the force that provided the fundamental impetus of nature, the hopeful incarnation of the thrust of intellect's evolution.

But what Elise was playing was not simply a lament, because it was also a summons. It was a summons to Dionysus to approach that mirror, to look into it, to encounter his true self, and to discover the truth not only of what he was but what he might become, if only he had the courage and the determination, and the fortunate collaboration of the impetus of magic.

The aged Theano had doubtless played something similar on her own instrument hundreds of times, to accompany the initiation of her own people—including the Sileni and the Nymphs—and doubtless she had played it with consummate skill. Elise was young, and using an instrument of her own, doubtless not as well adapted to the acoustics of the cavern, improvising rather than following a traditional pattern—but she had the force of her innate magic to assist her, strengthened by the nexus of which she was a part.

I became aware that Mariette and I were holding hands, that we were physically linked—but I was also aware that the physical link was neither necessary nor vital, being merely symbolic in its significance. There was a much more powerful and intimate sense in which we had formed a nexus, within which the music that Elise was playing was becoming interwoven, in order that its harmony might be detected, and smoothed, and perfected.

Elise's adoptive mother and I, her adoptive mother's lover, advanced together toward the lacquered doors, still hand in hand—but the dadoukhos separated our hands and moved me gently aside, to a position from which, when the doors over opened for the first time, I would not be able to see what was within the kiste, although I would be able to see Mariette's face.

Mariette took up her position before the doors. The hierophant opened them.

I had tensed myself, expecting see a reaction of some kind in Mariette's features, but there was none—not immediately, at any rate. Mariette simply gazed into the space that was hidden from my view. She didn't make a sound, she didn't change expression, and the pallor of her complexion didn't alter. She simply gazed at what I presumed was some kind of reflection.

While she gazed, the hierophant, standing to one side, and the hieroceryx, standing to the other, changed the angle of the open doors in such a way that the lacquered surface nearer to me suddenly reflected light into my eyes, dazzling me momentarily, and startling me.

Then the doors were closed again, and Mariette and I changed places. That required us to pass very close to one another, to touch one another briefly with our fingers, and it allowed our eyes to meet.

The lamplight was uncertain, and the effect of my momentary dazzlement had not completely cleared, but I could see Mariette's eyes quite clearly, and the whole of her face. I had never seen her resemble so closely the picture that Charles Parenot had painted of her as Eurydice. Like the image in the picture, she had the texture of a shade, an inhabitant of the Underworld. And because she had provided the model, she resembled exactly the undoubtedly-false image I had in my mind of what Eurydice might have looked like—but Mariette was not Eurydice. As I looked at her, I saw, perfectly clearly, perhaps for the first time, that she was entirely herself, and I knew that in looking into my eyes, she was seeing herself reflected there, not as a mere visual image but as the object of my passion, my adoration.

She had to know, as well as I did, that the passion and adoration in question was perishable, that it could not last forever and probably would not last very long— but she also had to know, because she knew herself, that for the moment, for the present, it was entirely and vastly real.

There was no gratitude in her gaze. Why should there be? She didn't make a sound, but I heard a word nevertheless, and the word I heard was *adieu*; in this instance, however, it didn't mean "goodbye" as it had when Hecate had pronounced it, regretfully, on the last afternoon I had spent on Mnemosyne. Mariette meant it literally; she was confiding me to the care of a god, to Dionysus, whose was about to become, symbolically, Zagreus.

Her image was still filling my mind, with all its associated passion, and adoration, when the lacquered doors opened in front of me, and I looked into the Mirror of Dionysus, and saw my true self.

XV. The Evocation

It really was a mirror, although not a plane mirror. It was concave, and thus had a magnifying effect, given that I was presumably standing closer to it than its center of curvature, so the impression I received of looking at my image was that I was larger than I really am. But it was not just a mirror. I realized that the movement of the doors that I had observed had not been calculated to dazzle me, as I had naively assumed, but rather to cut off some of the lamplight reaching the mirror from without. At the same time as the doors shifted, some kind of lamp behind the mirror, presumably controlled by the movement of the lacquered doors, flared up, so that my vision shifted strangely, allowing me not only to see the magnified image of my own face but also to look through it.

At what?

In a sense, at nothing: at an empty space illuminated by a single gauze-filtered lamp. But that, evidently, was where the cyteon-assisted imagination came into play. That was where the unconscious mind was invited to supply images to the brain that was suddenly starved of the visual information that it was using to construct the magnified image of the face. The "magic" mirror was a device for inviting and enabling illusion, but the illusion had to be supplied by the observer, by the reflexive action of the observer's unconscious mind, by the part of the mind that normally supplied dreams and illusions.

What other initiates might synthesize in similar circumstances, I could only guess. I could only guess what Mariette might have seen. But I had been primed, and carefully. Madame had done her best, in her own subtle way, to guide what I might see…and what Dionysus Zagreus might see, with my collaboration, employing my eyes and my mind, because he had none of his own.

In objective terms, my vision lasted no longer than Mariette's. It could not last any longer than that; it was a matter of a few seconds. Like her, I hardly moved, and I doubt if my expression or complexion changed at all. Subjectively, however, my mind escaped from time completely. Possessed momentarily by the god, I acquired godlike vision and a godlike sense of duration.

I did not consciously see my "true self" in the mirror. That was never the point of the exercise. The whole point of my being there was to enable Dionysus Zagreus to make brief contact with his true self, employing me as a vehicle. Axel Rathenius was only relevant to the procedure because he had an artist's eye and an artist's passion, as well as a Macrobian legacy of experience, all of which combined to make him a suitable vehicle, or crutch. I did not, in consequence, see what I might make of myself in future, given the right effort and cleverness, with the unconscious assistance of a little wayward inspiration. I learned nothing of any vulgar practical use to me…but that is not to say that I was not enlightened.

I suppose that I could have concentrated my attention on the visual image that was still present, of my own face, writ large. Perhaps some initiates did. Most, I suspected, took the alternative course, striving with all their might to look through the mirror, into the uncertain and deceptive space beyond, searching for a better kind of sight. I certainly did. Ignoring my own bloated image, I plunged into that vague space behind the mirror, in company with the god, Dionysus in search of Zagreus.

When I say that I *plunged*, of course, I didn't actually go anywhere, physically. I simply stood where I was and never budged an inch. Dionysus didn't "actually go anywhere" either, because he wasn't actual, and wasn't in any particular place to start with; he only had to shift the focus of his attention and consciousness—because, in spite of not being actual, he was, at last for the moment, thanks to my collaboration, attentive and conscious. He really was Dionysus, and he really was the Dionysus that was discovering at that instant he was Zagreus, and what that implied.

So, although I wasn't actually there, and certainly didn't see anything, let alone do anything, I became aware of what was happening at the other celebration of the Mysteries, in Mnemosyne.

There had been no Cycinnis there, but there had been a dance of sorts, a kind of inordinately feeble parody of the dance of the Sileni and the Bacchantes. It had not involved the entire congregation, however; it had been a performance, executed by a limited number of bacchantes—more than nine but less than twenty.

There was a kiste on the low platform, but it did not contain a mirror. There was a kalathis, which did contain a lyre, but the lyre was only taken out for symbolic display to begin with; there was no one to play music upon it as Theano had played on the lyre in the Dionysian ceremony.

There was also an "altar-piece" of sorts behind the officiating hierophant and between the kiste and the kalathis, which was my triptych. I have to admit that it was very tastefully and effectively lighted. That cannot have been easy to contrive, given that the hall in the Mesmay manse was exceedingly crowded, containing several hundred people. There were, I knew, many more in the other rooms of the house and outside in the courtyard, but they were foot-soldiers, potential reinforcements. I presume that my would-be assassin was among them, but Dionysus Zagreus paid no attention to such trivial details as that.

The three panels of the triptych, I knew, corresponded to the three aspects of the mythical Orpheus represented by the nexus of which I was a part. Elise was Orpheus charming the animals and the stones. Mariette was Orpheus in the Underworld, charming the dead in an attempting to redeem and recover the love that he had banished there in a momentary fit. And I was the severed head, floating downriver, singing while the lyre continued to play: three panels, but all representing the same individual, the same personality, albeit fragmented at present and alienated from the god that he had once been able to embody, as I was embodying him now: Dionysus Zagreus.

There had probably been recitations, I thought, mock-prayers of a sort, but they were over. They had probably been intended to fulfill their original purpose, to imbue the participants in the ceremony with a sense of collective identity and common purpose—something direly necessary, because, although the faithful had been summoned to the celebration from various parts of the Empire, especially but by no means exclusively the Gaulish capital, in order to achieve agreement, to reconstitute a broken solidarity, there was discord, mistrust and opposition within the assembly. There was violence seething just below its surface, ready to burst forth volcanically at any moment.

If it did burst out, I knew, it might destroy the Cult of Orpheus, not merely in the simple sense of occasioning slaughter in its ranks, but breaking the solidarity of its surviving members permanently. But that was, in a broader context, a rather minor matter.

The importance of the Cult of Orpheus and its solidarity was not merely of significance to the cult itself. The Duc de Dellacrusca had been the chief of the Empire's secret police. Cleverly, albeit unwisely, in Madame's opinion, he had spent the greater part of his adult life deploying new technologies in order to improve his means of gathering information and transmitting orders. He had become an exceedingly large and avid spider at the center of a web, whose principal threads were telegraph wires, and he had become so bloated with his own success that he had come to see himself as the true master and shaper of the Empire.

His grandeur had been at least partly delusory—as Madame had said, no one person can really control an Empire, whether he sits on the throne or operates behind it—but the fact that he had wielded great power and influence was indubitable. It was doubtless the indubitability in question that had excited covetousness, treason and eventual murder. In all probability, had the Marquis de Mesmay's plan, reckless as it was, actually worked, then the Marquis might have been able to take over Dellacrusca's position, to become the spider at the heart of the web. But Mesmay had overplayed his hand. He had made the mistake of simply standing too close to his victim when he had sprung the ludicrously theatrical trap designed and operated by his witch-wife. He had lost what he had been on the very brink of winning, and suddenly, in the ranks of his own supporters as well as Dellacrusca's, there had been a competitive scramble to gain a position from which it might be possible to move to the heart of the web.

The present ceremony was a hopeful attempt to settle that question. If it failed, not only would there be chaos and bloodshed within the ranks of the cult, but the effects of that chaos would spread, through the web of Dellacrusca's machinations. Even if that web simply collapsed and disintegrated, the consequences of that obliteration would continue to spread out, disruptively. The Empire's stability was already rickety; the repercussions of a shock like that might awaken long-suppressed anxiety, covetousness and ambition in all manner of men, in widely disparate locations.

The forces of magic, however one conceived them—as gods, or demons or simply as some fundamental impetus that imparted movement, and perhaps direction, to existence—did not like chaos, confusion and disorder. But if it is difficult for a weak man to rule a petty Empire like the one that had been born in Rome nearly two thousand years before, imagine how utterly impossible it must be for a feeble god to rule a universe!

What would have be the chances of the ceremony organized by the Marquise de Mesmay and her associates actually achieving its end, either by magic or by fakery, and bringing about a negotiated settlement to the predicament in which the cult now found itself, even if that was what everyone actually wanted?

Slim to none, I judged. Tommaso and Lorenzo Dellacrusca had vendetta in their blood, but their vulcanism was merely one possibly ignition point among several. There had to be countless conflicting agendas in the room, and countless metaphorical fissures that no amount of travestied ritual and hypocritical prayer could possibly paper over. It would require far more than the meager apparatus of ritual that the degenerate cult still retained, even though many of its members still believed in that mysticism, and its associated magic. Perhaps their magic was not devoid of effect; perhaps the Marquise de Mesmay's belief in the possibility that she could work a magic spell, with the aid of the right ingredients, was not entirely unjustified—but what kind of magic would be unleashed in response to her appeal, and what would its actual effects by?

Even if she had had Elise, I thought, and Mariette; even if she had been wise enough to attempt to recruit me to complete the nexus associated with the triptych instead of regarding me as a wayward factor best removed from play, I could not believe that the Marquee de Mesmay would have been able to direct the resultant magic to her desired end—which was, after all, working contrary to the preferred direction and the preferred goal of magic itself.

No, I thought, in order to make anything of the potential that was in the triptych, and in Elise, Mariette and myself, our true selves had to be engaged, and not whatever roles the Marquise would have wanted us to play. To make anything whole and harmonious out of the separated fragments of Orpheus would require real magic, produces in association with a real catalytic nexus. It would require a virtual miracle, of the kind that only a god could contrive, and only with the right assistance.

And that was where Madame and Dionysus Zagreus came in.

Not that Dionysus Zagreus actually "came in," of course, in any physical sense, because the only physical presence he had was in an Underworld on an island in the middle of the Ocean...but he made his presence felt.

Behind the lyre, directly behind the hierophant—the role that the Duc d'Alectryon had reluctantly agreed to play—there was the triple image of Orpheus, including, to the hierophant's left, an image of his severed head floating down the river Hebrus, with a distant, fugitive, barely perceptible image of Eurydice still contained in his eyes. To the left of that image stood the hieroceryx, the role being played by the Marquise de Mesmay. The role of dadoukhos was being played by an aristocrat who was not one of the island's regular summer visitors, but he was standing on the far side of the triptych, beyond the empty kiste, and was only a marginal presence

By no means marginal, however, in front of the hierophant and the lyre, were the two mystes that the Marquise had recruited for her ceremony, in the hope of improvising a nexus of her own possessed of some connection with the magical triptych: Vashti Savage and Hecate Rain.

Vashti, I knew, was there entirely voluntarily, possibly having been delighted by the invitation to be initiated into the cult and quite probably, give that she had a remarkable capacity for obliviousness to her actual surroundings, having little or no understanding of the danger she would be running at such an assembly. Her unconscious mind had probably tried to warn her via her nightmares, but Vashti also had a remarkable capacity for misinterpreting the messages that her unconscious sent her in unusual profusion.

As for Hecate, I could not read her mind, and I did not know what means had been used to entice her there. I doubted that force or blackmail had been employed; it seemed more likely to me that simple curiosity had played a larger part than any mere inducement...at least consciously. I knew, though, that there as a sense in which Hecate was there because she had been brought there, partly by visions and partly by sentiments. She had been brought there to constitute part of a nexus—but not the Marquise de Mesmay's nexus. She was there for Eurydice, for the real Orpheus, and the real Dionysus Zagreus...and perhaps, just a little, for me.

Unlike Vashti, however, Hecate was perfectly conscious of the tension in the air and the possibility that repressed violence might break out at any moment, once the climax of the ceremony was reached. She knew too, when that moment would come: when she, as the first of the mystes to be summoned to initiation, touched the strings of the symbolic lyre.

Hecate had no ear for music at all. The Mother Superior of the Sisters of Shalimar had despaired of teaching her to play the marine trumpet—and that was why she had requested the Sisters of Shalimar to provide an accompaniment to support Elise in her planned performance of "Eurydice's Lament," and had set the stage for Dellacrusca's murder. She knew, and I knew, that she could not possible draw a tune out of the symbolic lyre, or even a chord. Indeed, knowing her as I did, I suspected that she feared that when she touched the strings, she would accidentally produce a hideous discord, like the one that Elise had somehow produced on the fateful night of Dellacrusca's murder.

Nevertheless, she had to touch the strings in order to complete her initiation.

Perhaps—I strongly suspect so—the Marquise de Mesmay had some contraption set up by means of which the lyre could appear to play, producing chords of her own choosing, and some additional contraption set up to produce a voice that would play the oracle and pronounce her edict...fakery with which, she hoped, authentic magic would collaborate in order to make the effect real.

In the meantime, though, Tommaso's and Lorenzo's hands were by no means the only ones already fingering the hilts of their daggers and the butts of their pistols when the ceremony of Mnemosyne reached its

274

ostensible climax, and the mystes were summoned. The hall was a powder-keg, waiting for a spark.

Hecate Rain stepped forward. Her face was pale; she looked like a shade strayed from the Underworld. She steeled herself, and she reached out in order to run her slender, delicate, lovely fingers over the lyre—but they never quite reached the strings. They did not have to; the symbolic gesture was sufficient.

The lyre of Orpheus began to play.

There must have been numerous people in the assembled throng who had expected that it would, and merely thought that whoever had triggered that hidden mechanism had simply done so a fraction of a second ahead of cue. The initial astonishment among the assembled throng, when the lyre began to play entirely of its own accord, was therefore very patchy and very muted. Among the entire audience, it is probable that only Vashti Savage and Hecate Rain were taken completely by surprise. Among the other members of the audience, the surprise started small, and only augmented by degrees—but augment it did.

The lyre was a symbolic instrument; it was not normally employed simply for playing music. It could certainly be played by human fingers, armed with a plectrum, just as it could be made to play a few notes, after a fashion, by some clever artifice, but it was probable that no one had bothered to tune it properly for a long time, and highly probable that the tune capable of being synthesized by trickery was elementary, or tokenistic.

This time, however the symbolic lyre played harmoniously, and it continued to play, insistently and artfully.

I can only imagine the electric shock that gradually began to surge through the members of the audience as their vague expectations and anticipations were defied and crushed by the evolution of the moment. I didn't even see the surprise on their faces, because I wasn't there in any physical sense; I just knew, and all that I knew was what the attention of Dionysus Zagreus singled out, and allowed me to know. I could not focus my own attention, although I certainly inferred more than I genuinely apprehended.

Perhaps, if it had only been the lyre, it would have had no significant effect on the assembly. Most of those present would have assumed that somehow, the trickery of the lyre had been cunningly enhanced, by the Marquise or one of her acquaintances, in such a way as to be able to play harmoniously. Many would simply have assumed that the music only appeared to be coming from the symbolic lyre by virtue of an illusion, and that the instrument actually being played was hidden from view. They would not have seen the event as supernatural, even though, insofar as the word means anything at all, it was.

But it wasn't just the lyre. Notionally, the head on the left-hand panel of the triptych was still singing, but thus far it had only done so silently, being nothing more than paint on canvas.

Now, it made its song heard.

To the accompaniment of the lyre, the severed head of Orpheus sang.

In theory, I suppose, that could have been a trick too, some deception rigged by the Marquise. She could have contrived a voice, just as she might somehow have twanged the strings of the instrument—but there was no way on earth that she, or anyone else on Mnemosyne or in the Empire, could have contrived *that* song.

The Marquise, of course, masked as the hieroceryx, never thought for an instant that the playing of the lyre or the song that it accompanied were the product of trickery. She knew from the very first instant that it was magic—but she was just as deluded as everyone else who made an assumption; she merely subjected herself to a different delusion. She assumed that it was *her* magic that was working, that she really was a magician, that she really was on the threshold of obtaining her foolish, futile desire, of winning control of the Cult of Orpheus, and, indirectly, the Empire.

A ridiculous hope, in so many ways!

But she did not suffer the corrosion of gradual but devastating disillusionment that she might and perhaps should have suffered. She had tried with all her will-power to make magic, probably only half-believing that she could, but magic had come, and she, more than anyone, knew it for what it was. And no one would ever be able to convince her that it was not *her* magic, *her* doing; no one would ever be able to convince her now that she was not a magician, and a great one.

The magic it worked was not the magic she had intended to work, but that psychological adaptation was easy enough to make retrospectively; as the magic changed her purpose, she adapted her purpose to the magic. More than anyone else in the room, she was ripe for conversion.

Orpheus—for it really was Orpheus, the genuine Orpheus, incarnated through the medium of my assisted artistic genius—sang his own lament in his own voice: the lament of his estrangement from Dionysus Zagreus, of his reckless, foolish betrayal, and his limitless remorse. He sang a denial of the slander that Dionysus had sent the maenads who had murdered him, and he sang the truth that his murder had been instigated by his own misguided followers. He sang the necessity of a reunion between his severed head and the salvaged heart of Zagreus, the necessity of their association in a new embryo, in preparation for a new rebirth. He sang his vision of what the human world might yet become, if only the effort and determination could be combined with the appropriate inspiration.

Nor did he simply sing to the ears of the bewildered, astounded listeners. He sang, primarily and essentially, to their hearts, to their true selves. The song, spilling miraculously from the work of art, guided by the music of the lyre and the passion of the singer, cut far more deeply than the conscious attention of its hearers, summoning the artistry, the music and the latent passion that lay deep within them, perhaps dormant and paralyzed, but nevertheless there, still accessible to regeneration, rebirth and renewal.

Orpheus sang, at the behest of his master Dionysus Zagreus, after thousands of years of silence and estrangement—and the stones, the beasts, the shades of the dead, the gods and the hearts of the living listened to him, and were moved.

He sang a lament, and a plea for reconciliation, and he sang it with such artistry that his plea was irresistible. No one who heard it could escape sharing his emotion, his passion, symbolized in a love that he had carelessly lost, but which nothing on earth could prevent him from trying his utmost to reclaim, in this world or the next.

And this time, he did not look back at the crucial moment. This time, he looked forward, into the Mirror of Dionysus.

And the world was transformed, and the Golden Age returned...

Well, no. Some things are beyond the scope of miracles. Politics is the art of the possible. And you have to remember that, from the viewpoint of the instigator, it only lasted a matter of seconds, on the Island of Dionysus. It lasted a lot longer than that on Mnemosyne, with the aid of magical perception, but even there, it was fleeting and temporary, as all things are in this ephemeral and ever-shifting world.

The gods are, in fact, very feeble. They can only make small and subtle changes, and even those are very often thwarted, by the refusal of human collaboration. So no, the world was not transformed. The Golden Age did not return; it was gone forever, unless a simulacrum could be painfully regenerated by thousands of years of effort on the part of billions of human beings. The surface of mundane actuality was not transfigured in any vast or sweeping fashion by the rite that Madame had orchestrated.

Nevertheless, small changes can sometimes have widespread repercussions, whose eventual consequences, in the fullness of time, can sometimes become enormous.

In the final analysis, all that Dionysus Zagreus could do, god thought he might be, when viewed in a certain fashion, with the correct illusory magnification, was to give the universe a tiny little nudge in the right direction, and hope that the small change might, with the aid of a little cleverness and fortune, occasion far reaching chains of inevitable causality, the sum of whose effects would contain a little more harmony than discord.

But the immediate objective was attained.

The members of the various splintered factions of the Cult of Orpheus did not steep their daggers in blood and started blasting bullets in all directions. Dazed and confused they undoubtedly were, but they still had presence of mind enough to decide, for once in their turbulent lives, that for now, at least, it was necessary to make peace—*and to want it sincerely*.

The Cult of Orpheus did not disintegrate that day. The Empire, rickety as it was, continued to maintain its ever-precarious equilibrium—sustained, amid countless other threads, by the network of telegraphic tightropes that the Duc de Dellacrusca had built so painstakingly. Hope still remained, not merely of its durance—a meaningless thing in itself—but in its maintenance of a precious hint of harmony.

And Mnemosyne, which I had loved so much although I had been obliged to leave it behind, was preserved from its own catastrophic disruption. Emptied by degrees of its aggressive incomers, their blades still sheathed, it was allowed to continue to function as the haven of peace and the cauldron of artistry that it had been for many years, subtly and quietly vital—at least in my opinion—to the health of the Empire and the human world.

It would doubtless be poorer from now on for no longer having Axel Rathenius in its midst, but it had done without him in the past and would doubtless survive his absence, even though Charles Parenot had to be recognized, by any true connoisseur, as a mediocre substitute.

I didn't see any of that, of course; I didn't even know the broad outlines of it until days later, but while I was collaborating with Dionysus Zagreus, I heard Orpheus play, just as the people assembled in the Mesmay manse heard him, assisted, I believe, not merely by Theano but by Elise, who added their own harmony to his long-rusty genius, and what I heard…was indescribable.

But it was beautiful, and it was passionate.

Above all, it was passionate, not with anger a thirst for vengeance, but with yearning and with love.

The last thing I actually *knew*, for sure, with the aid of the attention of Dionysus Zagreus, perhaps as a slight gesture of gratitude in my direction, was that Hecate Rain, as she withdrew her hand from the symbolic lyre, looked at her fingers incredulously, wondering whether, even though they had not actually touched the strings of the instrument, she was somehow playing a part in that incredible, overpowering, miraculous song of love.

And I imagined—for I could not possibly have heard it—Hecate's voice whispering, but not sadly this time: "*Adieu.*"

The lacquered doors closed again.

Elise's viola fell silent.

I was an initiate of the Cult of Dionysus.

I took my place beside Mariette.

The ceremony couldn't just end; there were rituals yet to complete, albeit summary ones. It only required a matter of minutes, through, for the hierophant to return to me, and—without removing her symbolic mask—to say:

"Is it finished?"

She meant the work of art: the Orpheus triptych. She didn't know. She had to ask me.

"Yes," I assured her. "This time, it is."

As we were walking back through the tunnel, all three of us hand in hand, led by Helen, still functioning as torch-bearer, Mariette couldn't resist looking at me over Elise's head and asking: "Did you see your true self in the mirror, Axel?"

"I didn't have to," I told her, "I already knew who I really am."

"I saw my true self," she said,

"I'm glad," I told her.

"Are you? You don't know what I saw."

"I know who you really are, too," I told her. "I have an artist's eye." It sounded arrogant, but that's who I am.

She didn't protest. She trusted me, now.

Elise squeezed my hand, without saying anything aloud, and I guessed that she was squeezing Mariette's as well. She was expressing the opinion that she was glad too, even though she didn't know exactly what either of us had seen. She was only a child, but a sensitive one. She knew that our true selves hadn't disappointed us, or Madame.

Outside, it was still raining, but not as heavily, and I was prepared to see the rain as the Sileni did: as the source of the island's life, it's vital fluid, without which nothing could exist.

I knew that the rain would gave way to the sun soon enough, and that the future would be all the better for the brief refreshment that it had provided.

www.ingramcontent.com/pod-product-compliance
Lightning Source LLC
Chambersburg PA
CBHW030354020726
47493CB00003B/810